ᵀᴴᴱ BADLANDS

KENNETH TAM

THE BADLANDS

THE **FIFTH** NOVEL OF ADVENTURE SET UPON
HIS MAJESTY'S NEW WORLD

KENNETH TAM

ICEBERG

Published in Canada by Iceberg Publishing, Waterloo

Tam, Kenneth, 1984-
   The badlands : the fifth novel of adventure set upon His
Majesty's New World / Kenneth Tam.
(His Majesty's New World ; 5)
ISBN 978-1-926817-11-8
   I. Title. II. Series: Tam, Kenneth, 1984- . His Majesty's
New World ; 5.
PS8589.A7676B34 2012   C813'.6   C2012-904153-X

Iceberg Publishing
55 Northfield Drive East, Suite 171
Waterloo ON N2K 3T6
contact@icebergpublishing.com
www.icebergpublishing.com

First international edition printing: July 2012

Photos: Men of the Princess Patricia's Canadian Light Infantry Living History Unit, Canadian Military Heritage Society: photographed by Kenneth Tam, Peter Tam, and Mikael Christensen. 'Gurkhas': public domain image. Additional stock images: istockphoto.com.
Cover Design: Kenneth Tam

For
my father,
who taught me early
that to solve a problem,
you need to understand it.

He's right.

And for
all the men who
fought with the RNR.

We won't forget.

ACKNOWLEDGMENTS

Once again, we must begin a story of new-world adventure with special thanks to the many people involved in making this series a reality.

The Princess Patricia's Canadian Light Infantry Living History Unit was, of course, instrumental in setting the visual tone for the new world. This organization, part of the Canadian Military Heritage Society, is preserving the memory of Canada's soldiers in the First World War. When we found that there were no First World War re-enactors for the Royal Newfoundland Regiment, the members of this unit agreed to step in and play the b'ys. The men of the CMHS demonstrate unmatched care for historical accuracy, and we've greatly benefitted from their participation and support. For more information about the PPCLI unit, visit www.newworldempire.com.

As I've indicated before, this series grew in many respects from the studies I undertook while completing both my BA and MA at Wilfrid Laurier University, in Ontario, Canada. Thanks to the work of many exceptional history professors at that institution, I've been well-equipped to confront the historical implications of this alternate timeline... though, of course, any errors are mine alone.

Mikael Christensen, who was involved in our original photo shoot for these books, continues to be a keen friend of this series. I remain indebted to him for his enthusiasm. By the same token, my good friends Peter Caron and Wes Prewer continue to lend their not-inconsiderable support to these adventures, and to all of the work we do at Iceberg. As ever, I'm grateful to these fine gentlemen for their efforts and engagement.

Again I must thank award-winning Iceberg author John Fioravanti, who brought his editorial and historical expertise to the launch of this series. John, many thanks once more.

Now, as usual, I conclude with a nod to the Iceberg team, my parents and business partners Jacqui and Peter Tam. We are presently in the midst of Iceberg Publishing's tenth anniversary, and I know there are many changes soon to come. None of this spectacular decade of work would have happened without your incomparable support. My thanks.

Atlas too.

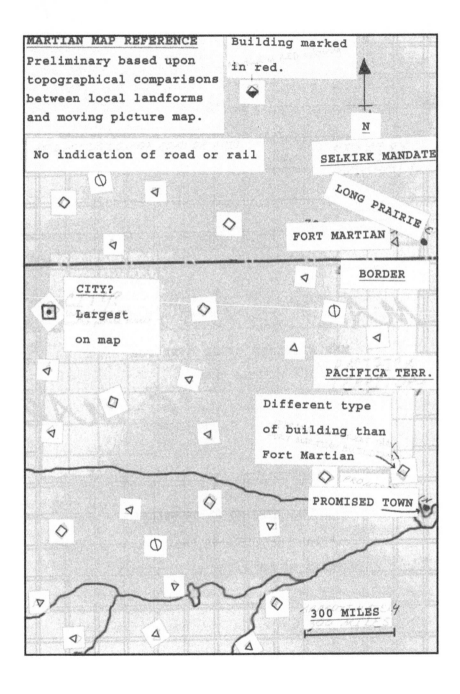

MARTIAN MAP REFERENCE
Preliminary based upon
topographical comparisons
between local landforms
and moving picture map.

Building marked
in red.

N

No indication of road or rail

SELKIRK MANDATE

LONG PRAIRIE

FORT MARTIAN

BORDER

CITY?
Largest
on map

PACIFICA TERR.

Different type
of building than
Fort Martian

PROMISED TOWN

300 MILES

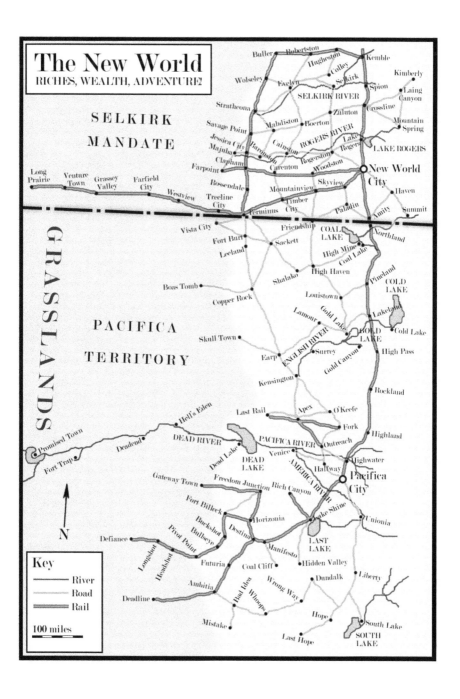

PROLOGUE

Deadline wasn't much of a town. Dry, craggy, lifeless, red, and filled with a sense of desperation... after being there for three days Smith felt about ready to move on. Most of the townsfolk had come to this place because it was their last hope — too far for collections men to follow them, or other sins to chase them. Only a few had the strength left to feel angry about their circumstances; most had given up.

It wasn't the sort of place Smith would have figured on spending his time, but the mission that had taken him out here was important. He was with soldiers again — the black Americans of the 25th United States Infantry — and that was reason enough for him to stick around. The townsfolk might not have agreed; few of them seemed to care much for the colored men who'd come to protect them from savages.

Savages who no one had yet seen.

Smith had ridden outside the palisade of this town twice over the past three days. It had been slow going each time, as the loose rocky slopes of the badlands all around were unkind to his horse. But in those mounted scout missions, he'd seen no sign of the beasts the 25th had been sent to face. It was too early to jump to any conclusions, but Smith figured either the original reports of danger had been over-excited, or the blue men had moved on.

Who would want Deadline anyway?

Those sorts of thoughts felt new to the drifter. He'd never been one to judge the worth of a place so blatantly, but now he was feeling a difference in himself. Maybe it was caused by the aches he still felt from the beating he'd gotten from the Murdos in Ambitia... maybe it was the direness of this alien landscape.

Smith didn't like where he was, but he'd stay because being around soldiers was right for him now. Eventually, he'd find his way back north, and maybe reunite with the Newfoundlanders. They were his tribe, he reckoned.

As Smith and his trusty Appaloosa mare rode through town, drawing near the train station, thoughts of the Newfoundlanders were front of mind. It was good timing, because the drifter's ears began to pick up voices as he approached the platform. A train was idling there — one locomotive had been keeping its steam up since the arrival of the 25th in Deadline, to provide a quick escape if an overwhelming horde appeared.

The voices were those of soldiers, some of whom Smith was coming to know pretty well, and they were asking for news. Telegraph lines ran along the rail line, meaning the town's wire office stood beside the dusty platform. Perhaps the commotion meant there was word of something important going on in another part of the new world.

Turning his mare, the drifter rode closer to listen.

The black American Captain Adams emerged from the telegraph shack just as Smith and his horse arrived. Easing his mount to a stop, the drifter laid his hands across the pommel of his saddle and waited for whatever news the officer might have.

"Alright, alright, calm down now!" Adams bellowed, and his soldiers — who seemed uncommonly eager — did as he commanded. Up and down the street, Smith saw some of the local folk stopping on their porches and boardwalks, curious about the spectacle.

Adams didn't make them wait: "This is from General Pershing. It's news from north of the line, from General Byng."

There was a slight ripple of noise when Byng's name was mentioned — he was known to the men of the 25th because Sergeant Turner had shared his words from their encounter after Promised Town.

"The Newfoundlanders went out on a mission over 700 miles to the northwest, and they found a prison containing captured soldiers from the dragon army that's fighting the blues. They broke them out, and brought them back. We now have dragons on our side!"

It didn't take long for those words to generate a loud cheer — the Newfoundlanders were well-remembered by the men of the 25th, even more warmly thought of now than they had been during the mission to Promised

Town. Time and distance tended to make people think more fondly of the good folks they'd left behind.

So the fact that the Newfoundlanders had marched out and done something great was welcome news to the Americans — and it was good news to Smith too. He felt a second of regret for not having been with Waller and the b'ys on that mission, but he reckoned he'd see them again.

For now, he wondered what the dragons were like, and if their discovery would change matters 1,000 miles to the south, in this dire place.

Smith didn't have answers to those questions, but he didn't mind thinking on them for a while. After he was finished with that, he turned his mare away and rode about town for the afternoon. There wasn't much to see, but he saw it all again anyway.

CHAPTER I

"I should be sitting with Emily."

Tom Waller's objection was an increasingly familiar one, and as he muttered it — ostensibly to himself — Major Bert Miller looked up at him. The two were standing side by side on the platform at New World Station, which had been cleared of civilians and roped in to control the crowd it was soon to receive.

No one else was within earshot so the Skipper decided to answer his young superior: "You sure use up a lot of the air in her room, don't you?"

It was a needling question, asked in a mostly kind fashion. The Skipper of the Newfoundland Regiment remembered what it was to be in love, though lately he was getting more reminders of it from his Colonel than he liked.

"I open a window."

Despite his preoccupation, the young commander of the RNR managed to quip sharply in reply to his Major's observation, and Bert Miller smiled and patted Waller's shoulder, "That's thoughtful, b'y."

Waller managed to chuckle, though only once before sobering. It was fair to say he was spending every free moment in the hospital room of the savage-born Lady Emily, who had so recently been shot by his bastardly brother-in-law. She was recovering well — her savage constitution, perhaps unsurprisingly, was responding quickly to the treatments of New World City's leading physicians. Her wound and been sufficiently irrigated with anti-bacterial solution, the bullet carefully removed with sterilized tools, and just this morning they had closed the hole in her abdomen.

It was all very promising, but Waller would not be satisfied until she was back on her feet, running circles around him. Until then, he'd spend as much time as he could absorbing the air in her room.

"This is the best place to be right now. Think of how happy you'll be to see the General."

Miller interrupted Waller's thoughts with that comment, and the Colonel tried to admit that his Major had a point — it had been a year since the Newfoundlanders had left Afghanistan, but the fine soldiers they'd learned so much from there were soon to arrive in Selkirk, part of the Empire's reinforcements in the face of the mounting blue man threat.

And fortunately, Baldwin had not been appointed to command them — that disgraced man was now hiding on some estate in England, as far as Waller had heard. No, the General coming to the new world this morning was probably the finest fighting officer Waller had ever served under... though to be fair, he hadn't been through quite so many fights with Byng to be able to compare the two.

A train breached the entrance of the tunnel that led back to Earth, hissing and slowing as it emerged into the morning sunshine of the new planet. The first troop train at last... and just as it puffed up the track towards the station, Waller heard boots clacking on the platform behind him.

"Evelyn Hughes is making quite a fuss," Sir Julian Byng greeted Waller with that less-than-welcome statement, and the Colonel contained some choice words that would have made an excellent response.

General Edwin Alderson and Colonel Currie were both with Byng, and at Waller's silence, the latter man managed to smile dryly, "Yes, we don't give a damn either. I don't think anyone will listen, but keep aware, Tom. He is a powerful foe, when no actual fighting is involved."

It was a wise warning — the Newfoundlanders had made a dangerous enemy when they had embarrassed the son of a politically-connected fool (who was, of course, himself an idiot). There would be no consequences in the short term, because Hughes had no credibility on the new world, but one could never assume that trouble would simply fade away.

Still, it was good to tell off foolish bastards from time to time.

Or shoot them, as many fine citizens of New World City had done to Waller's brother-in-law after he'd put a bullet into Emily's abdomen.

Stopping himself before those thoughts could make much progress, Waller turned his attention back to the train as it came to a stop at the platform. Behind it, three more strings of carriages were already arriving, being slotted to side-tracks for the moment. This single wave seemed to be bringing one whole brigade — a powerful formation of elite soldiers, with three more on the way.

"Been looking forward to this," Byng said to himself, thrusting his hands deeply into his pockets. "Never hurts to have good men around."

That was true, but before Waller could voice any agreement, one of the doors on the car behind the nearest locomotive swung open. After a few seconds, a leather-skinned man appeared, squinting in the light as he put his hat on to shade his eyes.

Unlike the officers gathered to receive him, the new arrival was clad in British tan — the sand-colored cloth favored in India and on the Northwest Frontier. The cut of his uniform was identical to Waller's, but instead of being topped by a hat in the style worn by troops from Newfoundland, Canada, and the British home army, a tea-colored pith helmet protected his scalp from the sun.

Unmistakably, the Indian Army had arrived.

As this Major General stepped down from the train, his eyes quickly scanned the station, the trees beyond, and the sky above. It was a cool and fresh new world morning — typical for the place — and that fact didn't seem lost on him.

After a second's thought, he turned towards the officers on the platform and made his approach, a wry smile appearing on his face as he neared them, "Well, it doesn't seem all that different."

"You'll find it's more green than tan around here, sir," Waller replied immediately, almost surprising himself with how easily he fell back into his old repartee with the man.

"So this time we're the ones who dressed wrong for the party, eh Tom?" The tan General's smile grew as he covered the final few steps separating him from the welcoming committee, and instead of saluting, he extended his hand to the Newfoundlander, "Good to see you again, Colonel Waller. Congratulations on getting the b'ys to yourself. And on all the work I've been reading about."

It was a warm and familiar greeting — far warmer than the average person might expect without knowing the history between the two. But for those who knew that the Royal Newfoundland Regiment had learned to war in Afghanistan, under the command of a certain Major General, there would be no surprise.

This was Sir Andrew Skeen, a man who appreciated good, intelligent soldiers. The Newfoundlanders were some of the best he'd seen, and he was happy to be heading into the field with them again — particularly considering the enemy on the new world was so mysterious.

"Thank you, sir," Waller shook Skeen's hand, then stepped back, blading his body slightly to indicate his current commanding officer. "May I present, General Sir Julian Byng."

"No need to present anyone, Tom. The man has a reputation," Skeen replied, turning his hand in Byng's direction. "Is it true you never take your hands out of your pockets, Sir Julian?"

Byng considered Skeen for a moment before smiling too, "Yes, Sir Andrew, I'm afraid it is."

That reply was greeted by a laugh, and then with no pageantry at all, the two men shook hands. There would be no undue tension here — this was not Evelyn Hughes, or any other stuffed uniform inflicted upon the new world by politicians. Like Byng, Skeen was a veteran of the British Empire's frontier wars, and he bore no misapprehensions of his own abilities, or of the qualities that made for good soldiers.

A proper General, commanding a fine division of elite fighting men, had come to the new world. This was a great day for the Selkirk Mandate.

Skeen was introduced to Alderson and Currie in turn, and the greetings remained warm until the Major General at last turned to Miller. The Skipper's eyes were narrow as the tan-clad General met them, and then with a severe look Skeen shook his head, "You know, I almost believed you'd be dead, Skipper."

Miller nodded, and then patted Skeen on the forearm in a decidedly elderly fashion, "No one ever said you was too smart."

That was enough: Skeen let out a sporting laugh, and Miller smiled.

"By God, I missed having you b'ys around," the General said. "And now I suppose we'll have to learn some things from you. Different war out here, from what I read."

Waller nodded, "Yes sir. But the same fundamentals. We survived on what you taught us…"

Before the conversation could progress any further, the doors to the remaining train cars opened and the unloading began. It was enough of a spectacle to draw silence from anyone observing.

When b'ys piled out of a train, they stretched and grumbled. They were usually good-natured, and anyone watching how they handled their weapons and looked to each other for instruction would have recognized they were good fighting men.

But when Skeen's men from the Indian Army disembarked, they did it crisply. They took pride in every step, and led by their officers and NCOs, with chests puffed and shoulders back, the Sikhs who had been occupying the other cars of Skeen's train began to march onto the platform.

The platform vibrated in a uniform rhythm beneath the feet of the veteran Selkirk officers, as Indian boots fell in perfect time. This was parade ground perfection, and it was impossible not to be impressed as the men wearing turbans formed their ranks.

From the other trains came Punjabs, and of course the Gurkhas too. All of them were fearsome, disciplined soldiers, and Waller was glad of their arrival.

"So, I hear we may be too late," Skeen lowered his voice and looked to Byng with that remark. "Past the point where rifles will make a difference against the blue men?"

Byng's hands were again thrust deep into his pockets, his eyes travelling over the perfect ranks of the new arrivals. He didn't answer for a moment, and then he shook his head before looking back to Skeen, "There are complicated problems to sort out, Sir Andrew. But good riflemen are always useful."

Nodding, Skeen turned to look back at his men.

"Well that's good," the General said. "Because I brought 20,000."

He had indeed.

The Selkirk Mandate was suddenly a more formidable territory.

CHAPTER II

The cattle didn't seem to want to move as their handlers whipped them towards the pen in the middle of New World City's main park. A dozen dragons were watching the beef arrive, and as Captain Jimmy Devlin stood nearby with folded arms, he guessed the animals had noticed the presence of the giant lizards. Perhaps they instinctively knew they were to be meals for the dragon contingent for the next few weeks.

His personal appreciation for steak not withstanding, Devlin supposed he might have felt badly for the steers... but it was better that cattle fed the dragons, instead of dead savages. Or people. It was still tough for many of the b'ys to reconcile the fact that dragons actually ate man-shaped meals, even though it was obvious that they were friends. Hopefully time would make their diet easier to overlook; for now, cattle served as a common food for both races.

Sass, the first dragon the Newfoundlanders had met on their mission to the prison camp, was suddenly in front of Jimmy. He blinked in surprise at her silent arrival; he was still adjusting to the fact that a creature the size of a whale could appear and disappear as quietly and quickly as a salamander.

"Morning Sass," Devlin greeted her with a smile, and then waved his hand towards the food. "Some prime steaks for you."

Following Jimmy's outstretched hand towards the herd, Sass began to nod, and showed an upturned palm. Then she said something — hissed it, really — but there was no way Jimmy could understand her, and she knew that. Verbal communication was probably never going to be easy between their two species, though one of the dragons was meeting daily with a schoolteacher in an effort to learn more about the letters that made up the written English language. The dragons were very smart, and if they could decipher human writing, it would be immensely helpful.

For now, messages were relayed via pantomime gestures and pictures.

That in mind, Sass pointed her claw from the cattle to her mouth, and seeing the gesture Jimmy nodded, then turned up his palm. After a second, he pointed to the beef as well, then pointed to his own mouth, then patted his stomach and said 'mmm'.

Sass tilted her head slightly, then bobbed it from side to side in what everyone was now certain had to be dragon laughter.

Smiling, Jimmy nodded. And then the conversation stopped. Neither of them knew how to make hand gestures about the weather, or any other subject that might have made for polite small talk under the circumstances, so they just stood there, only a little awkwardly, as the pen was closed behind the beef.

Then the drivers of the cattle stood around for a while too, unable to resist the urge to stare at the massive lizards who were going about their own business inside the park. As long as they didn't do anything daft, Devlin had no intention of driving off the gawking men. Besides, Sass and her commanding officer, Sask, didn't seem to mind being observed... which was just as well, because trying to keep such large creatures out of sight would have been impossible anyway. They had spent the past few days setting up a camp in the park, with their men... dragons... sleeping inside the two aircruisers they'd taken from the prison camp. They had nothing to hide, and probably were as interested in watching the humans of New World City as those men and women were interested in watching them.

Glancing back towards the aircruisers, Devlin saw a couple of dragons on all fours, staring thoughtfully at a pile of silver equipment pieces they'd pulled out of the captured craft. It seemed to Jimmy that they were wondering what the hell to do with the scraps they'd scavenged. They'd probably find something useful.

While Jimmy was distracted, Sass was not. Her finely-tuned senses began detecting a rhythmic drumming... the sound of thousands of feet marching in unison, still a little ways off but coming nearer. She looked down at Devlin, who hadn't seemed to hear it yet (his ears were comparatively quite small), and then glanced back towards the second ship with a quick hiss of alert.

It sounded to Sass as though more of the freed attackers — 'humans'

— were marching through. For a second, she wondered if perhaps soldiers were coming to surround the Saa camp, but nothing in Sass' instincts suggested any danger from these small creatures. Unlike the attackers of the Hubrin — the 'savages' — who they so resembled, the humans had been entirely civilized, if somewhat technologically crude. Surely they wouldn't turn on their new friends now.

No, it was more likely that the marching humans were newly-arrived troops, making their way to their billets in this settlement. In Saa culture, rhythmic marching tended to mean a formal occasion, so if they were coming near, the lady dragon supposed a salute might be in order. She hissed to the Saa on duty, and without delay they appeared silently beside her, forming a line.

As Devlin frowned at the sudden arrival of new dragons beside Sass, he finally detected the sound of troops on the street behind him. Turning, he watched as a column of tan-clad Sikhs came into sight, steps perfectly in sync as they marched to the beat of a nonexistent metronome.

Skeen's Indians had arrived, and Jimmy Devlin smiled broadly as he saw them.

The discipline of the Indian Army was its own sort of spectacle. Devlin had watched troops from other parts of the Empire well-drilled when it came to ceremony, but never had he come across any so sharp as those he'd seen in India and Afghanistan. These men knew how to soldier properly — and to block out all distractions on parade.

Which made it quite amusing when, upon realizing the towering lizards standing straight-tailed behind Devlin weren't statues, virtually every eye in the Sikh column turned left to stare at them. Not even the Sergeants — Havildars in Indian Army terminology — barked against the roving gazes. They stared. They had to.

Devlin contained a chuckle as he watched the reaction, "What would Skeen say to that…"

The question had been muttered for his ears only, but in just a few seconds Jimmy Devlin realized he'd have his answer: a party of officers entered the park from the street side, headed by Waller and including the tan and pith helmet-clad General from the Indian Army.

"By God, it's Skeen!" one of the b'ys from Sergeant Halloran's section called in a friendly fashion at first sight of the General, and hearing mention of his name, Sir Andrew reached up and lifted his helm in salute.

"Following you b'ys around, apparently," he called back to the fifty-odd Newfoundlanders who were hanging about the dragon camp.

They kindly replied to him with a cheer; the men of the Newfoundland Regiment liked Skeen for the same reasons they loved Waller. Though the General hadn't personally led them into fire, he'd never appeared unwilling to get his hands dirty, and his attitude in the field had been as uncompromising as it was professional.

When the Pathans wanted a fight, Sir Andrew always gave them one... and he never failed to figure out a way to outfox the tribesmen in their own damned hills. He was smart, a good soldier, and a brave one. That made him popular, and he seemed to have as fond a memory of the b'ys as they did of him.

Devlin was very glad to see Skeen too, and as he realized the General was coming directly at him, he straightened up slightly and adjusted his hat.

"I recognize you," Skeen addressed the Captain as he slowed. The fact that he was singling out a junior officer before taking time to gape at the dragons was another sign of his character, and Jimmy appreciated it.

"Captain Devlin," Waller stopped beside the General with the introduction. "When you last saw him, he was a Lieutenant."

"Of course," Skeen nodded. "He was the poor chap always following you on your errands, eh Tom?"

"Still am, sir," Devlin answered for his commanding officer, and Skeen laughed.

"Good man. Introduce me to your friends, will you?"

By now Byng, Miller, Currie and Alderson had all closed in as well, though the Generals were content to let the Newfoundlanders who knew Skeen do the talking.

Turning back to Sass, Devlin looked up to her and then waved, "This, sir, is Sass. She's the first dragon we met, and she managed to turn a Martian lorry engine into some sort of bomb that single-handedly wiped out a horde."

Hearing the sound the humans used to refer to her, the mighty starship engineer looked down from her position of attention. The newly-arrived freed attacker was clad in a different color, and had a differently shaped headdress, but he seemed to be from the same military as the others. Perhaps he was from a different branch of their armed forces.

He was here with the senior officers, which likely meant he ranked high in their system... perhaps the commander of the new arrivals, though his hide was not the same color as theirs. Given the common differences in color found amongst the ranks of the Saa, Sass had been wondering whether the humans sorted themselves out by skin tone.

Devlin was waving to Sass, and after a few seconds of interpretation she realized he was indicating that she should come down to ground level. Stepping back silently, she lowered herself onto all fours and brought her face into close proximity with the Newfoundlander, who stood aside so Skeen could get a clear look.

"That's incredible," the General said. "I'd expect them to be... heavier. Clumsy, even."

"Deft like lizards," Byng observed with a nod. "And damned smart. One of them is learning to read and write English with a local schoolteacher. For now we speak with gestures, and a good share of intuition."

Skeen pulled his helmet from his head and tucked it under his arm, then approached Sass' face, "You said she's a she, Devlin?"

"Yes sir. Told me herself, after some figuring."

Nodding, Skeen stepped right up to Sass, then leaned gingerly forward and put a tentative hand on her snout, "Pleased to meet you, ma'am."

"Touchin' a girl on the first date, b'ys. Sir Andrew still got the way with the ladies!"

That holler from one of the spectating Newfoundlanders drew some laughs, and Skeen grinned. He'd have to get re-accustomed to being around merciless senses of humor. His Indian Army soldiers were immensely funny, and he was skilled enough with languages to often know what they were joking about, but they were too disciplined and professional to swipe at him when he was within earshot.

The Newfoundlanders... he'd probably encouraged their familiarity with him too much in India, because he'd found it such a relief during tense days in the Khyber. Now he'd have to endure it again.

"B'ys, don't spoil my chances with loose talk," he countered instantly, drawing laughter from his audience. Then he turned his attention properly to Sass, "Ma'am, pleased to meet you. And despite what these fellows might have told you, my intentions are quite honorable."

Almost immediately Sass began bobbing her head from side to side, which was quite a shock to Skeen. He stepped back in a hurry, withdrawing his hand and looking over his shoulder, "What did I do?"

"Made her laugh," Waller answered.

Skeen frowned, looked back to Sass and detected a feeling of levity from her simple, silent movements.

"Hear that b'ys. He makes her giggle — he's right on track!"

Byng was by this time casting some glances at the b'ys, rather surprised by the ease of their jeers. He was a soldier's General, and he appreciated a joke, but it was getting to be a little much now.

Skeen didn't care; his frown remained as he turned to Waller, "How did she know we were amused?"

"Intuition, we think. How do you know when a dog is happy, or a horse is calm?" Miller stepped up beside his Colonel, and Skeen stared thoughtfully at the Skipper for a moment before turning back to Sass.

"That is remarkable," he said. And he was right.

He understood a giant dragon, and she understood him. It would be easier when the alphabet was at their disposal, but for now, this was quite a connection.

The humor from the crowd tapered off as Skeen's expression revealed he was in a more serious mood. Everyone stood by silently as he stared at Sass, and Sass stared back... then eventually he nodded, reached out to pat her snout, and finally returned his helmet to his head.

"Pleased to meet you," he said again, and then with a nod, he wheeled back to the officers who'd escorted him from the train.

Sass stood up silently as he turned away, and he didn't even realize she'd done so until he glanced back. Completely silent, the dragons were.

"So far the relations are very good," Byng said as Skeen returned to his host group. "And considering what the blue men have on their side, I'm glad to have them on ours."

Skeen nodded, aware that he'd need to tour the aircruisers that were landed in this park as well.

But for the moment a single question came to his mind: "So, what do we do now that they're here?"

A smile came to Byng's face, and he glanced at Waller, who shrugged.

"We don't know yet. But between them and your Indians, I rather wish we could go out there and give the blues a surprise."

There was much left to decide, but at least Selkirk was well-equipped for the moment.

CHAPTER III

Convalescence was not something at which Emily excelled. Lying in a hospital bed, watching the sky outside her window and, thanks to her savage ears, vividly hearing the sounds of life in the city, she was immensely frustrated at her lack of mobility.

But any attempts to move brought pain — less now than before her wound had been sutured, but still considerable amounts. She had been shot, and she simply had to take the necessary time to ensure her body recovered before she could begin considering new adventures.

At least her savage strength seemed to be helping. The doctors were most impressed by the rate at which she was healing, and by her seeming resistance to infection. Much irrigation had been done to eliminate the bacteria in her wound before it was closed, but there was always a chance of complication.

Perhaps she could take heart in the fact that she would return to action sooner than any human in her situation… but that was small consolation as the days went by.

There were dragons in this very city, and according to the voices her savage-strength hearing had detected, a new division had come to town as well — Indian Army troops, under General Skeen. Tom had spoken many times of those men, and the wily ways of war they had relied upon in Afghanistan. Emily was most interested in meeting them.

But not like this. Not from a hospital bed.

She did all she could to keep her frustrations off her mind… but wasn't entirely successful. And chief among her concerns was the fate of her lost sister Caralynne.

Emily was certain her elder friend still breathed somewhere on this world. She had to get out to the grasslands if there would be any hope of finding her, but that was impossible now… and the longer she lay, and the more pain she felt as she shifted in her bed, the harder it became to wait patiently for the moment she could launch her search.

Her mind told her it was essential to wait... but waiting was torture. As that thought occurred to her again, she met it with a heavy sigh, drawing a somewhat disapproving glance from her visitor for the day.

Sitting in the chair beside her bed was Annie Devlin. As Emily's former maid, the young woman was perhaps the savage-born Lady's closest remaining friend, Tom Waller excepted. Annie had visited regularly over the past few days, making sure that when Tom was away with duty, Emily never found herself alone in her room for an extended period of time. Solitude might encourage some sort of rash behavior, which wasn't to be tolerated.

Deciding that Emily had been brooding too long, Annie interrupted the room's silence with an observation from the paper she was reading: "The editors are wondering how the 20,000 new soldiers who are arriving will be fed. That is quite an addition of mouths."

Emily refused to make eye contact with Annie — she knew what the girl intended, and was agitated by the fact that her former maid thought she possessed the ability to distract her. It was even more frustrating that Annie was asking such advanced questions — she was taking her promotion to the social status of 'Captain's wife' very seriously, and though the growth should have been very heartening on one level, the current circumstances thoroughly reversed Emily's appreciation.

Admittedly, the question was an interesting one: the infusion of reinforcements from Canada in recent months had meant brisk business for the cattle ranchers and farmers of the new world, many of whom had been accustomed to selling back to the old world, and thus incurring greater transport costs.

Would those farms and ranches have enough crops and livestock to feed the fighting men who were now in Selkirk? There would be a logistical challenge as the new men were situated, their barracks either allotted or built, their daily needs met. Would the Indians be staying in New World City or moving on to the massive camp at Terminus, Byng's chosen launching point for action?

Emily's mind was starting to spin off into the possibilities before she caught herself. Damned Annie and her rapidly-growing sophistication.

"I am not interested in such questions just now. Not until I can get out of here and look an Indian soldier in the eye, and ask him how he's finding our beef."

To Annie the reply sounded petulant — an almost sure sign that the question had been as effective as she'd hoped. As maid, Annie had seen Emily in some of her worst moments, and clearly the current circumstances placed this convalescence in that category. Hopefully it would end soon, because without the ability to run in the grasslands, to seek her dead friend and demonstrate her powers to the world, Emily could rapidly become her own worst enemy.

Shaking her head, Annie turned her eyes back to her newspaper, and allowed Emily to continue to stew. Only time and patience could improve this situation.

"Did I read that Lady Lee was shot by a drunk?" General Skeen removed his pith helmet as he stepped into New World City headquarters, and Waller nodded as he pulled off his own hat and followed.

"My drunk brother-in-law, sir. Man abandoned my sister in British Columbia, she came here to join me, he followed, and Emily intervened," Waller had made enough peace with those events to be able to repeat the story without too much self-directed anger, and Skeen shook his head as he crossed the lobby and came to a stop.

"Bloody bad luck," he said quietly. "It's always that one moment when your vigilance slips. Happens to everyone, even the best of us. Glad Lady Lee will recover though. Should like to meet her when she's up and about."

"Would be my pleasure to introduce you," Waller nodded, and then Byng arrived beside him.

"Sir Andrew, scotch in the cigar lounge?"

"Excellent!" Skeen agreed, and Byng led the way.

Waller took a step to follow, but Miller, who had been last in line with the group, caught his eye: "I'll get back to the b'ys for now. You have a good drop with the Generals."

Though the Wall outranked the Skipper, Tom Waller knew well when Bert Miller was right, and thus when to defer. Nodding, he replied: "Thanks Skipper."

The little old man set off, nodding to Currie and Alderson as he went. Alderson then followed Byng and Skeen to the lounge, while Colonel Currie moved over beside Waller.

"I'm sure the Major would have been welcome," the Canadian said.

Waller tipped his head slightly, "I've never known the Skipper to drink too much, so I expect he'll be more comfortable this way."

"Not forced to make idle conversation with a bunch of lofty officers?" Currie asked, reading somewhat between the lines.

Waller shrugged, "Given the choice, I'd be sitting with Emily, sir."

"And no man would blame you," Currie concurred immediately. "We'll have you on your way to her side again promptly, Tom. And there you'll stay. With Skeen's men on the new world, I expect we can let some of our hard-fighting North American troops rest a while longer."

With that Currie left Waller and headed for the lounge. The Newfoundlander stared at the Canadian Colonel's back for a moment, then looked around quickly. He was in the middle of the lobby, no furniture nearby. Hurriedly then, he knelt and rapped his knuckles on the floorboards.

As he stood back up, Lieutenant Crerar appeared in his vision, holding a sheaf of papers and wearing a frown, "Colonel Waller?"

"Just knocking wood, Harry. Not to worry."

The Newfoundland Colonel then hurried past the confused Lieutenant and prepared to drink scotch whiskey with the Generals in charge of the defense of the new world.

CHAPTER IV

Something felt wrong to Smith.

There had been no savage activity in all the time the men of the 25th United States Infantry had been at Deadline, and that didn't seem usual to the drifter. Major Krazakowski had shared some of the reports that had led to the 25th United States Infantry's deployment to this place... they told of hundreds of savages being spotted within miles of Deadline's walls.

And still no attack had come.

There were plenty of possible reasons for the silence. The reports could have been wrong, or misunderstood the savages' intent. An attack could be headed elsewhere. The presence of troops could have scared off a raiding party... there could be many explanations.

But the more Smith rode around the haunting town with its loose red rock and its craggy cliffs, the more profoundly he felt as though there was more happening than could be explained away.

With only a feeling to go on, though, the drifter decided to keep his thoughts to himself. He wasn't as comfortable with the officers of the 25th as he had been with the b'ys, so he didn't figure they would be disposed to listen to his instincts.

They'd probably be right not to.

Instead, Smith decided to settle his nerves by setting aside time to brush down his mare, who deserved and appreciated the attention. She had spent a long spell on the train getting out to Deadline, and though he'd looked after her rightly along the way, he reckoned she'd earned more care. He'd have provided it even if she hadn't earned it.

She was in the stable behind the hotel in which Krazakowski and his officers had set up their headquarters, the only horse attached to the entire US Army column. Smith didn't have too many interruptions as he worked, and that was appreciated, so he kept on in silence, and enjoyed the peace.

Unfortunately, the peace didn't last long, because his instincts had been right.

Smith was getting used to the sound of running soldiers, so the drifter was already turning towards the barn door when a black man in khaki slid to a stop, puffing for air with a wild expression on his face.

Before the wheezing runner could get out any words, the drifter asked: "Savages sighted?"

It took a second for the man to begin shaking his head, and then he gulped out his message, "Telegraph office... they dropped on Destina... got savages sighted near to Ambitia. We're cut off."

Smith stared at the runner for a minute, and pictured the Pacifica Territory in his head. Destina was the town — deep in the foothills — where the rail line south from Pacifica City split into two different legs. If the town was captured, the rail system for the entire south of the territory was in trouble.

And if savages were running for Ambitia, which sat just a couple of miles inside the foothills treeline, even more problems were about to ensue.

Smith turned back to his mare, patted her on the neck, and then left her and followed the runner to the telegraph office.

Major Krazakowski had a deserved reputation as being somewhat odd. He was earnest, a good soldier, and dedicated both to his men and their cause as black soldiers... but he seemed to take certain kinds of news in a way other men might not. That wasn't a problem as far as Smith was concerned, but it did make for some unique conversations.

When the drifter reached the telegraph office, Krazakowski was there with Captain Koster, the second in command of the very under-strength 25th, and the Mayor of Deadline, who was also the owner of the hotel, and the barkeeper at the hotel, and part-time clerk at the general store. He was called Mulligan, and had the remains of an Irish accent.

The telegraph machine was clattering, and the operator was writing down words that were being sent in a hurry, then tearing sheets off his pad and handing them back for reading. News must have been coming from Ambitia... as Smith had experienced before, real-time news of an attack in progress, so many miles away.

"There is no more response from Destina... Ambitia is using the south line to alert Pacifica City..." Krazakowski read the most recent note.

Smith moved over to the officers as he listened in. Though most telegraph wires in the American territory followed the railway, there was a line that ran from Ambitia to Pacifica City through the southern trail — the same trail the drifter had ridden when he'd been going to and escaping from his friend Shylock's place.

He'd parted ways with Shylock in Ambitia. Hopefully Vonn, Miranda, Stephanie, Bo and Cameron Kard had left that town by now.

Steering his mind away from such thoughts, Smith returned to the mental picture he'd formed of the Pacifica Territory.

If the savages overran Ambitia, all the wire connections from the south of the territory to the north would be cut, rendering the defenses of half the new world blind to whatever the blue men had in mind. Based in Pacifica City, General Pershing might be able to get word from towns like Bad Idea and Whoops, but he'd have no way of knowing where savages and blue men were operating anywhere south of the Dead River.

The fall of two poorly-defended towns on the frontier could undermine every defense the United States could mount.

As Smith realized that, he felt a brief moment of regret for not being with the Newfoundlanders — because it was British, the Selkirk Mandate was a well-organized and connected grid, with troops just hours away from any population center you cared to name. That's why the blue assault at Farpoint had been turned back.

Pacifica was a sprawling mess of settlers connected by trails, road and rail in a haphazard fashion. Much more free, but much more vulnerable... and it seemed the blue men had figured that out. Smith didn't know exactly how the creatures would have gotten wise to the weaknesses, but if he could figure it out based on just a few pieces of information, and a bit of brainwork, he didn't doubt the Martians could manage the same.

The question was what they intended to do, now that they were free to roam the southern badlands.

It was while Smith was wondering about those plans that Krazakowski glanced back over his shoulder and noticed the drifter's arrival, "I must apologize, Mister Smith, but I fear we've led you into another cut-off town."

The drifter tilted his head, "I reckon if you'd left me in Ambitia, I'd be dead. This is preferable."

The Major turned completely away from the telegraph machine and earnestly considered the drifter's words, then nodded, "Mister Smith, you make an excellent point."

He then turned back around, just in time for the clattering to stop.

"Ambitia has stopped sending, sir," the operator reported, and there was no mistaking the dread that came with the news.

Krazakowski nodded, and Smith's eyes lowered. Ambitia had seemed a fine town, with good folk. But it had no troops as a regular garrison, and no sheriff because the last one had died trying to talk the Murdos out of killing Smith, the Shylocks and Cameron Kard. Not that one man could have stopped a horde... still, a dark piece of news.

The blue men were sending their savages to war again.

Krazakowski took a severe breath, and then turned to the Mayor of Deadline, "Sir, we have many difficult decisions ahead of us."

The Irish Mayor stared at Krazakowski, digested those words, and then said something less elegant: "No shit."

None at all. Deadline was cut off, and Smith was again on the wrong side of a blue man assault. It didn't feel any better the second time.

CHAPTER V

It was lunchtime before Waller was finally able to make his way to the hospital, and Emily was itching for news by the time he got there.

"The Indian Army has arrived?" she asked as he came through the door, pulling his hat from his head.

Blinking in mild surprise at the abruptness of the question, Waller nodded, "General Skeen and his men are getting situated here in town. Don't know how long they'll be staying with us... Byng might move them down to Terminus."

As he finished his explanation, he reached the chair on the opposite side of Emily's bed from the one that Annie was occupying. Young Missus Devlin was looking up from her paper, and then as Waller nodded to her, she realized her shift had ended.

"I'll see you later, Lady Emily," she said smoothly, then she picked up her hat and left the room.

Both Waller and Emily watched her go, and the Colonel shook his head slightly before looking back to the Lady, "Jimmy sure knows how to read a woman. She's no average maid."

"Really," Emily was far less complimentary towards her tormentor, but she had no appetite to waste Tom's time with a discussion of that subject — particularly when there was more interesting news at hand. "Tell me of the Indians!"

The eagerness for outside news wasn't really a surprise to Waller — Emily was, at the best of times, hungry for information and experience, and recent confinement had made her appetite more voracious.

"A full division from the Indian Army... the regiments are ones I know from Afghanistan. Excellent troops they've sent us, which makes sense since Skeen is leading them. They'll have some learning to do, as we did, but they're made from stern stuff. Should be good in any fight."

"Are they wearing green or tan?"

Waller blinked, then realized Emily was looking for far more than just an assessment of fighting character. Frowning in thought, he offered what he could, "Tan. As a rule, they're a well-turned-out bunch, though I've seen them looking rough after time in the mountains. They have a variety of hats as well... the Sikhs wear turbans, for instance. The Gurkhas wear their slouch hats... like Australians."

That was as much as he could think to say, but Emily was still staring at him, so he scrambled for something more.

"Skeen's wearing a pith helmet, though I expect he'll put on a hat soon enough," he added.

"The General is as you remember... think he'll fit in well here?"

Waller first interpreted Emily's question as a military one — asking whether Skeen would be comfortable fighting on the new world, which he would be — but he quickly realized there was more that he could speak to. Skeen was, after all, another soldiers' General.

"He and Byng have different ways about them, but similar principles. Between the dragons and this new division, they have more options now than they've ever had before... and I think they'll find good ways to make use of the resources. Skeen's exactly the man for that job — he always prided himself on outsmarting the tribes, and hitting them when they least expected. He should get along quite well with the fighting officers here. Better than Hughes did."

That last tacked-on thought was certainly correct: Major General Evelyn Hughes could now charitably be referred to as a laughing stock in New World City, the newspapers having done a great deal of damage to the man's reputation. His own attempts at recriminations clumsily added to his image as a political buffoon.

Skeen held the same rank as Hughes — remarkable, given their widely different experiences — but had a hard-won reputation of soldiering to back his command. Yes, Sir Andrew would fit well here — teamed with men like Byng, Currie, Prescott and Lapointe, the Indian Army officer would make quite an impression, and perhaps would find ways to let the Imperial soldiers of Selkirk strike out purposefully against the blue men, even in spite of their mechanical disadvantages...

"Tom."

Waller blinked, realizing he'd gotten lost in his thoughts. Emily frowned at him, "I know those thoughts you're getting lost in must be terribly interesting, so please do continue to indulge in them. Just speak while you're doing it."

Her frown as she made her complaint revealed some of her frustrations, and Waller reached out and wrapped his hand around hers, "Sorry. I'm sure I'll get better at describing things that I've seen that you haven't yet had the chance to see."

"Probably figure it out just when I'm getting out of here," she protested in a soft mutter, and Waller smiled.

"You're optimistic."

"Am I? So glad to hear it," she seemed in no mood for his humor, but somehow that petty petulant air — so alien to the woman Waller had come to appreciate — triggered his smile.

"Under the circumstances, and considering where you've come from, I think this is excellent progress," he said gently.

Emily fixed a mild glare on Tom, "You mean I could be more depressed?"

Shrugging, Waller let go of Emily's hand, "It's not a suggestion. Just pointing out that you've been civil this whole time, however frustrated the circumstances have left you. I can hardly imagine what it would be like to be in your place."

"You better not try to find out," Emily seized upon Waller's last point. "I'm strong enough to survive a shot, but you may not be. And with me not out there protecting you as I should very well be, you better not try to learn what my condition feels like."

There was no mistaking her agitation with those words — Emily certainly perceived herself to be Waller's personal guardian, and part of her malaise no doubt came from the fact that her wound had been incurred not in the protection of her lover, but because she'd been so engrossed in her own doubts when she'd remained behind during the Newfoundlanders' last mission onto the grasslands.

Surely a lesson for the future: abandoning one's duty was a dangerous business, which would lead to regret.

"Well if you hadn't stayed here last time, my sister might be dead," Waller interrupted Emily's thoughts at that moment, seeming to be able to track her reasoning even though she didn't voice it. "So I won't get myself shot, as thanks for your help with that rather important situation."

It was not exactly what Emily wanted to hear, but then, there was little more Tom Waller could say. She decided to force herself away from the subject before she dwelled too long on what still could happen while she languished.

She moved on to a new question: "What about the dragons. Do we know much more?"

Accepting the turn in conversation, Waller shook his head, "Nothing particular. The schoolteacher hasn't made much progress on the English lessons... and I put that down to her, not the dragons. They seemed generally accepting of the arrival of the Indians."

"The Indians have already seen them?"

"Marched down the street beside their park. Never seen so many good troops fail to keep their eyes front, but there was no panic."

"Hardly expected them to start shooting at each other," Emily's counter to that was slightly extreme, and again unexpected. "I'm sure your Indians are good men, but I can't imagine they'd survive that fight."

That was true; Waller had seen Sass single-handedly dispatching a small horde of savages, and while the blue men's minions were not so well armed as the soldiers of the British Empire, there was little doubt in the Newfoundlander's mind that a dragon would be incredibly difficult to slay.

It would require concentrated fire from very accurate and fast-tracking 18-pounders, probably... the notion that a sword could do it, as in the old medieval stories, was quite fanciful. Some newspapers analyzing the creatures had brought up such weapons nevertheless...

But so far there were no signs that violence would ensue, which made Emily's question all the more unusual. Immobilized as she was, it seemed likely she was feeling enough pent-up anger to launch her into all sorts of thoughts... but any notion of war with the dragons had to be taken seriously.

Of course it was rather difficult to communicate complicated concepts between the two species — both Byng and Sask, the dragon commander, had seemed to reach that conclusion very quickly. But as two wise leaders, they had decided it was better to wait for a written language before trying to ask tough questions, or solidify alliances.

Because an alliance had been the objective of rescuing the dragons in the first place. They'd been trapped out there in that camp to be used as training victims for savages, as far as anyone could tell. Now they were in friendly territory, with food and goodwill aplenty. Hopefully that would be a strong foundation for a relationship.

If the humans of the new world could become useful to the dragons — become, as some of the tribes in Africa and India were, allies of the greater force — then there would be the potential for powerful help against the blue men. Allying with the enemy of one's enemy was often a good strategy... though it was risky. It hadn't worked terribly well for the Indians of North America. Still, it was better than letting the blue men call in fleets of aircruisers to stomp Selkirk and Pacifica off the map.

An alliance with dragons... so many interesting possibilities, but the costs would have to be weighed. Hopefully the dragons, who had been such pleasant guests so far, would continue to be gracious and agreeable.

Only time would tell.

"Tom."

Emily's voice knocked Waller out of his musing again, and the Newfoundlander instantly donned a sheepish expression, "Sorry."

With a resigned sigh, Emily shook her head, "I need to get out of this bed. A few more weeks of this and I'll be intolerable."

Waller began to nod, but then stopped, "You give yourself that long?"

Her eyes jumped to him, a well-sharpened glare scraping across his face, "That long for what?"

The Colonel of the Newfoundland Regiment knew trouble when he found it, and though he was renowned by his men for leading from the front, and standing tall against certain death, he decided now was not the time for a humorous assault against all odds. Emily wanted to know if he thought she was intolerable now.

But he was the man leaving his regiment and fellow officers behind daily to spend time with her; it was important she realized he was on her side.

"You think you'll be in bed for weeks?" he pivoted, and Emily looked away and then nodded.

"So the doctors tell me. No strenuous activity, at least."

Waller nodded slowly, then sat back in his chair, "Well you won't be the only frustrated one."

He meant to make her smile; he managed only to intensify her glare. Emily severely disliked her situation, and that feeling was becoming more obvious with every passing hour.

CHAPTER VI

The guards on the walls of Deadline had been doubled, and all the men and boys in town were carrying rifles by the time Smith walked through its streets, heading for a meeting at Krazakowski's temporary headquarters. There hadn't been much action since the wires had gone quiet at Ambitia, but Smith knew silence couldn't be mistaken for good news.

Last time he'd been in a town cut off on the end of a rail line, it had ended up with Caralynne dead. The drifter knew this wasn't the same, but it was like enough to warrant the remembering. At least now, thanks to the honesty of Shylock's wife, and Smith's own recognition of his grief, it wasn't as painful to remember that loss.

He couldn't dwell, though. Between the 100 settlers in Deadline, and another 600 soldiers from the 25th, there were close to 700 rifles guarding the town. But even if every one of those was a crack shot and well-supplied with ammunition, Smith knew it wouldn't necessarily be enough. If a horde came through looking to burn the place down, as had happened to the Cape Breton Highlanders at Farfield City, then this defense would be too small for hope.

Smith wasn't sure what Krazakowski would do in that situation. The American Major had proved himself a capable soldier at Promised Town, but Smith hadn't taken much time to get to understand the way his mind worked. Waller was a known man, but Krazakowski and his somewhat odd mannerisms were still a mystery.

One way to take care of that.

Smith reached the Deadline Hotel, then climbed the stairs to the porch and stepped inside, removing his hat as he did. The light within was dimmer than the late-afternoon sun, so the drifter squinted for a moment before seeing that the tan-clad officers of the 25th were in the card room, having taken it over for their important meeting.

Smith moved in that direction, noting the men inside the room as he recognized them. There was Major Krazakowski of course, with Captain Koster, the second in command. Then there were a half-dozen Captains, including three Smith knew: Vogel, Insetta, and Adams. A few Lieutenants were there as well, and Sergeant Turner.

Most were talking amongst themselves when the drifter came to a stop and leaned against the doorframe, backlit by the windows of the lobby. No one noticed him, so he stood silent and tuned in his hearing: some men were talking about food and water, others ammunition and machine guns, others fortifications. One man was wondering about an escape by train.

All in all, they were concerned, and that seemed wise.

Finally, after a few more minutes of conversation, Krazakowski turned to the room full of officers and called them to order, "Gentlemen... gentlemen, we must discuss this situation."

The men fell silent immediately, and as they gave Krazakowski their full attention, the Major nodded to them, "Thank you very much, gentlemen, I appreciate your focus. As you all know, we have no contact with any part of the Territory, because Ambitia has seemingly fallen to the blue men. This is of course a shocking development, and I'm sure we are all rightly disturbed by it."

That was a fair observation, if a seemingly pointless one. Still, Smith didn't figure he should second-guess the words of a proven Major when it came to his own officers.

"This leaves us many questions. Our mission here was to seek out signs of Martian or savage activity and to report to General Pershing. It appears that we are now redundant, and we must decide what our next responsibility to the union should be. We can hold here, and protect this town to the best of our abilities against whatever danger presents itself. Or we can attempt to return to Ambitia, to fight our way through if necessary, and to assist in the defense of our Territory against what must indeed be an enemy attack."

Krazakowski's assessment seemed solid to Smith — the two options were to stay or go, and because unlike the once-besieged Fort Martian, Deadline was not an important town (maybe not even to the people who lived there) leaving was one of them.

"Gentlemen, I welcome any thoughts you might have, as we make this gravitious decision," Krazakowski ended on that note, and Smith frowned, unsure of the second-to-last word, but reckoning now wasn't the time to ask if it was real or invented.

Silence greeted his invitation for comment, none of the Captains in the room feeling terribly comfortable with the options being presented to them. Either staying or going could lead to certain doom, depending on what the blue men were up to. Smith reckoned someone just had to take a gamble, or maybe get more information and then make a choice.

Both trails, or neither, might lead to death.

"No word on the state of Ambitia, sir?" Captain Insetta asked after the silence had worn on for long seconds, knowing the likely answer to his question but deciding to pose it anyway.

Krazakowski shook his head, "No. I do think there may be utility to sending the train back, perhaps just with one car, for a reconnoiter. If the way is clear, that might influence our choice considerably."

A good point, and there were nods from the assembled officers. Adams spoke in support of the notion, "Yes sir, if we got a look at the town we'd have an advantage."

"And the tracks back," Koster added, looking to Krazakowski. "If they tore up the tracks somewhere, better to find out before we all try to use them."

Krazakowski was nodding as all of these suggestions were made, and then he folded his arms and grasped his chin with his right hand, frowning thoughtfully.

"Gentlemen, as usual, you provide a true bedrock of wisdom upon which sound military decisions may be made," the Major said, looking up. Then he caught sight of Smith, leaning in the doorway, and completely changed track: "Ah, thank you very much for joining us Mister Smith, your presence is most welcome!"

With that declaration, every man in the room looked back towards the drifter at the door. Smith's eyebrows went up and he nodded, "Happy to. I'll go on that scout train, if it'd be a help."

The drifter figured it made sense for him to get a look at the trouble behind them, because he might be better equipped than some to see the details of the problems they'd face. Maybe that was giving himself too much credit, but he still reckoned it'd be preferable to see the situation with his own eyes, then make his suggestions to the soldiers after that.

"Excellent. Captain Adams, are your men ready for a mission of this sort?" Krazakowski turned his eyes to the black officer, who nodded.

"Yes sir."

"Good, you'll accompany Mister Smith. Return to within sight of Ambitia, but take as few risks as you may. If the place is abandoned, and you can send a message to Pacifica City, please do. But we have few men and yours will be needed later, so please be cautious," Krazakowski was, as usual, quite earnest.

Adams nodded again, "Not to worry, sir."

"Very good," Krazakowski clapped his hands together. "You'll depart at first light tomorrow. Don't want you going on the rails in darkness, and don't want you gone if we face a night attack. Gentlemen, you may return to your posts."

The meeting ended on that note, and Smith stood aside as men began filing out of the card room. Koster, Adams and Krazakowski remained to speak about the particulars of the morning's mission, and Sergeant Turner from Adams' company hung back too, though he moved nearer the door so as not to be in the way of the discussions.

The drifter nodded to the Sergeant, and Turner answered the gesture with words, "Mister Smith."

"Major seems to have a good handle on the regiment," Smith observed in a quiet tone.

Turner answered: "He's been with us a long time. He's trusted and he's good."

Neither of them mentioned that he was also a little odd from time to time — seemed irrelevant. The bottom line was that he knew his job, and was a better soldier than a man like Robinson, the Custer-like Colonel they'd buried at Promised Town.

Turner had been a relatively quiet man on that previous mission, so it surprised Smith when the Sergeant continued speaking, "Haven't found another Colonel who wants us, since Robinson. Even with what we did at Promised Town."

There was bitterness in that tone, and Smith could understand why. The 25th was built of good men, and an opportunity for any good officer to lead real soldiers… but racialism, political problems and fear of commanding a perpetual ditch-digging unit probably kept away many promising officers.

Smith tilted his head and nodded, "Seems wrong to me, that you men don't get resupplied. But at least you don't have a bad leader."

"True," Turner agreed.

After that the two men stopped talking, and waited for the officers in charge of the mission to sort out their plans. Smith let them do that work without his interference; all he needed to wonder was whether he should bring his horse, or just his rifle. He'd wait to see what Adams and Krazakowski had in mind.

The engineer of the train that had taken the American troops to Deadline wasn't terribly enthusiastic when Krazakowski and Adams explained the mission to him. Unlike many train engineers the buffalo soldiers had encountered in Pacifica, this man seemed to have no problem with their color, but he did have considerable reservations about driving his engine 100 miles back through treacherous terrain, for a possible run-in with a horde.

"I ain't see the purpose to it," the man, named Bridey, protested after Krazakowski explained himself.

Smith watched the exchange, and as he expected, the American officer took absolutely no offense from the objection. Instead he answered like a school master, explaining his intentions more slowly and enunciating his words a with a little more clarity, "Sir, if we are to know how best to resist the blue men, it will be very important that we know where they are. Out here we are exposed… if there is an opportunity to reach Ambitia, we will have many more options."

Krazakowski didn't quite sound patronizing as he explained that, but Smith could have imagined a man getting upset at being told some simple facts like those. But Bridey wasn't the type to get riled up, so instead he wiped the sweat from his nervous brow with his sleeve and crumpled his dirty hat in his hands.

"I suppose... there's gonna be soldiers on with me right, though?"

"One carriage attached to your engine and coal truck. Captain Adams and his company will be aboard — close to fifty men."

Smith had heard that part of the plan back at the meeting, and again he was reminded that American regiments had a very different structure to British Empire ones. One of the Newfoundlanders' companies was 200 men, a platoon being fifty. But the United States Infantry hadn't joined up with the European models, and while things like company size didn't factor much into the chances of success on a mission like this, other purely American military ideas — like scattering regiments to posts across hundreds of miles — were probably aiding the blue men now.

Smith wasn't an expert on the subject, but he knew help was probably a lot farther away than it had been when he was trapped at Fort Martian...

"I'll does it," Bridey finally agreed with a nervous nod.

Krazakowski clasped the man on the shoulder, "Courageous fellow, my thanks."

With that, the Major turned from the engineer and saw Smith standing a few paces away, "Mister Smith, you still keen to join Captain Adams?"

"I'll go," the drifter answered. "I'll leave my horse."

"She will be well cared for, I assure you!" Krazakowski replied ardently, then grabbed the brim of his hat in salute before turning back to Adams.

"Your mission, Captain. I leave it in your capable hands. See me in the morning before you depart!"

"Yes sir," Adams saluted. Krazakowski did the same, then headed back towards headquarters.

As the Major left, Smith approached Adams, both men simultaneously adjusting their hats to shade their eyes against the sun that was lowering in the west.

"Appreciate you coming along, Mister Smith. We'll need every set of experienced eyes we can get," the Captain said evenly.

Smith considered his answer for a second, then nodded, "Reckon it's the right place to be. No telling what we'll find."

Adams was silent for a moment, then let out a sigh, "Trouble, probably."

Yes, that was likely.

There was no point repeating the danger, though, so Smith remained silent. The sun went down a little while later.

CHAPTER VII

Nights in New World City had an electric quality. Perhaps that was an obvious way to describe the atmosphere, considering the town featured electrical lighting on most of its streets, but Jimmy Devlin figured it was very apt: after dark the capital felt rife with a modern sort of excitement that never failed to uplift him.

Annie Devlin contributed to that feeling as well; her arm was looped around his, and as they made their way from the fine restaurant where they'd enjoyed a good meal, she shone as brightly as any of the lamps lining the street, happy to be with her husband.

People noticed the pair as they strode along easily — Devlin was a well-recognized officer now, and Annie had made her own impression on fashionable society. Neither of them let this mild celebrity go to their heads, though... in the end, he was just a Captain in one of the best regiments ever assembled, and she was just the former maid of the savage-born woman who was changing the conventions of what it meant to be a Lady.

Both of them were happy to have a small place in the events that were changing the course of history.

Which, as Devlin thought it, did actually seem a bit more heady than he perhaps wanted it to. No matter, he knew he'd keep his feet on the ground, whatever people said about him. Annie wouldn't let his ego swell.

Theirs was a silent walk — apart from the occasional 'good evening' to passers-by, they said nothing to each other. They didn't really need to speak; their happiness was contagious and evident to anyone watching. It was obviously mutual, and obviously deep.

So instead of talking, they enjoyed the atmosphere of activity that was able to thrive in defiance of the night, thanks to the presence of the street lamps and the two moons that shone overhead.

Devlin was basking in this environment when he noticed a uniformed figure hurrying up to the cable office ahead. The fellow looked awfully like Harry Crerar, Byng's trusted staff officer, but even with the electric lights it was too far for the Newfoundland Captain to make a certain identification.

He said nothing to Annie about the observation, though when he tensed slightly and his stride altered, she looked at him.

"What did you see?"

She knew him well, and he glanced at her with a sheepish smile, "I think that was Harry Crerar hurrying to the telegraph office."

Annie frowned, recognizing both the name and the possible significance of that destination for that particular man. Word of trouble? People could receive telegrams for all sorts of reasons — it didn't have to be bad news. But somehow it felt like this had to be a serious development, and as Annie turned her eyes forward and watched the office grow larger with their approach, she felt her own tension increasing.

Jimmy noticed his wife's growing anxiety and regretted causing it... but he still wanted to know what Crerar was after.

Slowing outside the telegraph office, Annie and Jimmy both peered through the building's open door and saw Byng's staff Lieutenant at the counter, having an urgent-looking discussion with the operator. The man behind the counter was shaking his head, and Crerar's hands were planted on the table, his head bobbing slightly as he spoke in a firm manner.

It definitely appeared to be serious, so Jimmy came to a stop, Annie keeping hold of him and halting too.

They waited, staring in the doorway for a few minutes and trying unsuccessfully to eavesdrop until Crerar finished his discussions and turned to make his exit, putting his hat back on his head. As he made his way to the door, the Lieutenant spotted the Devlins outside and tugged his hat's brim in salute.

Jimmy returned the gesture, "Business, Harry?"

Crerar frowned and shook his head, "Just been hearing rumors that the American telegraphs are down. People haven't been able to get through to the rail towns south of the Dead River, out in the badlands down there. Sir Julian is wondering whether it's something on our end, or theirs."

That did sound unusual, and a frown creased Jimmy's brow, "What'd the operator have to say?"

Crerar offered a very slight shrug, "He says their end. Which would mean the wires went down somewhere along their line."

Such a development might be entirely innocent, but it seemed an ominous turn of events. The blue men had proved relatively adept (if not masterful) at cutting the wire along the British rail line when they'd launched their reprisal against Selkirk months before. This could be their work again.

But surely if there was an attack, the Americans would have contacted their northern allies immediately. Such was the nature of the special relationship the Empire and the States had constructed since the discovery of the new world...

"How long have the wires been disrupted?" Annie surprised Jimmy when she put that question to Crerar, but the Lieutenant didn't miss a beat in answering.

"This morning, we think. It's probably something simple... a tree down on the line, or maybe bandits making mischief. We've had no word of trouble from Pacifica City, just routine messages."

"Probably a good sign," Devlin suggested, and Crerar agreed.

"Indeed. Anyway, sorry, but I must report to Sir Julian."

"Of course," Jimmy nodded, and then Annie delivered the parting words for both of them.

"Good night, Lieutenant Crerar."

The staff officer smiled, again tugged on the brim of his hat, and made his way past the pair. As he moved off, the frown began to lift from Jimmy's brow... but it didn't vanish entirely. Considering the side of her husband's face, Annie asked the question to which she didn't necessarily want an answer: "Worried?"

Captain Devlin of the Royal Newfoundland Regiment took a breath, then nodded, "I believe I am."

There was something unusual going on, and he didn't know what it was. If it was dangerous, though, chances were good that he and the b'ys would find themselves in the middle of it.

But there was nothing to do about that for now, so he finally smiled and nodded down the road ahead, "Let's not waste the night over it."

With a smile of her own, Annie fell into step beside her husband again, their arms still interlocked.

Sass was trying to restore the sub-orbital sensor array from one of the two Hubrin ships they'd captured, but it wasn't proving easy. Part of the problem was simply the scale: her claws were massive, while Hubrin hands were tiny. When it came to work at such a miniature size, she wasn't nearly as deft as she wanted to be.

Perhaps in time, some of the humans could learn enough to offer their assistance, but they'd need a common language first. That wouldn't happen overnight, so for now she was stuck trying to needle controls with the tips of her claws. Slow work — but important.

The run-down transports that had served the prison camp were like most of the Hubrin's other resources on this world: dilapidated and out of date. This planet was in a rear area, after all — useful to the blue creatures for attacker training, but not deserving of any real combat resources when four Saa armadas were forcing action against the dominant Hubrin star systems light years away. Had this place in fact been a major priority to the Hubrin, the humans would long ago have been wiped out.

Many concerns came with that revelation, and Sass and Sask had spoken of it numerous times since landing in the central human settlement. These freed attackers had the resources to fight their unfree counterparts quite effectively, but a single orbital bombardment could probably render their entire colony in the foothills to ash.

It was up to Sass to find a way to contact her own fleet command — and to do so before the Hubrin managed to move a warship into this part of space. Using whatever she could scrape together from these two ancient, run-down prisoner transports, she had to build an interstellar comms array... and come up with any other technology that might help her party of survivors, and the humans who were their hosts, against the sparse military resources that the Hubrin *did* have on this planet.

Sub-orbital scanners would be a major first step, since the humans lacked any sort of air-search capability beyond sight. Even a simple sensor array could let them all know if the Hubrin were using some of their remaining transports and med-jumpers to drop attackers off for strike missions…

If the equipment would work.

It really was slow going, and Sass finally decided to take a break, putting the tiny unit down beside her tail while she looked skyward again. She was very far from home, but at least she was alive. Most of her ship's crew had perished in its destruction… for a time, she'd believed them to be the lucky ones. Had the attackers been able to kill her for their training purposes — a death that would have been truly agonizing — then her lost fellows would indeed have been more fortunate.

But now she was alive, and her fortune seemed to be improving.

She'd somehow find a way to build a transmitter that could send a signal all the way across the galaxy. She had the equipment salvaged to send a message, but she lacked the power supply to send it very far… If only they were closer to home.

But there would be a solution. There always was.

As Sass thought those words in her native language (which would have been incomprehensible to both human and Hubrin) her hearing senses picked up the sound of a familiar approach. The soldier called Devlin was nearby.

Turning away from her work, Sass looked in the direction of the street as Devlin and a female of the species appeared, walking arm in arm. Both seemed to carry a little tension with them, and Sass wondered what they might have experienced to warrant such a reaction. Obvious language barriers aside, she decided to try to find out.

"The dragons are just in there, aren't they?" Annie whispered as she and Jimmy began to pass the park in which the aircruisers had landed.

The Captain nodded, "Just…"

Sass was suddenly, silently, right at the edge of the park, her head extending out into the street and craning to look directly at the Devlins. Annie stopped with a jolt of surprise, her arms tightening around Jimmy's for a second.

"Evening, Sass," the Captain just barely kept his wits, and then smiled nervously. "When it's dark, you come out of nowhere even quieter!"

Sass still couldn't quite break down the language of the humans — some words, like names, were comprehensible when said in isolation, but the entire combination of sounds remained quite alien. However, it seemed obvious that her rapid appearance in the darkness had startled both the soldier and the female who, Sass assumed based on smell, was his mate. That in mind, she lowered herself down to try to look less like she was looming, then nodded in a human-style greeting.

Annie had yet to properly meet one of the dragons, so she considered the massive creature with somewhat wide eyes, "She's very... silent."

"I know, like a lizard," Jimmy agreed, and then they ran out of things to say.

Sass, similarly, had nothing she could say — she looked forward to having a written form of communication, but for now she shifted her gaze between the two humans, then rotated her head sideways — almost ninety degrees to the left — hoping to imply that she was asking how their evening was.

"She has a very flexible neck," Annie observed as Sass made this gesture, and Jimmy nodded.

"Yes... I think... well when a dog does that, I think it's a question. So..."

Annie frowned thoughtfully, then picked up the message, "We're having a lovely evening, thank you for asking."

As she said that, she smiled and nodded in an exaggerated fashion, pulling herself even closer to Jimmy so that it was clear she was enjoying his company.

Sass studied the body language carefully before leveling out her head and presenting an upturned palm. Saying 'yes' probably wasn't quite the ideal response, but it was as close as she could get to indicating her pleasure that they were enjoying themselves, and the humans seemed to pick up on the gesture's positive connotation.

"I think she's approving," Jimmy nodded to Sass in thanks.

Then he frowned, a question occurring to him. With his free hand, he pointed to the dragon, then to his wife. Then he pointed to himself, and pointed at the empty space beside Sass. Annie followed the gestures with her eyes, and discerned the meaning: did Sass have a husband?

Considering the motions for a moment, Sass thought quickly about their meaning. It seemed likely Devlin was asking whether she had a mate, which she did. She therefore showed an upturned palm, and for some reason, the smiles on the faces of both Jimmy and Annie grew. Perhaps it was their joy at the evening they'd spent together, or the fact that their communication was proving successful, but either way, they found the answer pleasing.

Sass spared a second then to think of her mate, who was very far away, a medical practitioner on one of the central colonies. Almost surely he would think her dead, but she believed now she would see him again. It was a warm feeling, and she appreciated it.

But this was not the time for dwelling on such things. She would see him sooner if she could get the Hubrin technology to serve the survivors here, and support the freed attackers. That in mind, Sass rose from her four feet to her full height, Annie and Jimmy watching and marveling at the whole process.

Then the dragon dipped her head in a sort of bow — a gesture similar to one she'd seen humans make — and gestured back towards the park. Both Annie and Jimmy bowed back, and then Jimmy touched the brim of his hat.

Recognizing that was a parting gesture, Sass vanished in silence, back to her work on the sub-orbital sensor unit.

Jimmy and Annie stayed still in the street for a moment after that, and then they looked at each other. It took only seconds of a shared gaze for the excitement to erupt from Annie: "She's marvelous!"

"She is," Jimmy agreed with a smile, enjoying his bride's warm reaction.

They began walking again, slowly making their way back to their rented house, but Annie was still affected. She shook her head, "And a mechanic of some sort, you said?"

"We think so… she sure is working on the blue man machines a lot," Jimmy confirmed.

"Incredible."

It was indeed. The dragons had been marvelous guests so far, and though Jimmy knew things might change when written communication became a reality between the two races, he figured there was a good chance that first impressions would bear up.

For his part, he had no interest in shooting a dragon in its brain. And that, he knew, was as good a point as any from which to build a friendship.

Captain Devlin and his wife Annie forgot their concerns about the loss of communication with American towns, and walked home through the electric night.

CHAPTER VIII

Breakfast was ready by the time Waller reached the kitchen of his rented house. Alice Walters — now Alice Waller again, by her own choice after the death of her no-good husband — was still staying with her brother, and despite the shock of everything that had occurred, she remained a Newfoundlander to the core: she knew the value of a good breakfast, and she made certain one was ready.

Tom appreciated this effort — it was a reminder of home, and his younger days when Alice had always been nearby and looking after him as best she could. Since the shooting of Emily, he'd spent relatively little time with his sister, but breakfast was one thing they continued to share, and he valued it.

"Morning," he greeted her as he entered the kitchen, and Alice looked back to him.

"Eggs are almost ready."

Waller nodded as he moved towards the kitchen table and picked up the newspaper that lay there. One of the front page stories bore the headline 'American Telegraph Service Breaks Down', and that brought a frown to his face. He walked with the paper over to the pot of coffee that stood on the stove, then read the first few lines as he pulled a cup from its perch and began pouring the hot brew.

"What started you on coffee?" Alice asked as she pulled the eggs from the stove, and Waller blinked and glanced at her.

"Promised Town, I think," he replied before setting the pot down again and taking his cup back to the table. "Still don't like the stuff... just necessary."

Alice raised an eyebrow as she shifted the eggs to a plate for him, "Yes, keeps you going through those long hours in the hospital."

Waller didn't notice anything unusual about his sister's tone, and that was just as well. His focus was on the paper when he returned to her side to collect his plate, so he didn't realize he had neither fork nor knife until he sat down again. Alice appeared with both a second later, and then eventually joined him at the opposite side of the table.

He was frowning at the report in the paper as he began to eat, and Alice studied his face, "Something interesting?"

Waller didn't respond for a second, considering what he was reading carefully before coming to any conclusions. The American telegraph lines to the south of the Dead River seemed to be down... no one could get any response from Destina or Ambitia. Having never travelled to those parts of the Pacifica Territory, Waller could picture neither town, but he recalled both locations from the maps he'd seen of the new world...

Interesting places for breakdowns to occur, and the author of the article seemed to be quite concerned. Silence meant businessmen with interests in the southern parts of the settled new world territory couldn't check in on their investments... and that no one could report on any savage movements in the badlands to the south of the river.

It was the last point that stuck in Waller's mind... surely the Americans had to be concerned about that gap in their defense.

A visit to headquarters on the way to the hospital might be in order.

"Tom?"

Alice's voice pierced Waller's musing, and he looked up from the paper, "Sorry. We've lost wire contact with some of the southern settlements in the American territory. It's unusual."

She frowned as she ate, then between bites said: "Would the Americans tell us if there was trouble?"

It was probably meant as a rhetorical question — at least partially — but it was one that struck Waller oddly. Would the Americans admit if they were under attack?

Waller hurried through his breakfast.

"It's damned unusual," Currie was saying when Waller arrived in Byng's office. The Colonel was speaking to Skeen, who was the first to see Waller arrive, and who nodded to him as he entered.

The Indian Army General had indeed switched from his pith helmet to the tan version of Waller's own drab green hat, but the man's uniform remained otherwise unchanged — the tan-khaki version of the British Army's overseas service dress.

Turning his eyes back to Currie, Skeen nodded, "You'd expect if there was trouble, we'd be their first call. The Yanks must know we have far more resources, and far better troops, than they do."

Waller had arrived in the middle of a conversation, but already he was picking up the strands, and as he approached the two men standing near the office's window he decided to join in, "I know they have at least some good troops, sir. But they're scattered all over the territory. Very poor arrangement for defense."

Currie recognized Waller's voice and nodded back to him in acknowledgment of his arrival, then added some narration for the Newfoundlander's benefit: "Sir Julian just went to the communication office to call General Pershing on the special telephone."

Waller began to nod, but then stopped, "Special telephone?"

Seeing the flash of confusion, Skeen smiled, "That was my reaction. Apparently there's a telephone line directly from here to Pershing's headquarters. Put in after your foray to Promised Town, in the interests of close communication between allies."

"Serving the special relationship," Currie added, and Waller offered a single, silent nod in reply. Sounded sensible.

"We think there's trouble down there?" the Newfoundland Colonel asked, and Currie shrugged.

"It's suspicious. The blues haven't attacked in months, and considering the difficulty we gave them, they might have decided to go after our weaker cousins."

It would make sense. There was no mistaking the fact that the scattered American settlements were far more vulnerable than any place in Selkirk — some towns were nearly two weeks from help, and were only reachable by horse, not rail. That made for an obvious contrast: most towns in the British mandate were connected by rail, with troops invested in them, and reinforcements just hours away.

The fact that rancher blue men had been able to overrun Promised Town, while the blue man military had been driven back during its attack on Farpoint, was probably a clear signal to the creatures about which quarter was weaker.

But were the Martians attacking? So far it was just a breakdown in communications, and those could happen for any number of reasons.

Hopefully Byng would have an answer for them soon.

Waller, Skeen and Currie continued their speculative conversations for a few more minutes, only falling silent when they heard the boots of Sir Julian Byng in the corridor beyond his office door. They all turned to face that entrance as the mustached General clomped in.

He looked not at all calm.

"Gentlemen, savages were dropped by aircruiser on Ambitia and Destina yesterday. The Pacifica Territory is under serious threat."

Waller blinked.

Currie's jaw dropped.

Sir Andrew Skeen folded his arms and said: "I believe someone needs to explain this special relationship to me."

"I have a hell of a lot more to explain to you, Sir Andrew," Byng replied darkly, moving over to the map table that stood on the far side of his office. The three officers joined him without delay, and as Byng unrolled a new world map that showed Pacifica, he let out a throaty growl.

"Pershing is keeping word of the attack as quiet as he can. He doesn't have any idea where the savages are going to come from, but apparently aircruisers like the one you saw at Fort Martian, Tom, dropped a few hundred each on Ambitia and Destina. No warning, and neither town had a garrison anyway. God only knows why they didn't drop the savages straight onto Pacifica City... but now they've disrupted all communications with posts in their grasslands south of the Dead River."

As he explained the situation, Byng began gesturing to the area in question with an open hand. The Americans had never strayed too far out into the grasslands by rail, and what half-hearted attempts had been made were down far to the south of British territory. Rail speculators had guessed — correctly, as it turned out — that the British line running closely and efficiently near the border would attract any American travelers wanting to go west in the northern part of the explored new world. That in mind, they'd built their lines far to the south, where there was no competition.

And as a result, they were far from help.

With Destina and Ambitia fallen, all of those places — cities like Deadline, Defiance and Gateway Town — were cut off. The savages could come at Pacifica from any approach they liked, and no one would see them until they were two-thirds of the way to the American territory's capital.

It was a defensive disaster, and Pershing had precious few troops with which he could do anything about it.

All of these truths were readily apparent to Currie, Skeen and Waller.

"Because he can't protect everything, Pershing is trying to keep the story quiet... avoid panic. Don't know whether I'd do the same in his place, but that's no matter right now," Byng continued his explanation, moving his finger to the dot that marked Pacifica City. "He has to hold the capital. If the blue men take it, they get access to a tunnel to the old world."

That, of course, was the greatest danger of all. For all the battles fought here on the new world, none were important compared to the fate of the old mother Earth. If savages were able to break out onto the North American continent, with its countless plains and prairies, there would be no containing them. That was why the tunnel entrance in New World City was so powerfully protected, and why the exit on the Canadian side — back in Alberta — was similarly fortified.

But Waller had never seen Pacifica City's defenses... he had no idea if the settlement was equipped to stop a horde. The thought made his pulse quicken, but Byng kept his attention away from thoughts of possible horror.

"Black Jack's collecting all his reserves... close to 19,000 men... around Pacifica City. Now look here, their capital sits in the middle of a 'V' made by two rivers, the America River to the south and the Pacifica River to the north. He's going to make those rivers his line, considering how much trouble we know savages have in fast-moving water."

Skeen leaned forward at the reference, his eyes scanning the still-unfamiliar map to see precisely where Byng was indicating. He then frowned, "The American River is thirty miles from the city. And it's nearly

200 miles long. He'd need ten times as many men."

Byng nodded, "I mentioned that. I also told him that since the savages can be transported in the air, a river's useless as a defensive line. He's working with what he has."

That didn't sound terribly optimistic, and as the four men at the map table fell silent, Waller stared at the rivers too. Only to someone who hadn't fought savages could Pershing's deployment seem at all hopeful... but even Skeen was seeing through it. With or without the support of an aircruiser, the blue men could undoubtedly find an unprotected crossing somewhere. Or perhaps they could build a bridge.

Either way, Pacifica City was in grave danger, and because its fall would jeopardize Canada as well as the United States and the Selkirk Mandate, that was suddenly a British Empire problem.

"Obviously we have to do something," Byng said with a growl, and then looked up at his officers. "I'm open to suggestions."

The first thought that leapt to Waller's mind was straightforward: a new division was on the new world, and Skeen's 20,000 men could at least stiffen the river defenses of the American territory's capital — and put an experienced commander in charge to support Pershing.

But as Waller's eyes rose from the map to scan Skeen's expression, it seemed obvious that Sir Andrew was seeing the map differently.

"So they landed only a hundred on each town..." the Indian Army officer said quietly. "Perhaps their transport is limited. Otherwise they'd have landed more."

"They could have landed more since the wires were cut," Currie pointed out, and Skeen paused and then agreed with the Canadian's point.

"Of course. But that would be quite an operation. If they could move hordes by air, this mandate would have been overrun last year. They could have moved in more aircruisers since then... but perhaps not..."

As was his habit, Skeen was thinking out loud, but Waller was so out of practice in briefings with the man that he couldn't get ahead of the thought train quickly enough.

Skeen didn't make him wait: "Sir Julian, they attacked those two towns to blind Pershing to moves in the badlands... which suggests to me they're doing something out there."

Byng's hands were thrust deep into his pockets, but he pulled one free now to brush his mustache, "You want to go find out, Sir Andrew?"

The Indian Army officer narrowed his eyes a little hungrily, and Waller immediately recognized the expression: Skeen's gut was telling him he'd figured his foe's agenda, and now he meant to counter it.

"I studied photos of the badlands on the long trip out here. Familiar ground for my division... all those heights and cliffs can't be good for hordes, but my men know how to fight in them. If we could find them out there, without any civilians nearby to concern ourselves with, we could make their lives hell."

It was an impossibly ambitious boast, and both Currie and Byng seemed to stiffen slightly at the prospect. Just weeks before, Evelyn Hughes had been similarly convinced of the power of his lorries to cross the grasslands... Indian Army troops were good men, but did Skeen really think some uneven ground would allow him to stop a horde?

Waller stared at Skeen as that question played in his mind, and the Newfoundland Colonel was distinctly aware of the thoughts he should have been having — that this was foolhardy, that Skeen didn't know what he was in for, and that despite the merits of engaging an enemy far from the towns of the foothills, it would be an inevitable disaster.

But those weren't the thoughts Waller was actually having. Because somehow he believed Skeen.

"I think... he's right," the Wall almost blurted that out, drawing surprised gazes from both Currie and Byng.

"Tom?" the latter General asked, and the Newfoundlander nodded once, his gaze meeting Skeen's.

"We have air travel available to us... we can ask the dragons to take us down there for a look, and see what's coming," Sir Andrew spoke again, a plan quickly forming in his mind. "If we can find some advantageous ground, we can do some damage."

Byng blinked, looking from Waller to Skeen and back again, "Or you could lose a whole division at some blasted imitation of Isandlwana."

Or that.

Waller's pulse had quickened, and he was beginning to remember the thrill of briefings with Skeen. The General had never let anxiety or fear slow him down... his was a game of sensible, calculated risks. He was never impetuous, but he knew which days warranted ambitious action.

And looking at a map shrouded in mystery, he felt such a moment coming on.

"What about a compromise?" Waller blinked himself from musing, and looked to Byng.

The military governor of Selkirk remained surprised by the candor — the very notion of a Lieutenant Colonel negotiating between two General officers was silly.

But owing to Waller's storied experience in fighting the blue men, Byng listened. So did Skeen.

"I'll see if I can talk Sass into taking us down to the badlands for a look. General Skeen can go to Pacifica City with his division to reinforce Pershing... but if we find an opportunity out in the badlands, we can collect his division by air and take advantage of it."

In that moment, it did not even occur to Waller that he was volunteering not only his b'ys but the dragons for a dangerous, potentially one-way mission. Currie, however, had not missed the obvious: "You want to take your b'ys out again, Tom? We could hold them in reserve."

Waller paused at that offer, but looking back to Skeen he knew no other regiment would be as well suited for the scouting job — they knew the dragons, they knew Skeen's Indians, and they knew the blue men. It had to be the Royal Newfoundland Regiment.

"We're best suited, I think," was his answer.

Byng listened to Waller's words in silence. His eyes fell back to the map, crossing the hopeless defensive lines at the America River, and then travelling out to the vast emptiness of the badlands. Surprising the blue men out there, with veteran mountain-fighters... it would show the Martians a British Army they'd yet to face, and it could be a success.

Worth the risk?

"No more than one brigade, Sir Andrew. If you find a place out there to do them harm, take no more than a brigade to do it. If you need more men than that, the risk is too great."

It was indeed a compromise, and Skeen would take it, "We'll find good ground, Sir Julian."

"I'll count on that. Make preparations to move your division by rail to Pacifica City. Edwin can help with the logistics, when he gets here. Tom, you sweet-talked yourself into one powerful Lady's good graces... good luck doing the same with Sass."

Waller hadn't been ready for the comparison of Sass to Emily, but he supposed it made some sense. In any case, he hoped the dragon lady would understand this opportunity.

Hopefully it *was* an opportunity...

CHAPTER IX

There were sounds of commotion outside Emily's window. As her savage-tuned hearing fixed on the noises, a frown crossed her brow; soldiers were getting prepared for some sort of urgent deployment.

What could demand such haste... an attack?

Alice Waller was sitting beside Emily's bed, but her normal hearing, and the fact that she hadn't spent months in the field with an infantry regiment, kept the sounds from meaning anything particular to her.

She was reading the same paper that Annie had abandoned the day before — a new one had yet to be picked up — and seemed to be paying no attention to the world beyond the room, or Emily for that matter. The already fragile relationship between the two women had become strained, but that didn't stop Tom's sister from fulfilling her obligations to sit with her brother's Lady.

Another noise joined the commotion, this time from within the hospital. Emily recognized it instantly: the thud of army boots on the floorboards, and from the tempo Emily knew Tom was coming. He was hurrying... Something serious was definitely afoot.

And Emily was convalescing.

Turning her eyes down to her abdomen, now bandaged and no longer hooked up to irrigation tubes, she wondered briefly if she could get to her feet. If the circumstances demanded action, could she force her way out of this hospital and join the b'ys?

She started to sit up, but the strain that simple act placed on her torso muscles sent a dagger through her, and with a grimace she eased herself back. Dammit.

By the time Waller came through the door, Emily had cleared any sign of discomfort from her face. Alice looked up casually, then read her brother's expression and immediately lowered her paper, "Tom?"

The Colonel nodded to his sister before turning his eyes to Emily. His frown conveyed most of the message before any words managed to emerge: "The blue men seem to be assaulting the American territory. Pershing has virtually nothing in place to stop them. General Skeen is looking for an opportunity to ambush the Martians as they come up, so we have to get out there with him to help find the best location."

Emily had been prepared for worse news — that a fleet of aircruisers was only minutes away, perhaps — but this was still bad enough.

"Why... do you have to go protect an American city?" Alice asked the question, and given her recent arrival on the new world it was a very sensible one.

Turning his eyes to his sister, Tom Waller shook his head, "They have a tunnel home, just the same as we do here. If that falls, we could have savages roaming the American west... and if they make it there, we'd never be able to contain them."

Alice blinked, then nodded, "Right."

Tom's eyes were already turned back to Emily, and immediately his sister realized she was an unwelcome imposition in the room. Though she couldn't quite fathom why her brother was so dedicated to Emily, she knew the question wasn't hers to ask, at least for the moment.

"I'll go see if Annie needs any help... with... cooking... for the b'ys..." she plucked a somewhat plausible excuse from the air, then rose from her chair and left the room.

Neither Emily nor Waller seemed to register her departure.

"You said Skeen wants to ambush the blue men?"

Waller shook his head slightly, "If there's an opportunity. Pershing is drawing up static defense lines against an attack he doesn't have information on. Skeen knows it's better to take the fight to the enemy, out in a place where there aren't civilians around to be put at risk."

The certainty in Waller's voice deepened the frown that was forming on Emily's brow — he was talking about a fight in the open against savages and blue men, which inherently seemed risky. But he wasn't at all reluctant... his bearing suggested he was even eager...

"So you know what's coming. You're not just planning some sort of ambush somewhere, sometime?"

The disapproval in her tone was sharper than she intended, but it was as honest as Byng's skepticism had been. Waller recognized it immediately, but refused to let it frustrate him. People who hadn't been with Skeen in Afghanistan just couldn't understand...

"We'll only stage the ambush if it makes sense. We're hoping the dragons will fly us down for a look, while Skeen's division takes the train to Pacifica City. We'll collect Sir Andrew and a brigade, if there's a good opportunity for offense."

Those words did little to satisfy Emily: "You meaning the b'ys. You want to take them by air into the unknown, to go after blue men you don't know exist? What if they're waiting for you?"

Prudent questions that reflected just a few of the many criticisms Waller knew could exist. But again, Skeen was always right about these moments... about finding the times to attack. His foes never saw him coming, and this would be no different. Waller just knew it.

"I'll see you when I'm back. And I promise I'll be back," he halted any further questions with that simple assertion, and Emily's mouth fell open in surprise at his dismissal of her concerns.

"I—"

Waller stopped her with a kiss, deep and proper. It was an unfair tactic, but effective enough. As soon as he drew his lips back from hers, he turned and hurried from her hospital room.

And Emily stared at the empty doorway after he went. She barely recognized the man who had come and gone... how was it possible that Skeen could have so undermined his reason?

The savage-born Lady didn't know, but as the reality of his determination settled in, her frustration began to grow exponentially... along with her fear. Tom Waller was chasing off into the unknown, seemingly blind to the dangers he was so often aware of...

And she was in bed, because the last time he'd been sent into the field, she'd been too sorry for herself to follow him.

Forcing her head back into her pillow, all she could do was stifle a frustrated scream. She was left behind again... and this time she knew Tom would truly need her.

CHAPTER X

Bert Miller was staring up at Sass and Sask as the two dragons hissed to each other with a completely incomprehensible cadence. The commotion of men getting ready to march had not escaped the notice of the giant creatures, but they didn't seem too agitated. Miller had managed to convey to them that an attack wasn't coming towards New World City — at least as far as anyone knew — but beyond that, it was tough to communicate mission orders through hand gestures.

Looking down from the dragons and their hissing, the Skipper wondered where that schoolteacher was. He'd sent Kennedy to fetch her and all her picture cards, and whatever else she was using to try to convey written English to the dragons... surely she'd arrive soon. Waller couldn't be far away either — his distractions with Emily simply couldn't absorb him on this afternoon.

"Any sign of Missus Lewis?" the Colonel abruptly arrived at the Skipper's side with that question, and as the little old Major turned he found his young superior looking quite focused.

"Been to the hospital yet?" Miller asked, wondering if distraction was ahead or behind.

"Yes. Why?"

The Skipper considered his answer for a second, then decided there was no point elaborating, "Glad you're all set."

Waller frowned at the Skipper's words, but then decided simply to nod, "Yes. Well. The schoolteacher? Or have the dragons managed to intuit our intentions?"

Miller smiled at the last question, then shook his head: "Afraid they haven't asked if we need them to fly us to an unknown location in the American territory to join a Skeen ambush against an enemy we haven't found yet."

"How inconsiderate of them," Waller smiled, and that expression tipped Miller off to the Colonel's state of mind. He was eager for a fight.

"Think Sir Andrew has the blue men figured out already?"

Smile fading at the question, the Wall looked down at the Skipper, wondering if the RNR's dad was doubting this venture. Miller knew Skeen's ability — knew what he'd accomplished so many times in Afghanistan. It was never easy, and often bloody, but Sir Andrew had consistently bested his opposite number. And no man could say beating Pathan tribesmen in their own lands was simple.

Could he be doubting, as Byng and Emily had?

"The b'ys were sure he was right as soon as the messenger came," Miller shook his head. "Would have been easier if they'd heard it straight from you first, but important thing is they trust Sir Andrew. Even when he hasn't seen savages. And they trust you for agreeing with him. So as long as you're sure, I'm sure."

The Skipper was feeling cautious, but he'd been with Byng at Farpoint — knew savages weren't invincible, and that their blue men masters could die too. He'd seen Skeen in action, and knew Tom Waller was a fine officer... so this mission made sense as long as Waller was fully present in his own mind for it.

"I'm sure," the Wall said evenly in reply, and studying the young Colonel's face, Miller decided it was the truth. He might have stopped at the hospital before coming to the start of the mission, but that was no matter. The Wall was here, and so was Skeen. And they both believed in this march.

The two men fell silent for a few moments, and then in a bit of a production, Lieutenant Kennedy arrived with the teacher in tow. Missus Lewis was not a particularly specialized school mistress... she just happened to be the one Byng's staff had first encountered when seeking someone accustomed to breaking down the English language into learnable pieces.

Linguists from Canada and Britain would soon arrive to replace her, but in the meantime, she was the closest thing they had to an interpreter.

"I certainly hope your soldiers who abducted me do not shoot any of my students!" Lewis protested as soon as she recognized Waller from his picture in the papers. Her protest made absolutely no sense, and the Colonel did not receive it sympathetically.

"We don't make a habit of shooting children," he answered. "I've never had a fondness for teachers, though."

Staring back in open-mouthed shock, Lewis puffed up to protest, but Miller interceded.

"Now Missus, we're preparing here for a mission about the fate of the new world. So if you mean to say anything rude, I'd suggest you wait until you're alone."

Lewis turned her glare onto the Skipper, but the little old man had seen far worse, and he was unaffected. Turning halfway, he waved his arm towards the dragons, just as Saan, the one who'd been working on written English, noticed Lewis' arrival and approached.

Hissing something to Sass and Sask, Saan came down onto all fours so he'd be closer to the relatively small images Lewis had to offer. The other two dragons remained at their full height, but fell silent as they waited to hear what was happening.

Turning to Lewis, Waller began, "We need to convey the fact that a blue man attack is coming in Pacifica."

Setting aside her frustrations, the teacher opened her satchel and withdrew a thick bundle of cards, each about the size of a typed sheet of paper.

"You don't have anything bigger?" Waller asked with a frown, and that earned him a glare. Instead of replying, Lewis flipped to a page with a photograph of one of the captured blue men pasted to it. She held it up towards Saan, and he hissed something that almost sounded like 'human'.

What it sounded like didn't matter. Lewis was already hurrying to the next card... a heroic sketch of a soldier with a bayonet fitted to his SMLE as he fought a savage. Waller recognized the picture as being one from a newspaper account of the battle at Farpoint. Underneath the image in capital letters was the word BATTLE.

Whether that was the best word for the picture, Waller didn't know — he might have thought of fight, or combat, or a number of other words... but he wasn't a teacher.

Saan hissed something else back to his superiors, and as Waller turned his eyes up to Sass, she nodded. So far there wasn't too much to work with.

Next, Lewis produced a map of the new world, which promised riches and adventure. Waller had seen it before, and thought it to be a rather unimpressive mapmaking effort — the sort of thing a cheap publisher would provide in assembling a pamphlet to draw prospectors to Selkirk. Nevertheless, it showed the disposition of the world, and it appeared Lewis had used it with Saan before.

Pointing to New World City, she nodded towards Saan, and the dragon raised one hand and pointed his claw at the dirt beneath his feet. He knew where they were.

Lewis then nodded and moved her finger down to Pacifica City, before pointing again to the previous two cards, which were lying in the dirt beside her feet.

Saan looked from the cards to the map and back, then hissed something else. As soon as the sounds emerged, Sass was on all fours as well, moving with her customary silence. She studied the map, then hurried away.

Waller didn't understand the dragon's departure at first, but then he realized she might be seeking a different sort of information to clarify this brief. Scale was probably the most important missing piece at the moment — the dragons likely had no concept of what a mile was — but if Sass could find a map on one of the aircruisers' moving picture screens, perhaps she could figure out how far away the battle was from her current location.

So far, at least, the communication was working.

"Alright, we need to ask them to fly us to the badlands, while other troops move by train," Waller turned back to Lewis, and she scowled.

"We don't have functional writing yet, Colonel. I have to play this game of charades!"

The protest didn't seem entirely connected to the order, and even if it had been, Waller remained unimpressed by the woman's tone.

"Give me the cards and get out of the way," he said directly.

Lewis' jaw dropped, "I was appointed to this duty by the staff of Sir Julian Byng!"

Waller turned to her and stretched out his hand, "I was appointed to this mission by Sir Julian himself. The cards, please."

Miller shifted his weight from foot to foot at the cold words. He'd heard that Waller had gotten a bit unkind at Promised Town, and now it was happening again — increasingly of late, whenever he got onto a tough mission, he tended to get intolerant of ignorance.

The teacher huffed and handed him the bag, then backed away. Not knowing what she should do, she just stood there and watched as Waller started flipping through the available images. Some of the ones he needed were there, but not all.

"Kennedy," he said with a frown as he flipped, and the Lieutenant came over with a nod.

"Sir?"

"Go find me an Indian soldier. Or officer. Don't care who, just a man in tan who we can borrow for a moment."

With a quick salute, the Lieutenant hurried back towards the street, while Waller started drawing cards and handing them to Miller, "Could you hold these for me, Skipper?"

The Major did, looking at each as he took it. Waller was trying to explain the entire mission through sketches and photos...

"I had hoped we could have at least written simple sentences back and forth," the Colonel said, ostensibly to his Major, but aware that Lewis could hear him.

That was enough; she made a disagreeable noise and stomped away. Hardly a good example for the children she was teaching, but then, those poor youths were trapped in a schoolhouse with Sergeant Halloran, who apparently might shoot them.

"Bit hard on her," Miller leaned in close to Waller as the Colonel continued choosing his cards.

"I'm aware," Waller replied, and then Kennedy returned with three Gurkhas, all of them looking a little confused.

"Thank you, Shawn. You men stand over here..." Waller gestured to the space Lewis had vacated, and the Indian Army soldiers did as they were asked.

With them in place, Waller collected the cards from Miller and began laying them out. Saan followed the Colonel with his large eyes — for his part, the dragon was surprised that the woman with whom he'd been trying ineffectively to liaise for days had been so easily replaced with someone who could communicate much more quickly. It was certainly an improvement...

Sass returned as the cards were laid out, and hissed to him the distance between their current location and the point of attack, based on the geographical features — bodies of water, mainly — that could be observed on both human maps and Hubrin surface scans.

It was scarcely forty decas — a short flight away.

Waller finished laying out his pictures, then turned toward the dragons. Sass had settled down onto all fours again, and was looming curiously over the images as well, so the Colonel nodded to her.

"We have to send reinforcements to defend the American territory," he motioned towards himself, Miller, Kennedy, and the Gurkhas, then pointing towards Pacifica.

Sass and Saan both nodded.

"The Indian division will go by train..." Waller pointed to the Gurkhas, then pointed to a photo of a train — a device the dragons had seen come and go from the city in recent days.

The message made sense to both dragons, and as was his duty, Saan hissed it back to Sask in their native language. That done, Waller pointed to himself, Miller, and Kennedy, then to the dragons, and past them to the aircruisers, "And we were hoping you could fly us out there for a look."

He then waved his hand over the badlands on the map, gesturing to his eyes in a bid to convey the meaning of a reconnaissance mission. It was hard to say whether that set of gestures would be interpreted correctly, but he did have great faith in Sass' intelligence. Surely she'd see the wisdom of Skeen's strategy.

Saan and Sass both stood up as they deciphered Waller's message, and the Newfoundlanders watched with some apprehension as Sask came forward and the trio exchanged hisses for a few moments. All three of their tails were swooping back and forth thoughtfully as the basics were conveyed — from what Sass could tell, a Hubrin attack was being launched against the apparently less-organized southern part of the human territory, and the

Newfoundlanders and their new comrades were being deployed to locate enemy forces, and counter as appropriate.

Waller was hoping to take advantage of aerial surveillance, and probably deployment, to try to get ahead of the Hubrin forces.

Sask was a good officer, if somewhat cautious. He absorbed the information Sass and Saan shared with him, then sought their input with hisses of his own: how much of a risk would it be to put these two relics into the air again, without knowing for certain that the Hubrin didn't have anything available to shoot them down?

A definite risk, Sass conceded, but the fact that no human settlements had been bombarded to date suggested that, at the very least, there was a window of opportunity — a time during which they could do some proper scanning of Hubrin assets without air-to-air engagements.

That argument was apt, and Sask agreed. Assisting the humans in finding a Hubrin attack was worth some risk. That in mind, he proposed a single condition, which seemed fair to Sass. Turning her palm up to her commander, she wheeled back to the b'ys and came down to the dirt again.

Her palm remained upward as she began to nod, and after she knew Waller had seen her confirmation, she held up her left claw and raised one finger. She then raised a second finger, and turned her other palm down.

Waller followed her meaning immediately: the dragons only wanted to send one aircruiser. If the scout force found trouble, better not to lose both ships at once. And it was certainly preferable to leave one in New World City, available to Byng and the reserves in case of another attack.

Satisfied with the outcome, the Newfoundland Colonel nodded, and turned his own palm up, "Thank you."

Sass kept her palm turned up, which seemed the only way she had of saying 'you're welcome'.

"Suppose that settles it," the Wall said, glancing back to Miller. "I'll let Skeen know. Tell the b'ys to get ready to fly."

The Skipper nodded, and then smiled, "They'll be right thrilled."

Off to war again — and this time flying with dragons...

CHAPTER XI

There was no denying the excitement in the ranks as the b'ys prepared to launch their mission against the blue men. Such enthusiasm was not new to the wary men of Newfoundland, but due to the dangers they'd faced on the grasslands so far, it hadn't surfaced for some time. Now things were different — General Skeen was back, and no man from the RNR would ever doubt his ability to sniff out victory in the unlikeliest... or most dangerous... of places.

Some men, though, were less eager than they'd once been to simply launch themselves into the unknown. Certain officers had far more to lose now than had ever been the case in Afghanistan. Jimmy Devlin, for instance, hadn't had a wife to leave behind when he marched into the Khyber.

Annie was standing at the edge of the park as the Newfoundland Captain got his company in order to board the south-bound aircruiser, and as much as he tried to keep his eyes focused on the men of 'C' Company, she was infinitely more attractive.

The b'ys noticed this preoccupation, and since every man among them had been at the wedding, they were sympathetic.

"Alright Captain, we doesn't need a kiss from you, but she might!"

That call came from one of the rear ranks of the company, and at the words Devlin immediately reddened and puffed up. Such heckling was, of course, entirely inappropriate. The b'ys had gotten carried away over the past months, thanks in no small part to the Wall's repeated public displays of affection for Emily, and now Devlin was the target.

"When I find whoever said that..." Devlin began to issue his threat, but then ran out of words. Instead he shook his head and turned to Kennedy. "Get them in the damned aircruiser, will you?"

Kennedy was politely containing his smile, and he saluted at the order, "Of course, sir. Will you be kissing your wife in public while I do that?"

"I'll punch you Shawn, I really will," Devlin waved his fist with as much anger as he could collect. It was a feeble effort.

Abandoning any further attempts at verbal defense, Devlin then did precisely what Kennedy — and every b'y in the company — knew he was going to do: he hurried over to the edge of the park where Annie was waiting.

His bride didn't take any steps in his direction — the park was alive with activity as mules and carts rolled in with ammunition and rations that would keep the b'ys ready to fight for at least a month if they needed to wait in the badlands for an ambush. The dragon crew accompanying the b'ys had all just finished feeding on three steers each — according to Sass, that would be enough to keep them going for a comparable length of time. Annie was too sensible to get underfoot, just for the sake of a simple kiss.

Devlin negotiated his way through the chaos as quickly as he could manage, pulling his hat from his head as he finally reached the park edge, "We'll be launching soon."

"I thought so," Annie nodded as her husband finally came to a stop in front of her. She was no more used to this than he was, so she found herself staring at his chest instead of his face. Reaching out, she tugged at the lapels of his uniform, straightening them slightly. Then she brushed some dust off his sleeve.

"Everyone seems very excited for this mission. It sounds like Sir Andrew knows how to fight in the field," she observed, containing her own skepticism, though Devlin detected it anyway. "You will obviously take care of yourself?"

"The b'ys will take care of me," Jimmy replied evenly, reaching up to cover his wife's hands. "I'll take care of Tom, and Skeen will make sure we're where we need to be, when we need to be. He's like a mighty wizard at that."

Annie watched Jimmy's face as he spoke, realizing her husband was perhaps less confident than many of the other b'ys around her... but still, Skeen inspired much certainty. Where Evelyn Hughes had seemed to doom the last mission to failure — only the Newfoundlanders had managed to seize success — the Indian Army Officer was quite the opposite. Was he a man who could guarantee success?

Annie hoped that victory would come... and that when it arrived, it would be without a great price. She would be forced to wait and see, but while she waited she would have her own concerns.

"I'll look after Emily while you're gone. I'm sure she'll be delighted to be left behind."

Jimmy appreciated his wife's acceptance of that difficult mission, and the confidence she silently projected: "Good luck."

"You too."

With that, she and Jimmy finally kissed — a little awkwardly because neither were as comfortable with public affection as Emily and Waller. Even over the sounds of carts and loading, they could both hear a cheer. The b'ys of 'C' Company approved.

Promptly they parted, and Annie watched as Jimmy disappeared back into the commotion of the park to rejoin his men.

Skeen was leaving Byng's headquarters at the same time as Waller, so the two men walked together for a moment before stopping in the street outside the building. The Indian Army General was bound for the railway station, where his troops were now being loaded into the reserve trains that Byng kept on standby for rapid deployment to threatened areas.

"I intend on being established around Pacifica by this time tomorrow," Skeen squinted against the midday sun as he spoke.

The Newfoundland Colonel nodded. It was ambitious to think a 500-mile rail trip and then a field deployment could happen quite so easily, but again, it was Skeen and his Indian Army.

"We'll find you there as soon as we discover what we're facing," he replied.

Skeen nodded in silence, and then remained still for a moment before narrowing his eyes and glancing back at the Colonel from Newfoundland: "I'm not wrong on this, Tom? You wouldn't let me go off half-cocked?"

It was not a question Waller ever expected to hear from the General. Skeen had always been a pillar of certainty, or at least had seemed so whenever he dealt with his men in Afghanistan. But Waller had only been a Major then — perhaps not senior enough to be asked for his opinion. Now the Newfoundlander was the most experienced Martian-fighter in the British Army, and though Skeen's abilities had been proven in another war, he was prudently wondering if his calculations could be applied here.

He needed Waller's support — the respected opinion of a local expert.

"We haven't over-committed ourselves, Sir Andrew," said the RNR's Colonel. "One brigade, only if the b'ys can find good ground."

Skeen tipped his head. "Yes I suppose we're being prudent. But if we find ground that looks good, Tom... will the rules I learned to fight by match up here? You understand what I'm asking?"

Skeen was wondering if he was out of his depth, though he couldn't say as much in so many words. Waller knew the feeling, and shook his head.

"You've never fought savages, or blue men. Neither had we, a year ago. But we came with the experience you gave us, and made it work. We're confident that your penchant for surprising the enemy will come through for us again. And I haven't seen the b'ys this excited for a mission in quite a while."

That was as much reassurance as Waller felt he could offer. The words were supportive and Skeen appreciated them, though the skepticism didn't entirely leave his expression.

"We'll see, Tom. I'll rely on you to stop me making a mess of things."

Waller smiled, "So nothing's changed, sir?"

Skeen didn't seem to hear the riposte at first, but as soon as it registered he smiled, "By God, Tom, make you a Colonel and you're already taking stabs at your superiors."

The Newfoundlander extended his hand, "Only the good ones, sir."

Skeen looked down at Waller's hand, then took it, "I'll see you in Pacifica tomorrow. Find us some bastards to surprise."

With a final nod, Waller replied, "Yes sir."

Releasing their grips, the two men parted, heading in opposite directions to their transports.

Sass watched as the last of the Newfoundlanders came up the ramp of the southbound transport. Deeper within the large Hubrin-built craft, her two pilots were carefully running pre-flight diagnostics — they were taking the more robust of the two captured ships, but the maintenance regimen on this world had truly had been a disgrace. Keeping the thing in the air would be relatively straightforward, but if the Hubrin had any sort of air-assault capabilities nearby, the outcome would be decidedly unpleasant.

She decided not to dwell on that possibility, as there had been no sign so far that any such weapons were present. For now, there was no better option than to assist the humans — to work together with their hosts and rescuers, to turn back this latest attack, and to get a better gauge of what resources the Hubrin did have on this world.

Information was always vital in war, and Sass meant to collect some as soon as they got off the ground.

The loading of supplies continued even after the Newfoundlanders finished boarding the aircruiser. In itself, Sass found this a fascinating insight into the methods the humans used for war; the freed attackers needed food and water at much more regular intervals than did the Saa, and because they were using projectile weapons, they had many munitions to carry as well. Transporting so much was quite a logistical undertaking, and it was the reason Sass' race, the Hubrin, and most of the intelligent species of the known cosmos had ultimately abandoned such combat tools. Energy was available to be harnessed as a weapon just about anywhere... carrying projectiles was a needless inconvenience.

Well, except for the warriors of the Scourge. But they reportedly *grew* their projectiles from their carapaces, so perhaps that didn't count.

Sass stood by the ramp and watched as the loading teams maneuvered the last of their crates into the transport, then withdrew with the animals that had helped carry the supplies.

Only Waller was missing, and then Sass spotted him crossing the park quickly, his bearing altogether more confident than she'd seen before. Indeed, all the Newfoundlanders seemed to have a different air about them, and she wasn't certain why. This mission — doing reconnaissance ahead of a Hubrin attack — seemed no less dangerous than the one they'd last embarked on. Perhaps it was the presence of the soldiers with different-colored hides, and that new officer who commanded them.

Sass hadn't thought much of Evelyn Hughes, who had been atop the Newfoundlanders' mission to relieve the prison camp, but that new fellow in the tan cladding seemed to command a different respect. Even though his size, shape and bearing were nothing at all like that of a Saa, he somehow reminded Sass of a great Admiral she'd once served under, who now commanded the Central Armada. Was he here to bring the fight to the Hubrin? And if he was the great war-leader of the humans, would he lead them well?

Sass would only be able to judge with time. For now, Waller was hurrying up the ramp and meeting her with a positive expression, "Sorry I'm late, Sass. Ready when you are."

The words still meant nothing, but with a gesture Waller pushed his hand into the air, as if suggesting flight. Sass nodded slowly, then hissed to her command crew to close the boarding ramp. The poorly-maintained piece of machinery started to groan, but soon it achieved its purpose, and the aircruiser set off.

Taking the fight to the Hubrin...

CHAPTER XII

Smith's finger sat lightly on the trigger of his Winchester '92. There was a round in the chamber and the hammer was back, so any man familiar with guns would have told him to keep his finger off the trigger, lest he accidentally discharge the rifle. Normally, Smith would have agreed with such advice... but here he wanted to be absolutely ready to shoot.

As he walked up the main street of Ambitia, the drifter was overcome by a thicker, darker feeling than he'd ever experienced before. The last time he'd made his way through a town that had been overrun by savages, the place had been ghost-like — no signs of the people who had died in the attack, just the broken buildings that told a tale of woe. That had been Farfield City, where Caralynne had died...

Smith pushed past that thought, fast as he could.

Avoiding memories of Caralynne was easier, though, because unlike Farfield, Ambitia was a gruesome sight. Bodies left half-eaten in the street. Pieces of men, women and children lying in the dirt, untended and abandoned as though the savages had begun to gorge themselves, but then been summoned away.

Behind Smith, Sergeant Turner and a squad of his men from the 25th United States Infantry were barely containing their sounds of disgust at the sight. The smell itself was putrid — something the black soldiers were familiar with thanks to some of their more brutal experiences in the Philippines — but the visual gore was more disconcerting than anything even they had witnessed.

It was clear the people of Ambitia had been *fed upon*.

Smith was getting distracted by the horror, he realized, and that was no good. He needed to keep his eyes moving, otherwise he could be a meal just the same as those now dead. The purpose of him leading this mission into town was to make sure it was clear — the train with Captain Adams and the rest of his company was sitting on the rails half a mile down the track, steam up and ready to run if the place turned out to be infested with beasts and blue men.

If all was clear, Adams' men would come through to check the telegraph lines, and the trails leading out of town.

But only if it was clear.

Smith kept his rifle to his shoulder as he moved up the street towards the hotel he'd recently used for shelter, and the patch of dirt in the road where he'd nearly been killed. Hopefully returning to this place wouldn't give death a second chance to grab him.

"Looks clear to me," Private Marks was one of the men with Turner's squad, and the sharpshooter who had twice saved Smith's life — the second time on this very street — sounded cautious with that declaration.

Sharpshooters like Marks were known for being closely aware of their surroundings, so they could spot targets for their rifles. If he wasn't detecting savages, that was a good thing... but Smith still wasn't convinced.

Something about the town was wrong — and not just what had happened to its people.

"Keep ready," Sergeant Turner's caution was similar to Smith's own, and the big American kept his Springfield rifle with its fixed bayonet ready ahead of him. "Seeing much, Smith?"

Coming to a stop in the middle of the road, the drifter paused before answering, "It's different than Farfield City, the last place I saw cleaned out by savages. Too many bodies left around."

"Why would they leave them? In a hurry to get themselves out of here before we came up?" Private Preston, Marks' shooting partner, asked the question. He sounded anxious, which Smith reckoned was fair.

"Or they left them out to keep us distracted when we came in..." Turner suggested.

Smith didn't know if that would be a good tactic — what if men arrived here and stayed out of the town because of the signs of death? Anyone who'd been on the trail and hadn't heard about the attack would see the entrails as a reason to turn away... only soldiers or lawmen would be obliged to come in for a look.

That was definitely over-thinking. This display of gore could have
been intentional, or it could have been necessary because of circumstance.
No way to know — it was impossible to get inside the minds of the blue
men and savages that way. Or at least it was impossible for Smith. Waller
had been better at it, and for a moment the drifter wondered what the
Newfoundland Colonel would have made of this situation.

"When can we go back, Sarge?" Marks asked the question edgily, and
Turner seemed to sympathize.

"Smith... you reckon we can bring in the Captain?"

For a veteran Sergeant like Turner to ask that sort of question, he had
to be anxious. Turner had fought in jungles against men who had grown up
in them, but this place was different...

Or was it?

Smith remembered something Emily had told him about the time
they'd left Promised Town. The blue men had been able to plant doubtful
thoughts in her mind, and while she and everyone assumed she'd been
vulnerable to that because she was savage-born, what if...

Turning to the men of the 25th, Smith began to speak, "I think they're
trying to–"

The eight soldiers of Turner's squad were all staring at Smith. The
drifter, however, was looking past them to the end of the street... where
a line of blue men now stood. At least one Martian for each man in the
squad.

Smith stared at them for a moment, eyes moving left and right across
the line that he somehow couldn't believe was there. How... had they...?

More questions slipped into the drifter's mind, and he started to realize
there were too many doubts to be just his own. Those blues were getting
into his head, and Turner's, and trying to make every man here lose his
nerve. Before they got any closer to succeeding, Smith would have to do
something.

Aligning his '92, the drifter blasted the first Martian he could line up in
his sights.

The crack of the shot seemed to shake the men of the 25th back into
reality, and they wheeled too. Their .30-06 Springfields were all ready to

fire, and the buffalo soldiers surely knew how to use the rifles.

Marks put a bullet through a blue man's face, Preston another, and as Smith worked the lever of his Winchester and sent more .45 caliber lead down the street, the blue men seemed to realize that their deployment — standing in an open line as if going for a high noon showdown with veteran infantry — wasn't wise.

They began to scatter, but of the nine who had been standing, only three made it to cover.

"What the hell were they thinking?" Marks demanded to no one in particular as the squad ceased fire. By natural instinct, the men of the 25th backed into a circle in the middle of the road, pointing their fixed bayonets in every direction as the thunder of their shooting cleared.

There was no answer to Marks' question — no one here, aside from the surviving blue men, could have hoped to understand what the creatures had intended. Smith had seen their arrogance many times before, so it was no longer a surprise, but now the squad needed to move...

Before Turner could make that point, or give any orders, the whistle of the train blew in the distance. That was Adams' signal — if shots were heard in the town, the train whistle would blow a five-minute warning, and then the locomotive would run back to Deadline. If the squad didn't show up in that time, they'd be assumed lost.

And if savages closed in on the train, Adams might have to leave before five minutes were up.

"We're leaving. Watch the side where those blues ran," Turner ordered, tone far firmer than it had been a moment before. "Move."

He wasn't the sort of Sergeant who needed to yell to get attention; his cool words spurred his men to turn and begin jogging down the street, towards the fallen enemy. Smith followed, looking back over his shoulder and wondering where the savages were. Blue men without savages... smoke without fire.

But the blue men didn't have to make sense.

It only took a moment for the soldiers and the drifter to clear the streets of Ambitia, and dart into the woods on the left side of the tracks. The blue men who had survived the shooting were nowhere to be seen, but

Smith took no relief from their absence.

Something was wrong here, and he couldn't figure it.

Smith kept his finger away from the trigger of his Winchester as he went on through the woods — too many chances to stumble and yank it. He knew they were making good time, though, and would be back to Adams and the train in time for its departure.

Still, getting away without knowing what the blue men were up to would somehow be unsatisfying. Smith figured he might be better off staying, seeing if he could find the surviving creatures and get some information from them. Maybe he could find out what their plan was, and then he'd be able to better help the defense of Pacifica.

That seemed like a good idea — a good enough reason to stop running.

And he nearly did, before his complete lack of common sense struck him again.

But then he was forced to stop, because a lightning bolt cut through the forest, catching one of Turner's men and throwing him a dozen feet to his death.

"Down!" the Sergeant roared, and his soldiers didn't need any more encouragement. Dropping behind deadfall, the black men started scanning the woods for the source of the shot.

Nothing was obvious. It was like they were being taunted... like the blue men had expected them and were now doing their utmost to torment them. It was different than anything Smith had seen them do before... more calculating. These must have been different kinds of Martians.

Crouching behind a thick tree, Smith looked deeper into the woods, but his enemy remained invisible. They were out there... they had to be... but where? And what could be done about them? A break for the train would probably end in a lightning storm and death for every man... but what else could they do?

Surrender.

Smith blinked at the thought, because there was no fibre of his character that would have naturally produced such an idea. Maybe... maybe the thought wasn't meant to seem like his own. What if it was an impression from a blue man — an offer from that creature. Should he accept? Waller had once been prisoner of the blues, and he'd come away alright. But that was back in the beginning...

Smith's mind wasn't clear, and the thought of surrendering persisted until he heard movement of a familiar kind.

"Savages," he said it quiet and low, and Turner's eyes narrowed as he turned to follow the drifter's gaze.

"Many?" he asked.

The noise was getting louder, so Smith nodded.

Silence fell for a moment, and then the train whistle blew again — Adams had to go.

Turning away from the trees he was watching, the drifter fixed his stare on the men who were with him — now seven soldiers from the 25th United States Infantry. They were anxious, fearful, and yet he sensed defiance too. Nowhere to run if the train was gone, and nothing to lose by using up all their ammunition on whatever savages came for them.

Smith didn't know how long they'd last, but he reckoned fifty or sixty beasts would be killed before these men were taken down.

As if to confirm the drifter's thinking, Private Marks started pulling stripper clips of .30-06 ammunition out of his pouches and laying them on the fallen log in front of him. Faster reloading if he didn't need to fish them out later.

Turner met Smith's eyes with his own rock-hard gaze. He was ready to die as well, and his men would follow him to whatever end.

But Smith, a man who'd known his number was up a few times before in life, didn't feel as if that was the case now.

Surrender. This didn't feel like the place or the time for a last stand... for a fight to the finish.

The drifter watched the men of the 25th prepare to die, and wondered what he should tell them. After a moment he realized it was odd for him to not simply say what he meant, so he spoke plain: "I think we should give ourselves up."

Every one of the black soldiers crouched in the deadfall looked up at him in the same split second, their eyes wide with surprise. Smith was not the sort of man any of them would have thought a coward.

Reaching up and adjusting his hat, the drifter shook his head, "Don't know. I reckon... there's something unusual about this."

"What the hell happens to us if we become prisoners? Where will they take us, what will they do?" Preston was the first to voice those obvious questions, and Smith had no answer.

He just acted instead.

The drifter stood up and changed his grip on his Winchester. Wrapping his hand around the wooden hand guard, he turned and stepped around the tree, holding it over his head in a sign that he wasn't going to use it. As soon as he did, savages appeared twenty yards ahead of him, rising from deadfall with feral looks on their faces. But they didn't come forward, they just stared at him.

And then a blue man appeared among the beasts. The alien creature was stepping over the fallen deadwood and the underbrush of the woods with some unease, eyes cast down to make sure he didn't stumble. He clearly was not experienced in the bush.

Smith watched the creature advance, then noticed another four who appeared behind the savages, one of them with a lightning gun.

This really had been an ambush...

Movement sounded behind Smith, and the drifter looked back over his shoulder just in time to see Turner climb out from cover, his Springfield left behind.

"You better be right."

The men followed their Sergeant, and as they all appeared Smith nodded once. He needed to be right... though if he was wrong, they probably wouldn't be alive long enough to tell him so.

After another moment of careful walking, the blue man came to a stop ten yards away from the humans he had now captured. Two silver bands were wrapped around each of the creature's upper arms, which probably meant he held some significant rank. His silver gaze scanned over the narrowed eyes of the men, and then fixed on Smith's weathered face.

The drifter's mind suddenly felt a twist, and then there was a flood of pictures.

It was him, on his mare... riding to the glass building — Fort Martian.

Then riding at Promised Town. And then at Farfield City, standing in the street and watching Caralynne being taken away.

For a second he wondered if the images were his memories, but as they looped through his mind again he began to realize they couldn't be — he was seeing himself from the outside. Maybe the way he'd been seen by other people... or by savages, or blue men.

They had seen him before.

That thought needed a second to sink in.

Then it led to a certain realization.

The blue men knew who he was. They knew that he'd been there since the beginning.

Smith.

The drifter's eyes went wide, and the blue man with the silver bands tilted its head. This creature was some sort of special soldier, Smith could feel it. And now, either by chance or some sort of planning, he had captured what he considered to be one of the leaders of the humans who were causing all the problems.

Savages began closing around the captured party and the men tensed, reasonably expecting death. The blue man held up his hand, stopping the approach, then pointed to the Americans and gestured that they follow him. All through this, the fellow did not take his eyes off Smith.

Wherever the creature was about to take the drifter and the buffalo soldiers, Smith knew he was going to get a lot of attention. His mind was clouded, but his feet started moving. He was a prisoner of the blue men.

CHAPTER XIII

The grasslands looked very pleasant when one cruised over them from high above. Like an endless gold-green sea, the terrain that the Newfoundlanders had marched over several times in the past year stretched out to every horizon, and from the cockpit of the aircruiser transporting the b'ys south, Jimmy Devlin had to marvel at the scale of the place.

Of course the steppes of the new world seemed vast to a man out amongst them, but to be so high as they were now, and to see that there was still nothing interrupting the grass all the way out to the line where sky and land met... Even in the midst of this mission, the young Captain could pause to appreciate that scale.

"Think that's the Dead River coming up."

Lieutenant Kennedy was on the aircruiser's flight deck with Jimmy as they watched the terrain floating by beneath their craft's hull. Now the junior officer leaned over one of the boards of switches beneath the front window, and held his field glasses to his eyes as he looked down. Moving over to Kennedy's side, Jimmy raised his own glasses and scanned as well, quickly detecting the wide strip of water that stretched westward. The last time they'd been south of the border, the Newfoundlanders had been travelling on that river by boat, in company with the black soldiers of the 25th United States Infantry.

Now those elite Americans were somewhere else — probably helping set up the defenses of Pacifica City — and the b'ys were flying through the air on a giant magic carpet (that just happened to be the size of a building).

"Right, get the rest of the lookouts up here," Devlin lowered his glasses as the river disappeared under the cockpit. They were now passing into the sector of American territory that was unreachable from the capital, which meant the blue men could appear at any time. More eyes on the lookout increased their chances of sighting the enemy on the first pass.

"Be right back," Kennedy nodded to Devlin, and then headed to the back of the cockpit to descend the ladder down into the hold.

Sparing a look over his shoulder, Jimmy watched Kennedy disappear down the stair. The cockpit itself had no back wall — it was open at the rear, so even from the front-most position next to the switchboards and the windows, he could easily look back into the vast hold and see the small figures of the b'ys sitting relaxed on the deck. It was like being on the fire-escape platform of some massive warehouse... a remarkable feeling when the building in question could fly...

But that was a feeling Jimmy needed to set aside. Turning back towards the windows he raised his field glasses again and began sweeping the grasslands ahead. He had no idea how fast the aircruiser was moving, but as the river fell behind he was still seeing only grasslands, not the badlands about which he'd heard stories. This was supposed to be a rough area, not unlike Afghanistan... which was indeed why Skeen figured he could ambush the blues there.

No matter what sort of machines one had at his disposal, fighting in terrain like Afghanistan was always brutal, particularly for the side being surprised. Hopefully surprise would be on humanity's side...

For now, there was nothing. As he continued to sweep back and forth across the grassy steppes ahead, Devlin tried to contain his impatience. He did want to see the enemy, but even as high as he was up in the sky he figured it might take many sweeps of the territory to cover every possible approach. Human eyes could only see so far, even from this altitude, and he had to be ready for the possibility that they'd be looking for hours... perhaps even longer.

Patience. He just needed more patience.

Lowering his glasses again, Devlin paused to look left and then right. There were windows on all sides of the cockpit, but the view from all of them was the same: more grasslands, no enemy.

The only activity in his eyeline seemed to be coming from the control switchboards for the aircruiser itself; some of the switches were glowing, and there was a moving picture screen embedded in one board that seemed to be scrolling across a terrain map as the aircruiser moved along. That was an interesting feature in itself, so Devlin moved over to the right side of the cockpit and stared for a moment at the device.

The map seemed to be showing the Dead River falling behind the ship, but was devoid of many other details. If it was a topographical map in the midst of the grasslands, Jimmy supposed that made sense — it wasn't easy to identify one definitive landform over another.

He waited a few moments to see if anything else came up on the moving picture screen, but when nothing did he stepped back and turned again to the horizon. It remained far in the distance, without anything remarkable disrupting it...

But the ground had finally begun to change.

At first Jimmy wasn't certain if his eyes were deceiving him, but as he started to see the grass thin ahead of the aircruiser, he raised his glasses. The sight that greeted him was both welcome and dreadful: the soft steppes were being replaced by red gravel and rock — entire swathes of hard terrain that looked at once alien and familiar.

It wasn't a single discreet shift, as some grassy patches still managed to penetrate the rocky stretches, but as the aircruiser pressed on, Devlin found more and more red rock, and less welcoming grass.

This had to be the badlands, and even from above it seemed to earn its name.

"We into the..."

That aborted question marked the return of Kennedy to the cockpit; the Lieutenant didn't need to finish asking it as he arrived at Jimmy's side. Sergeant Halloran and his section were just behind, all set to assist as lookouts.

"Jesus, that's rough stuff," Halloran wasted no time in making his observation, and Devlin could only nod in reply.

The horizon was losing its straight edge, as high and low peaks of jagged rock started to climb out of the ground ahead of them. The sky seemed to lose its typical blueness... it was as if the red rock of the planet was bleeding its tones into the air, making for a yellow-red atmosphere that felt profoundly unwelcoming.

And below, there were plenty of signs of ground that would be suited for an ambush.

"It's like Afghanistan, alright," Kennedy shook his head and rubbed his brow. "But redder."

"Feels mean," Private King, one of the RNR's perennial runners, added his observation.

Jimmy nodded; it did feel mean, but for their immediate purposes it was also somewhat inconvenient. Certainly, there would be places on ground like this where even a handful of well-supplied mountain-fighters could make hell for a column of advancing infantry... but if the blue men were operating somewhere in this terrain, they might just as easily hide from the lookouts' eyes. Would they even be able to spot savages from this high, with so much disruption around?

Devlin didn't know, but if there was a chance that savages could be spotted, he had to get his men ready.

"Alright b'ys, we're going to have to look sharp if we're going to see these bastards. Everyone pick a spot, and don't blink..."

If only they had a way to see around corners... God help them if they had to spend a whole day cruising back and forth over these badlands, straining their eyes the whole time...

Sass considered trying to tell the Newfoundlanders that they didn't need to post lookouts, but decided it would be too complicated to explain. She also didn't mind redundancy in a ship this poorly-maintained; she was reasonably certain she'd gotten the passive scanners on the transport working before their liftoff, but right now the screens were all blank. That probably indicated the Hubrin were further south... but if it meant something wasn't working, she'd rather have Jimmy discover it, not learn about it when the pulse cannon started tracking her.

To be fair, she had masked the transport's signature reasonably well — not a difficult task, considering the pathetically low power-output from the big craft's power plant. Combined with their low altitude of travel, and the fact that the Hubrin seemed to lack an orbital detection network, she was fairly confident they were moving in secret. They'd literally have to overfly the Hubrin to be noticed, and with Jimmy watching from the flight deck, and her scanners going, that seemed doubly unlikely.

Sass hoped.

Standing with her two pilots at the auxiliary steering position she'd installed at the rear of the transport's hold, she opened and closed her hands uneasily as she waited for some sign — any sign — of the enemy she shared with the humans.

The Hubrin were out here somewhere... hopefully they'd be surprised when the Saa and humans dropped in on them.

CHAPTER XIV

"So it was an ambush?" Major Krazakowski's typically earnest question drew a nod from Adams, and then the Captain elaborated.

"We didn't see much, but there were shots, and then savages started appearing on the tracks between us and the town. We had to withdraw or risk losing the train," the black officer said bitterly. "Sergeant Turner and Smith were among those we left behind."

It was a grim loss, and Krazakowski shook his head in disappointment, "Nothing else you could have done, Captain. You would have lost men and equipment essential to our defense if you had attempted anything else."

That was undoubtedly the truth, but it was small comfort to Adams. He had achieved the rank of Captain in the United States Army by being one of the very best — too good to be ignored for sake of his color — and he had come through many ambushes in the Philippines without losing men. Having to chug away from a fight left a bad taste in his mouth, but the higher purpose of protecting Deadline had weighed too heavily on his mind.

Krazakowski held most of the burden for that subject, though; it was clear now that no escape would be possible, and that the town — as poorly positioned and equipped as it was — would have to defend itself until relief somehow broke through the blue man forces.

But what were those forces up to? Why were they holding Ambitia?

"No notion of their purpose in town?" the Major put the question to his Captain, and Adams frowned as he shook his head.

"Nothing more than guesses, sir. But they're still holding it... so maybe that tells us something about their intent. If they're still holding Destina too, maybe it's to secure the rail line... make sure reinforcements can't get out this way. Or maybe to make sure they can send more savages up the rail bed..."

That was a very good point, and Krazakowski nodded. The fact that the blue men had chosen to attack those two towns suggested they had strategic significance... but without knowing if other places had been similarly assaulted, it was impossible to understand the bigger picture.

All Krazakowski and his soldiers could really worry about now was their own survival. The savages had them cut off, and probably knew very well that there were living men out at Deadline... it was only a matter of time before a horde came.

Could they hold out?

Krazakowski stared at the map for a time, then took a breath, "Adams, can you find someone local who knows the lay of the land here? I need to speak with someone familiar with these badlands."

The request surprised the Captain, but after a second he nodded and left his Major's office.

Krazakowski continued to stare silently at the map, lost in thought.

Adams emerged onto the street outside headquarters and squinted against the afternoon sunshine. Somehow the sky seemed to have a redder hue than it did before the last mission, but he tried to ignore the seeming color shift — it was undoubtedly just his personal frustration tinting his view.

Captain Insetta was coming down the street as Adams put thoughts of his lost men out of his head, and as the white officer slowed, the black officer nodded to him, "Heard?"

"I did. Sorry too — Turner was a good man."

"All of them were," Adams agreed. "Major wants to talk to whoever from the town has the best local knowledge. Someone who knows the land."

Insetta's eyes narrowed, and Adams could read some of his counterpart's thoughts: what exactly did Krazakowski want to know about the local terrain? Was he thinking about establishing defensive posts outside the palisade, or was he thinking of marching out?

The latter option wasn't terribly appealing... but then sitting around and waiting to be overrun was equally distasteful. And there were only 100 people in this town, all of them hard-worn frontier types. They were probably as good as the men of the 25th when it came to moving over difficult ground, and looking after themselves.

Maybe escape was an option... or maybe Krazakowski was simply thinking of early-warning posts. Neither Insetta nor Adams would second-guess their Major at this point. While politicians like Robinson had come and gone from command of the regiment, the eccentric Polish Major from Baltimore had stuck with them, and fought some very nasty battles at their side.

"There's the Mayor... Mulligan. He's probably been out here the longest," Insetta said eventually, and Adams nodded, recalling the Irishman who was also a store clerk, hotel owner, and other things.

"I'll ask him," Adams said. He left Insetta to ponder the possibilities.

As Jimmy Devlin lowered his field glasses again he found himself shaking his head slightly at the prospect of trying to cross the badlands on foot. There were certainly a few sections that seemed passable, but those were hemmed in on all sides by what appeared to be razor-sharp cliffs, or outcroppings, or peaks... he lacked sufficient vocabulary to even describe what he was seeing.

Why the Americans had begun to send settlers out into such a mess, when there were perfectly lovely grasslands just a few hundred miles north, was a mystery.

Perhaps they'd thought that savage hordes would be less common out amongst the red rock — that in this difficult place, they were safer than they'd be to the north.

They'd have been wrong.

Jimmy Devlin had fought hard battles in a place much like this, and the only thing he could imagine being worse than facing a hardened Afghan tribe in such terrain, was facing even a handful of savages who could appear from behind any boulder, or leap out of any crevice.

It was the stuff of nightmares, and it did make the young Captain wonder whether an ambush in a place like this wouldn't be disastrous for both sides.

Though if the situation was too dangerous, he knew neither Skeen nor

Waller would take the risk. Both men were eager to bring the fight to the blue men, but neither was a fool. That's why the b'ys were so devoted to them.

By now, Devlin's eyes were beginning to ache. Too many long minutes staring through his field glasses, straining with all his effort to see signs of savages who just weren't there. Kennedy had rightly pointed out that a travelling horde would likely kick up a dust cloud, but none was evident.

Not that a whole horde could move over any of the terrain they'd seen. If the blues were coming in an organized fashion, they'd need to find a clear stretch of terrain... a pass somewhere that, like the Khyber in Afghanistan, let the savages move together in one column.

That was what the b'ys needed to find: a pass where the ambush could be safely set.

Unfortunately, nothing was immediately presenting itself. Deciding he'd earned a break, Devlin turned away from the front window and paced towards the back of the flight deck. As he went, he spared a glance out one of the side windows, and then he happened to see the moving picture screen he'd noticed before.

It was no longer showing a blank canvas. It was showing blue.

Sass watched the markers indicating a Hubrin column pop up on her improvised sensor screen at the auxiliary steering position, and assessed what she saw with quick efficiency. The passive sensors were only able to detect the power signatures from Hubrin equipment — particularly their ground transports and other aircraft — and it seemed both types were operating within seventy decas of her current position.

None were altering course to suggest they'd seen her transport, which was good news and a mark in favor of her emissions-masking routine, but the ground vehicles were certainly moving somewhere. She needed to get Waller.

Turning away from the auxiliary steering position, Sass began to move across the transport's hold, seeking the small figure of the Newfoundland Colonel. She caught sight of him just as one of the men who'd been on watch in the cockpit reached him, and started speaking in a manner that sounded urgent. Waller grabbed a piece of paper — probably one of his paper maps — and then joined that man in a fast walk towards the flight deck.

The sensor displays on that deck must have shown the same thing her own screen had revealed, but imagining Waller would have no idea how to interpret passive scan data, Sass knew she needed to follow quickly.

Arriving at the cockpit just after Waller finished scaling the ladder, she peered in through the open back of the compartment and hissed softly to announce her presence.

Waller had just been joining Jimmy at the moving picture screen when Sass arrived, and he turned back to his dragon counterpart with a frown, pointing to the screen, "Blue men?"

Recognizing the sound for Hubrin, Sass nodded. She then leaned back and held up her hands, so that she could count off the number of vehicle engine signatures she was seeing.

"Ten," Devlin followed the count. "Ten what?"

"Here," Kennedy interrupted at that point, drawing a couple of folds of paper from his pocket, along with a pencil. He moved over close to Sass' face, because the paper was quite small. "I'm drawing a savage."

He quickly did a stick figure of a savage, and held it up to Sass. She considered the crude rendering for a second, then realized she couldn't answer. There were probably savages with the convoy she'd detected, but because they didn't have detectable power plants, there was no way to be certain. And she couldn't risk active scans... if the active scanners were even working.

Her stillness caused Kennedy to frown and look at his drawing, "Maybe we need a better artist?"

One of the b'ys from Halloran's section started to make a joke about that, but Waller interjected first: "Try drawing a lorry. Maybe this just shows equipment, not people."

Sounded reasonable, so Kennedy quickly scratched out the rough shape of a silver Martian vehicle, then held it up towards Sass.

That was better for the Saa engineer, and she quickly sat back and nodded, then repeated her hand-count to ten.

"So that looks like ten lorries, moving east towards the foothills," Waller concluded slowly, turning his eyes back to the moving picture screen. But were there savages along?

Then he had an idea: they knew aircruisers had been sent to Ambitia and Destina, and there were two other blue markers on the screen. Quickly holding up the map he'd brought with him, the Newfoundland Colonel roughly matched those dots with the positions of the invaded towns, and concluded they were probably the same: the screen, and whatever powerful optics were behind it, had seen the vehicles all the way over in the foothills, hundreds of miles away.

Pointing to both of those dots, Waller turned back to Sass. The dragon watched his movements, then held up one finger.

"One... or one each..." Jimmy interpreted, and then looked to Kennedy. "Shawn, show her the stick man again."

Kennedy held up the piece of paper and pointed to his savage, and again Sass stilled herself. She understood what they were asking, but she didn't have a word like 'maybe' available.

But Waller understood. Waving to Sass, he used his boot to tap the floor of the bridge, then gestured to the entire aircruiser around him. Then he pointed again at the two icons near Destina and Ambitia. Sass nodded once more, and that confirmed it.

"She's able to spot their vehicles, but not savages," he concluded.

"How does that make sense?" Private Connolly asked the question, and Jimmy shot a frown at him.

"You're in a flying warehouse. Shut it."

"We know there were savages landed in Ambitia and Destina. If she's not able to answer about them being there, it means she can't know if there are savages with this column of lorries," Waller said thoughtfully. Then he wondered whether seeing these blue men meant the aircruiser had been seen, so he pointed to the icons, then his eyes, and then waved his hand to indicate the ship around him.

Sass had been waiting for that question, so she now shook her head and reached up to cover her eyes.

The Hubrin hadn't seen them — thanks, Waller suspected, to Sass' mechanical abilities. That was good and definitely provided the advantage he and Skeen would need. But the question remained: where would that advantage take them, and what would be the gain? Turning his focus back to the screen, Waller raised his map again, trying to use the position of water to orient himself.

Maybe...

"Jimmy," he asked after a moment's frowning. "Does it look to you like they might be close to... Deadline?"

The Captain of 'C' Company leaned in closer to Waller, to look at the map and then compare it to the moving picture screen. It was hard to tell with only landforms providing comparative scale... but Deadline was the only settlement near those markers, certainly. Perhaps the town was their objective.

"Worth a look?" he asked, and Waller's frown deepened. If the blue men knew enough to attack two cities that would blind Pershing to this entire piece of territory, they had to know that Deadline was probably nothing more than a collection of sticks in some rocky valley.

But if it was a valley the beasts were crossing through, and in it they suddenly discovered a brigade of crack infantry instead of a terrified bunch of settlers, it might be the place for Skeen to work his deadly magic.

Or it might be nothing at all.

Either way, Waller figured Jimmy was correct: "Worth a look."

The Colonel turned towards Sass and raised his map, pointing to the dot for Deadline, "Can we get there?"

Narrowing her massive eyes, the dragon focused carefully on the small terrain outlines, then realized she probably didn't need to be too precise. There was only one human settlement out in the midst of all these difficult cliffs, so she just needed to find it. Perhaps Waller had a plan to stop the Hubrin there... she just had to trust he knew what he was about.

With a nod, she turned and headed back towards her auxiliary steering position. As she departed, both Waller and Devlin looked back to the moving picture screen, and the markers on it.

"Ten lorries. Could be a thousand savages, or ten times that many," the young Captain observed.

Waller took a breath, "It will depend on the terrain. If the ground is good, we can face whatever's coming. If not, we run for the hills."

That was the calculation now: fight or withdraw.

CHAPTER XV

"You're fuckin' kiddin'."

Adams winced at the words of the Mayor of Deadline, but standing on the other side of the table in his adopted headquarters, Major Krazakowski seemed entirely unfazed by the sharp tone.

"I wish I were, Mayor Mulligan, but you must agree that there is some sense in trying to escape a known target in favor of a better-hidden location. And unlike the prairies to the north of us, these badlands might present exceptional opportunities for concealment."

Mulligan stared at the Major, eyes wide as his face grew steadily redder. He then glanced at Adams, "Darkie, he's serious?"

"The Captain's name is Adams, not Darkie," Krazakowski corrected, as if reminding a child to use his words. "And serious I most certainly am, Mayor Mulligan. You must know this land. The topography. There are so many craggy peaks within sight of us. They must conceal valleys, and washes, and perhaps even caves. Is there any route we might take that could shelter us from the air as we move towards civilization… or perhaps strike north? Any route with natural fortifications along the way, that we could take advantage of?"

Krazakowski was as earnest now as always, and the Mayor simply wasn't ready to participate in such speculation. The Irishman shook his head and began to turn to leave, but he found his way blocked by Adams.

"I suggest you answer the Major's questions, Mayor Mulligan. If we have to march out on our own to find the sorts of places he is inquiring about, your town will have no protection."

Adams' words lacked any sympathy, and Mulligan seemed to sober slightly at the big man's dour mood. Turning back to Krazakowski in a huff, he uttered an oath, then moved forward to the table that had become the Major's desk. A map was laid out there with some crude attempts at topographical features sketched onto it.

"This town is here because they were looking for coal. Badlands are supposed to have it, so they figured the badlands on the new world would be made of it. But the rock is different here. It's loose and it crumbles and it's shit. People gave up trying," the Irishman planted his finger on the map to the north of the town. "So there's a lot of hard-going areas around here, that's true. Twenty miles north is the deepest canyon of the bunch. Wide, too. Runs east and west, usually with steep sides. No caves, but water pops out of the loose rock and streams for a while, then goes back in for no reason. It's like nothing I've seen anywhere else. Might be something that way we could use. If we could get there."

Useful information at last, and Krazakowski nodded, "Twenty miles is your estimate? How is the ground between here and there?"

Mulligan shrugged, "It's the fuckin' badlands, isn't it? The problem around here ain't hordes, it's finding a way to get from one place to the next over the fucking rocks and washes and valleys."

Krazakowski tilted his head at the remark, then glanced at Adams. The fact that the terrain would make the assembling of any hordes difficult was certainly a help — though at the same time, it meant that small groups of savages could remain hidden while they prowled. Still, if they could get to the canyon, perhaps they could follow it to a point nearer a settlement that was still intact...

That was a long shot, to say the very least, but Krazakowski preferred it to sitting pat in a town called Deadline, waiting for the blue men to attack in organized force.

"You're not serious about leaving?" the Mayor repeated his senseless question as he tried to read the Major's thoughts through his expression.

Krazakowski raised his eyebrows, "I am serious about most things, Mayor Mulligan. Thank you for your help, I suggest you begin organizing your town for evacuation."

The Irishman wasn't ready for that, but he found the quickest way to cope with his disbelief was simple: he turned and left. This time Adams didn't step in his way; instead the Captain approached his Major.

"Better chance on foot, sir?" the black officer asked.

Nodding, Krazakowski took a breath and then spoke as earnestly as ever, "Captain Adams, I do not like the prospect of a field action in the midst of such a difficult situation, but we cannot stop an air assault. Good men with rifles, plenty of inaccessible heights, no room for a horde... better take our chances in the badlands, I think."

It was true — or at least it could be, if Mulligan's assessment of the terrain was correct. Until Adams saw it for himself, he couldn't be certain.

"We must get the men ready to march, Captain. I'll join you... we will have to requisition all the animals and supplies we can find. Wagons probably cannot go where we intend."

With a nod, Adams stood aside and allowed his Major to round the desk and lead the way out of the office. Both men hurried down the stairs of the headquarters building — which was, of course, Mulligan's hotel. As they crossed the lobby, they ignored the red-faced and disbelieving Irishman as he glared at them from behind the counter, then both men donned their hats as they stepped out the door into the late afternoon sun.

The town still felt bleak — even more hopeless than Promised Town, which had been fortunate to be surrounded by living woods. Here only the reddish rock of the badlands surrounded them, but the harsh landscape would favor them once they escaped into its midst.

"Whatever he says about streams bursting from the rock, I suspect water will probably be our greatest concern, Captain," Krazakowski observed as he looked north.

Adams nodded, pulling a pad of paper from his pocket, then a pencil with which he could make note of the priorities that needed to be handled.

He jotted down water, and finding the best barrels and transport for whatever supply could be drawn from Deadline's wells. Then he stood by and waited for the Major's next priority... but it did not come.

Krazakowski was looking to the northern sky with a frown — even more earnest than usual. After a moment of questioning his vision, he reached down to draw his field glasses from their case, then raised them to his eyes.

"Captain Adams, it is too late. Sound the alarm. Men to their posts."

Blinking in surprise, Adams followed Krazakowski's gaze northward, and then up. When his eyes settled upon the growing shape in the air, he realized what it was: a heavier-than-air machine without wings. A Martian air vehicle.

"To arms!" he bellowed.

"Anybody alive there is probably going to start shooting at us as soon as we're in range," Jimmy Devlin was standing beside Waller in the cockpit of the aircruiser, with Sass again staring through the compartment's open back.

Deadline wasn't far ahead now, and the dragon pilots were taking their craft in low and slow so the men on the flight deck could get a good look at the settlement before deciding if it warranted a landing. No horde was in sight, so it was possible that either the attack had already passed through, or that the blue men were still on their way. The dots on the moving picture screen were still quite a ways off...

But Devlin was certainly right: if there were scared people in the town, seeing a Martian aircruiser would probably cause panic.

"Any ideas how to let them know we're not savages?" Waller glanced at his Captain, and Devlin frowned.

"We should have brought a large flag. Though that might not have helped... knowing the Yanks, they'd probably fire on us for flying the Union Jack."

Appreciating Jimmy's attempt at humor, Waller managed a chuckle, "Yes, well, perhaps we'll be fortunate. The 25th could be down there."

"Ha, like we'd be so lucky," Devlin folded his arms. "Guess we just land far enough from the wall that we're out of effective range, then send a company up to say hello."

Waller liked that suggestion, but as soon as the words were out of his mouth, Devlin realized it probably wasn't the best thing he could have said. As the Newfoundland Colonel looked at him, the Captain of 'C' Company groaned and let his arms drop to his sides.

"Why yes, sir, I'd love to be the b'y to walk up to the Yanks and tell them not to shoot us or the dragons. So kind of you to offer."

"Don't say I never give you nothing," Waller agreed, then patted Devlin once on the shoulder before the Captain turned and headed for the ladder.

Deadline grew larger in the windows of the cockpit, and Waller watched the town, wondering what they'd find there.

Krazakowski reached the firing step on the northern palisade after a quick jog. Already Captain Koster and Captain Vogel had men deployed — nearly 120 rifles were pointed at the air vessel, though none of the men of the 25th had any idea whether their trusty .30-06 rounds would do anything against such a machine.

Behind Krazakowski was Adams, and as soon as both officers got a look at the Martian ship, the Major turned to the Captain, "Bring your men and Insetta's up here, rest of the regiment in reserve. If they land to the north and attack from that direction, we'll need plenty of firepower."

Adams saluted and headed towards his men immediately, leaving Krazakowski to approach the palisade wall and direct his field glasses at the machine. It was getting very low now, producing a roar that was undoubtedly deafening at close range, and pushing out a wind that shifted loose rock beneath it.

The craft had to be the size of a building...

Captain Koster appeared at Krazakowski's side, "How many do you think that thing holds?"

The Major kept the glasses to his eyes, answering only absently, "At least 2,000, I would guess. But of course there could be more."

It was impossible to be certain... but at least there were armed men ready here. Neither Ambitia nor Destina had garrisons protecting them. If the blue men were expecting as easy a time with Deadline, the men of the 25th would quickly challenge their assumptions.

Boots crashed into the gravel behind Krazakowski and Koster as more men arrived — Adams hurried his company up onto the firing step near the pair, while on the other end of the palisade, Captain Insetta led his men to join the defense as well.

Just about 250 rifles were in position, with 350 more ready to join the battle wherever needed.

Timely, because the craft was settling onto the ground.

"I put that at about three-quarters of a mile, wouldn't you say, Koster?"

Krazakowski lowered his glasses to gauge the distance, and his second in command nodded.

"I'd say so."

"Well then, prepare the men for volleys," the Major ordered, and Koster bellowed the necessary instructions.

The aircruiser made a soft and civilized landing.

Standing at the rear ramp as the noise of the engines began to die down, Devlin nodded to his b'ys: Lieutenant Kennedy and Sergeant Halloran were right up front, and the 200 b'ys of 'C' Company were all standing edgily behind. Twitchy American trigger fingers could have them all in a spot of trouble, though realistically it seemed unlikely that a full-on firefight would break out... unless the townsfolk here had a serious problem with the British Empire.

As Devlin contemplated that possibility, one of the dragons at the auxiliary control position turned back to him, then showed an upturned palm. As soon as the gesture was made, the ramp groaned and began to lower, letting in the bright afternoon sun. Squinting as his eyes adjusted to the glare, Devlin led the way to the ramp's edge, and then down it onto the foreign rocky ground.

The landscape was alien for this world — the loose rock with an orange-red hue...

"Jesus... it's like the rock on Trout River Pond," Corporal Crocker blurted within earshot of the Captain, though Devlin didn't know what the young soldier was referring to.

As the company began to form up behind the shelter of the aircruiser, Devlin crept to the corner of the big ship, then leaned sideways and poked his head out, looking towards the town.

He half expected his hat to be shot off — only his hat if he was lucky — but there was silence.

They probably hadn't seen him. Taking a moment to fish his field glasses out of their pouch, he held them to his eyes, wondering if he could make out anyone on the town's walls. This concern for not being shot would be grimly unnecessary if the savages had already come and gone, leaving the place the same way they'd left Farfield.

Quickly sweeping the wall, he looked for clues... and then he came glasses-to-glasses with an American officer.

He stared for a second. Then he frowned. Then he stared again. Then he pulled his glasses away and held them up with a wave.

Captain Koster lowered his glasses, then raised them again. Then lowered them, then held them up in a wave.

Standing beside his Captain, Krazakowski frowned at the sequence of gestures, "Captain?"

Koster was frowning too — looking quite confused, in fact, but he managed to narrate what he was seeing for his Major, "Sir, I'm positive that I've just seen Lieutenant Devlin of the Newfoundland Regiment looking around the back of that vehicle."

Krazakowski's answer sounded entirely unsurprised, which was in itself quite confusing: "In fact, he was recently promoted to Captain."

Koster looked at his Major, then looked back towards the craft. But...?

"Hold your fire!" Krazakowski called out to his men, and as the private soldiers on the wall didn't have the benefit of field glasses, the order earned him some surprised looks. "It is the Newfoundland Regiment."

That earned him even more surprised looks — not least from Koster, who was wondering if he was seeing things. Could there be savages behind... Captain Devlin...?

Leaning back around the edge of the aircruiser, Devlin looked to see who was closest. It was Lieutenant Kennedy, with a slight frown on his face.

"Good news? Bad?" the Lieutenant asked, and the Captain shook his head.

"No... I just. Go find Colonel Waller. Tell him... it is, in fact, actually the 25th. Captain Koster just waved at me."

Kennedy's head dipped slightly and he blinked, but that was the extent of his reaction. He hurried off to find Waller as Devlin peeked back around the corner, raising his glasses again to be sure.

Yep, it was Koster. And Krazakowski with him.

Deciding he no longer needed to hide, the Captain stepped out around the aircruiser and waved his b'ys to follow. A reunion was about to happen... and then, Devlin supposed, the blue men were going to get a nasty surprise.

CHAPTER XVI

Waller had been expecting another settlement like Promised Town, with at least some signs of prosperity, even if it was of the criminal variety. Deadline did not meet that lofty expectation: it was barren to the point of seeming barely alive.

For all its alien feel, though, the red craggy peaks around the town did indeed remind him of his past in Afghanistan, albeit with a slightly different texture.

"At least it doesn't seem as damned dusty," George Tucker observed in low tones as he, Miller, Devlin and the Colonel led the way to Deadline's wall, the entirety of 'C' Company following them at the ready in case savages popped out of the ground.

Waller nodded in agreement. One of the most oppressive things about the Khyber had been the pervasive dust, unlike anything he'd seen anywhere else in either world. These badlands were rockier, and they also bore a slightly different atmosphere. It was as though the craggy heights around them had eyes and were watching with some malevolence.

You shouldn't be here, they were saying. Hopefully there were no snipers to reinforce the message...

The b'ys were picking up the same feeling — there were too many places for marksmen to be lying in wait for them.

"Well the good news is if blue snipers shoot lightning at us, we'll be able to see where they're shooting from," Devlin pitched in with a little extra volume, making certain to remind his b'ys of the advantages they'd have in this terrain: no one would be able to spot their sniping positions.

Smokeless gunpowder had made its debut in the Boer War at the turn of the twentieth century, and it had made snipers particularly deadly in that conflict, because unlike in past wars, counter-fire couldn't be directed at the smoke spouted by a sharpshooter's rifle. If he was well hidden in rocks like these, a man could empty a magazine without being spotted — a benefit any Martian firing bolts of lightning wouldn't enjoy, thanks to their conspicuous weapons.

That was small comfort as the b'ys crossed open ground to the town of Deadline, but it was enough to allow the rest of the short march to pass in silence, and the closer they drew, the clearer the many black faces peeking over the wall became, their tan field hats bright in the afternoon light.

It really was the 25th — Waller recognized some of the men from their fight at Promised Town the year prior.

The Newfoundlanders were heading for Deadline's northern gate, and as they neared it, the large doors creaked open, then expelled three tan-clad officers and fifty men — an American-sized company.

It was Krazakowski, leading Koster and Adams, and within moments they met the Newfoundlanders beneath the walls.

"Colonel Waller, welcome to Deadline," Krazakowski greeted his counterpart warmly, and Waller had to smile in reply.

"I was just joking with Jimmy — thought it would be too much to hope to find your men out here. Though I suspect it hasn't been a laughing matter for you?"

"I rarely laugh, I'm afraid," was Krazakowski's answer. "We were sent to Deadline after reports of savage activity. We found none, but perhaps that's because the savages moved past us."

It was a familiar sort of circumstance, and Waller had to nod, "Know precisely how that feels. But help is at hand." With that, Waller turned slightly and indicated his officers, "The rest of our regiment has arrived, Major. This is Bert Miller. We call him the Skipper."

Miller nodded to Krazakowski at the introduction, and the American replied with typically earnest words, "It is an honor to meet more men of your fine regiment. Major Miller, welcome to Deadline."

The Skipper wasn't accustomed to such formality, but he accepted it with an easy smile, "Very pleased to meet you as well."

It was as much time as could be dedicated to pleasantries; looking back to Waller, Krazakowski turned his mind to the circumstances: "Were you sent here to relieve us? By your surprise at seeing us here, I suppose you haven't come under orders from General Pershing."

Waller shook his head, "The General didn't inform us of the troubles he was having until we realized something was going on. Savages landed in Ambitia and Destina, so we've moved reinforcements to Pacifica City..."

"They haven't pressed any further so far?" Captain Koster interjected for the first time, and Waller shook his head.

"Not by the time we'd left. Pershing is rallying his defenses at Pacifica because he expects them to come that way next, but they hadn't moved yet. General Byng sent our reserves to join his, but we wanted to get a look down here to see if there were signs of the blue men's plans."

"Were there?" Captain Adams was the next to raise a helpful question, and Jimmy took his turn to help explain the situation.

"We spotted a column of blue vehicles coming this way... we think they cut off communications at Ambitia and Destina, so they can safely move up their main force."

It was an interesting conclusion, and it brought a frown to Krazakowski's face, "Coming in this direction?"

"We think. We're getting that from some... *new* reconnaissance tools," Devlin decided not to try to explain the dragons and their moving picture screens just yet.

"Wherever they're headed, though, our mission isn't just to see them, Major," Waller chimed in again. "Selkirk was just reinforced by men from the Indian Army... the men we fought with in Afghanistan, and our best General from that campaign. They're fine soldiers for ground like this..."

Waving his hand towards the unforgiving surroundings, Waller watched Krazakowski's eyes narrow thoughtfully, then his head tilted as he replied: "You mean to ambush the blue men, taking advantage of the terrain?"

"If we can find the right place," Waller confirmed. "And now that we find you here, perhaps we can work together to see if such a place exists."

Krazakowski began to nod very slowly, "Quite similar to something we were ourselves considering, Colonel Waller. With you here, a move into the badlands would not be one of escape, but of offense. I believe we have much to discuss."

They did indeed, so without wasting further time they turned for the gate and made their way behind the walls of Deadline.

**

Sergeant Halloran was grinning at his b'ys as the gates swung shut behind 'C' Company. They'd found the 25th — and it was a funny thing to see the American buffalo soldiers so soon after being reunited with Skeen.

As soon as the b'ys were put at their ease, reunions began. They were warmer than some might have expected, given the reluctance of the black men of the 25th to trust the Newfoundlanders back at Promised Town. Halloran didn't consider himself to be a particularly wise man, but he knew that sometimes time apart could make old adventures seem better than they were... and make people appreciate good company even more.

So whatever had happened between Promised Town and now, the men of the 25th had fond memories of the b'ys, and the b'ys had similar sentiments towards the black soldiers.

"What the fuck they figurin', sending these big fellers out here to this hell?" one of the b'ys was asking loudly, and his comment drew laughter as handshakes were exchanged.

Halloran was looking for one man in particular — his counterpart, Sergeant Turner — but he wasn't around. That was odd, since he'd seemed as attached to the black Captain Adams as Halloran was to Devlin, and they were amongst Adams' men at the wall. Halloran recognized a few of them with nods.

Spotting the American officer standing and speaking with Devlin, Halloran decided to ask. He arrived beside Jimmy just as the Captain was shaking his head and talking about the battle at Farpoint — explaining how Sir Julian Byng had led men into a cloud of smoke and dust to fight the beasts. Adams was listening closely, as Byng was an officer of some interest to him — a good general, which was rare in his experience.

Halloran just stood aside while the story ended, and when conversation briefly paused he interrupted, "Excuse me, sir, I was just wondering about Sergeant Turner?"

Devlin hadn't seen Halloran come up, so he glanced back at his veteran NCO with a frown, "He's the fellow Sir Julian spoke to at Highwater?"

Nodding, Halloran turned his eyes back to Adams, and Devlin did the same. Both therefore saw the uncomfortable expression that came to the

Captain's face.

"We lost Turner and his squad when we tried scouting Ambitia. Mister Smith too…"

The Captain kept speaking after that, but neither Devlin nor Halloran heard another word.

Mister Smith?

"Smith? Smith was here?"

Waller had been surprised enough to find the men of the 25th at Deadline, but the moment Krazakowski made his apologies for the loss of the drifter, the Colonel's eyebrows shot to the top of his head, and he began to question what brand of providence was intervening in this mission.

Of course Krazakowski seemed completely oblivious to the surprise: "Indeed, he joined us as we came through Ambitia on the way out here. We arrived just in time to save him from a band of outlaws who were set to kill him."

Outlaws? Smith? Ambitia?

Waller couldn't keep up, and somehow he didn't think it was too unreasonable for him to be slightly behind.

"He volunteered to lead the scouting party that went back to Ambitia, because he'd spent days in that town recently. Captain Adams sent Sergeant Turner with him… some hard losses there, but there was nothing to be done."

This had obviously happened, because Krazakowski was telling the story and making apologies for it, but Waller still wasn't digesting the words.

"I must particularly apologize, Colonel, because I believe Smith's intention was ultimately to return to Selkirk, and to rejoin your men. A loss for both our commands, without question," Krazakowski's words were genuinely regretful, and he cast his eyes down for a moment.

Waller just stared in silence.

He thought for… but. Wait. Smith had been here. He'd ridden south after Caralynne's death, had crossed outlaws, and then ended up with the men of the 25th, only to be killed when scouting for them?

Smith had been here. And now he was dead.

Waller let out a long breath and just barely shook his head.

This seemed an unfitting end for the drifter... but then, few ends for men seemed fitting. Waller could only hope that one day his own demise was befitting his notion of how it should be...

While the Colonel of the Royal Newfoundland Regiment was gathering his thoughts, the Skipper knew it was necessary to keep things moving: "We appreciate you telling us that, Major Krazakowski. Best now to put the thoughts behind us, though. What about the blue column coming this way... you've had no sign of it?"

Those words dragged Waller back, and Krazakowski raised his eyes from the map, "No sign at all. Though this landscape makes it rather difficult... and indeed, I must ask, do you believe they are passing through this town?"

Waller shook his head, "We don't know their precise route. But they're moving close to here."

"You think there's a natural path they might be taking to get around all these cliffs?" Miller pressed a little more helpfully, and Krazakowski looked down at his crude local map again.

"Just before you arrived, Captain Adams and I were speaking to the Mayor of this town, wondering whether the local terrain might provide us escape in case of a horde coming this way. He suggested a canyon, roughly twenty miles to the north of here, that runs east and west."

Both Newfoundlanders let their eyes settle on Krazakowski's map, but unfortunately the crude piece of paper did little to clarify the location of any such pass. Still, it sounded promising.

"If it's the path they're taking... and it's a proper canyon... there could be potential there," Waller said quietly, casting a glance at Miller.

The Skipper's brow was creased as he considered what he was hearing, but then he gently agreed: "Worth a good look. If it has steep sides and is deep enough..."

Koster was in the room as well, though he'd been silent. Now he looked between the Newfoundland officers with a frown, "You b'ys really think you can go out there and meet a horde?"

Waller looked up from the map to the Captain, not taking any offense at the question, "Not alone. But with General Skeen and a couple of Indian regiments, plus the ability to withdraw by air... at the very least, we might be able to give them something to think about, and Pershing more time to draw reinforcements from the other side of the tunnel."

"Always better to fight savages far away from civilian populations, too, I should think," Krazakowski's agreement sounded thoughtful, and he slowly folded his arms as he spoke.

Silence endured for a moment, as the four officers considered each other, and the map spread out between them. Koster was clearly the most skeptical, but as the Major of the 25th United States Infantry thought more on the circumstances, a certain clarity seemed to be reflected in his expression.

"Gentlemen, if you mean to go and fight the savages in these badlands, my men will accompany you."

It was a solid pledge, and though he looked immediately surprised by it, Koster did not discourage it — it would hardly have been appropriate for him to do so.

Waller considered Krazakowski's face as the American Major spoke, and saw determination that reflected the history of the regiment he led. The buffalo soldiers had been sent to Deadline because they were the unit that received the thankless jobs... but now, with the Newfoundlanders, Skeen, the Indian Army and an aircruiser, perhaps they had a chance to be a part of more important work, just as they had been at Promised Town.

"I think somewhere, a blue man just got a chill down his spine," Skipper Miller replied, since Waller was too lost in his musing to speak.

There would be four regiments contributing to the ambush, provided the pass was the place. Tom Waller found himself hoping very much it was.

CHAPTER XVII

Smith didn't figure any man should know what to expect when he surrendered to creatures from another planet. Waller had been taken at the beginning of the clash with the blues, but that had been before the fighting. After the losses the British and American forces had caused the Martians, it would probably be fair of the creatures to treat prisoners badly.

So far, though, these particular blue men hadn't.

The fellow with the two silver bands on each arm stayed close to the prisoners as they climbed up uneven goat trails into the deep woods east of Ambitia. Smith was first in line as they made their way up the track, Turner right behind him. Every so often, the drifter looked back over his shoulder and found the black Sergeant's expression to be taut and uncomfortable, though still stern.

Savages were always close by, in sufficient numbers to convince the prisoners that making a run for it wasn't a wise idea... but the pace was quite slow, because the blue men weren't sure-footed. A few beasts were carrying the rifles surrendered by the soldiers, which didn't make much sense to Smith. Did the Martians want to study human firepower? Why would they even care? The drifter didn't know, but it did grant him some comfort to see his '92 was still somewhere nearby, even if there was no way he could get hold of it.

Their fate remained a mystery... and the long walk just meant more waiting, and more time to grow anxious.

Nevertheless, Turner and his men kept their composure. No matter what they were marching towards, they were professionals, and the same way they'd been willing to stand and fight with a horde climbing all over Promised Town, they were willing to keep to their discipline now.

How long would they have to wait to learn their fate?

Smith caught sight of something ahead — a glint of light reflected off of a shiny surface. It was the sort of sign that men inexperienced in being stealthy could often give away, by failing to dull down a belt buckle or a button.

But the reflective surface was much bigger than a button; as Smith continued up the track, following his blue captor, he saw a wide silver panel... and as he came closer still through the trees, he was able to make out the shape of an aircruiser.

Moments later, the prisoners emerged into a grassy clearing that was just wide enough for the large machine. Smith recognized the design as being like the one that had rescued the blue men from Fort Martian, after the Farpoint attack. It was bigger up close than the drifter would have thought... could probably hold 200 savages inside its frame.

Coming to a stop at the edge of the clearing, Smith watched the blue man approach the machine, and saw a trio of other blues who were sitting on silver barrels beside it, working on lightning guns.

Immediately Smith got the feeling that he was looking at soldiers — real fighting Martians, who had probably seen action before. He'd never been skilled at reading Martian body language, but something about their movement, and the way they looked over him and the men of the 25th, conveyed the impression that they were serious types... more like the ones he'd seen in Farfield City than those who had attacked Promised Town.

After meeting in silence with the seated blues for a few moments — undoubtedly communicating with them via the psychic language they used — the blue man with the bands returned to his party of prisoners. Raising his hand, the creature pointed to the humans, then waved towards the craft.

It didn't take much interpretation to figure his meaning: they were to be imprisoned inside, so when it moved, they would too.

Smith chose not to think about how far away that aircruiser could take him, he just looked back to Turner and nodded his head towards the machine. Better to get inside, get a look at the place. Maybe if they could find an arsenal of lightning guns, and figure out how to work the aircruiser, they could do something to turn the tables on their captors.

The soldiers began to move, but before Smith could follow them the blue man... perhaps best dubbed an 'officer'... blocked the way, his eyes locking on. Again Smith's mind began to twist, and the drifter felt his brow crease at the uncomfortable feeling.

Pictures started flying into his head, delivering a message: if they cooperated, they'd be left unharmed. Smith recalled sending a similar message to the blues captured at Promised Town. It wasn't as good being on the receiving end of such ultimatums, but the drifter wouldn't complain at the notion of not being killed.

As long as he was still breathing, he reckoned he had a chance. Maybe he could even learn something, and get it back to people who could use it.

Smith realized the blue man might be able to read those thoughts from his mind, but there was nothing he could do to prevent that. Only thing left to do was try to talk back, so he focused his thinking and put a question to his captor.

He pictured a soldier, and then pictured this officer and his comrades at the aircruiser. Then he pictured the blue men who'd led the attack on Farpoint, who had been evacuated in an aircruiser like this one. After he got the mental picture of those creatures into his head, he pictured a man sitting behind a desk, writing lists.

As the images appeared, the blue man with the bands seemed to take an interest — perhaps it was no surprise to the Martian that this man, who had been involved in numerous engagements so far, understood how to crudely communicate his questions.

What was more interesting to Smith was the blue officer's answer.

Pictures flashed back through the drifter's mind... this blue officer on a world with a red sky, fighting lizard men — lightning bolts crossing back and forth, and savages swarming around in organized chaos. The officer was standing in the midst of the battle, coolly directing the action of his other blue men, and of savages. As a result, victory was secured... or at least that's what the officer wanted Smith to believe.

Before the drifter could decide whether or not he was convinced of the blue man's ability to bring victory, the pictures began to change. Returning to the image of the blue men who had mounted the attack on Farpoint, and then escaped by air, the blue officer established that his next message would be in relation to those individuals. He then placed those creatures in an office similar to the one that the Newfoundlanders had used at Fort Martian, except with more moving picture screens in the walls.

The message, it seemed, was that this blue man was a veteran of combat — a professional soldier in the way Smith expected — while the officers who had come before had belonged behind a desk, or worse, had been Custer-types.

Smith supposed that made sense — as it was true for the Americans and the British that there were inferior men holding posts of authority, particularly on the far reaches of their territory, the blue men could suffer from the same challenge.

But if the reason the humans of the new world had been able to survive this long was because the blue men had only sent their most inferior combatants, things didn't bode well for the future. If the blue in front of Smith now was a real soldier, and his men were actually good fighters, this handful alone could be the biggest danger the British or Americans had yet seen on the new world.

At one time in his life — a time not far behind him — Smith might have taken that possibility as a sign he should just move on, to avoid trouble. This time his immediate reaction came as a slight surprise to him, even though it made sense: he would need to find a way, with Turner's help, to stop this blue officer and his aircruiser before they had the chance to prove their skill.

The officer might have picked up on that thought, but if he did, he didn't show it. Instead he pushed a new question into Smith's mind: a picture of Smith, with silver bands around his arms. He was asking if the drifter was in a similar military position... a leader of the troops. Made sense to ask, since Smith had been on the sharp end of most of the scraps between savages and humans since the two species had been violently introduced.

Smith considered answering with a lie, because it might be helpful if the blue thought him to be a lofty soldier... but the drifter had never been any good as a liar, and he figured he'd be even worse at it when trying through telepathy. He thus honestly pictured himself on his horse, riding alone for years, and only coming to the fight against the blue men because of the Newfoundlanders.

As the blue man processed those pictures, his head tilted. He pushed back a picture of a man with silver bands around his arms scouting ahead of troops, but then later standing in line with them. Smith shook his head, and pictured himself riding away from the Newfoundlanders. He wasn't one of them, even though he had a beach rock from a place called Middle Cove in his pocket.

Again, the blue officer struggled with that picture — Smith got the feeling that he had no notion of people joining a military operation of their own independent will, and then being allowed to leave. It was pretty irregular in the world of humans too, come to think of it, but that didn't matter.

After a time, the blue officer seemed to resign himself to the lack of clarity. To reinforce his initial message, he again pictured Smith and the other prisoners behaving themselves, and being left in peace within the aircruiser. Smith replied with the same picture, which he hoped indicated his understanding.

It seemed to satisfy the Martian, so with that the being broke eye contact and turned towards the craft, gesturing for Smith to enter it. The drifter didn't need any prodding; he took easy steps across the grassy clearing, counting how many were needed to reach the machine from the treeline.

Inside, another hard-looking blue soldier waved him to go left, and he found himself entering a plain silver compartment, the men of the 25th already settling in on the cold metal floor. The door shut behind him, and Smith looked back quickly to make sure they were alone.

"Fifteen yards from the door of this thing to the edge of the clearing," Turner offered the same information Smith had collected, and the drifter nodded in reply.

"My count as well."

"Probably too many of the savages there to try to get through... and without knowing where they put our rifles..." Private Marks made that observation a bit uneasily. He was a fine sharpshooter; to strip him of his weapon was as bad as taking one of his hands.

His remark was hardly wrong, though; the savages were all over the woods, and if Smith was right about the size of this aircruiser, there could be a couple of hundred of them. Not too many for a company to deal with — a British-sized cómpany, anyway — but far beyond the ability of eight unarmed men.

"Think we could steal this thing we're in, fly it away?" Preston asked, earning only blank looks in reply. No one had any idea how the machine worked, or how its switchboards might operate. Shaking his head, the Private leaned back against the wall and let his head hit the alloy, "Didn't think so."

"I got some pieces from that blue one who took us," Smith spoke up next, drawing his hat from his head and studying it as he thought again about his conversation, if that's what it could be called. "We'll be treated well if we don't cause a fuss. I think that's honest, but I don't know where we'd end up."

"I'd rather get killed than end up in some city of theirs," Turner said sharply, and Smith agreed with a nod.

"The other thing I got is that this blue man, the one with the four bands on his arms, was an officer in their wars with the lizards. He showed me pictures of himself in the field against them. Looks to me like he and his men here are probably the most professional soldiers they've put against us."

Smith let those words hang for a minute, looking up from his hat to watch the faces of the men as they heard the news. They traded glances, and eventually all eyes turned to the Sergeant. Turner voiced the question that came to mind, "He's their General?"

"Maybe. Or a Colonel. He's important enough to command this ship, and to lead it into our territory."

Turner digested the importance of the statement for a few seconds, then came to the obvious conclusion, "So if he and his blues didn't make it into the next battle…"

"It'd probably hurt them some," Smith agreed.

Turner and the men fell silent. These were professional soldiers who'd worked harder than most in order to get recognition for being good at their jobs. They were smart, and skilled, and they weren't afraid to risk their lives for bad missions.

The chance to risk their lives now for a useful purpose — to potentially get rid of one of the blue leaders — was appealing... even if trying to kill an officer who had shown them mercy was distasteful, and also a certain death sentence for them.

Worth thinking about though, because it could make a difference.

Silence settled over the cell for a while, and eventually Smith sat on the cold floor too. They had a lot to figure.

CHAPTER XVIII

Word of the loss of Mister Smith had done much to dull the good spirits of the reunion between the Newfoundland Regiment and the 25th United States Infantry. As men from both units clustered around the gate through Deadline's northern palisade, the mood grew quieter and more solemn.

Jimmy Devlin was far from immune to this feeling, though he was still having a difficult time believing the drifter had been killed, despite Captain Adams' belief.

"I really am sorry," the American was saying again, though the repetition of the apology did nothing to convince Devlin.

"Just... hard to get to grips with," the Newfoundlander replied, shaking his head.

Smith had always seemed the sort of man who could make his way out of any fix, but then he was also the sort to remind any man that mortality was a fact of living... that no man was going to survive everything life threw at him.

Could he truly be dead? Jimmy Devlin still didn't believe...

But before he could question Adams any further, a new friend who had attached herself to the Newfoundland Regiment decided to intervene. Of course Devlin didn't hear her approach, because dragons are silent, but when he noticed Adams' eyes suddenly climb into the sky, and his jaw drop, he realized what must be happening. With a quick turn, Jimmy set eyes on a trio of dragons.

Sass and the two pilots were standing up on their back legs, looming over the palisades of Deadline. Their eyes traveled over the tan-clad American troops with some interest — unlike the other differently-colored soldiers Sass had seen in the Newfoundlanders' base city, these humans had slightly different equipment. Another faction, perhaps... but they seemed to be principally similar to the Newfoundland troops. That made sense, she supposed — the different clans of a species would undoubtedly learn their warfare methods from each other.

They were all quite surprised to see her, of course, but none seemed to be aggressive. She got the feeling they had already heard of the existence of the Saa... so communication between these two factions was effective enough. That was good to know too.

Devlin immediately started waving, so Sass moved sideways along the settlement wall and stopped at the point right outside the entrance gate. The ground within was too full of troops for her to step inside, so she simply leaned down to get closer.

"Sass, may I present Captain Adams," Devlin gestured to his American counterpart, and the dragon nodded in reply.

"He's very... large," Adams said, holding up a hand to wave at the massive lizard.

"She, actually. That was awkward," Devlin corrected.

Adams blinked and looked down at the Newfoundlander, then shook his head, "You Newfoundlanders... you surround yourselves with all sorts of women, don't you?"

Jimmy Devlin might have laughed at that, but instead he thought of the loss of Caralynne, and the convalescence of Emily and only managed to smile thinly as he replied, "I suppose we do."

Not certain what was being said, Sass simply straightened back up, wondering what would come next. Would Waller join with these new troops to mount a counter to the Hubrin column that was near? Aggression seemed their intent, but had anything changed?

"So General Skeen is confident of his abilities to fight in this terrain?"

As Waller, Miller, Krazakowski and Koster made their way back towards the northern gate, they were continuing to discuss the options for ambush in the badlands. Although Krazakowski's determination to involve his men in any combat had not waned, he was asking prudent questions.

"It's hard to explain, Major... but yes. He's one of the best fighting Generals we've ever known, and a master at outwitting his enemy — in his enemy's own country. I suppose the timing couldn't be better for him to turn up," Waller's own enthusiasm for this mission — whether appropriate or not — was trickling into his words, though Krazakowski didn't receive it poorly.

"It sounds as though you're most eager to let him at the blue men."

"I am," Waller agreed. "And this is the right place for it."

Krazakowski nodded at that point — his own notion of escaping into the badlands in the first place reflected his similar appreciation of the advantages of the terrain.

"If this canyon is deep enough, and steep-sided enough, we could consider an ambush. But it's risky," Koster remained the least convinced of the group, and as he spoke he looked to Krazakowski.

Both the Major and his counterpart Colonel nodded, but it was Miller who recognized the tension in the American's voice, and addressed it head on: "There won't be an ambush unless we find the right spot, Captain Koster. But in a place like this, I expect we'll find that sort of spot."

"And we can go find out for certain quite quickly," Waller added. "We'll evacuate your men and the townsfolk onto the aircruiser, then go look at this canyon. If there's no real opportunity, we all return to Pacifica City to wait for the blues."

Koster was still taking time to get comfortable with the idea, but Krazakowski already had it well in hand. His were the final words on the matter: "It is as prudent as one can be in war. Let us all hope a good opportunity does present itself."

That was it — there would be no further discussion of the ambush until they saw the pass. After a few more moments of walking, the quartet of officers reached the edge of town, there discovering that Sass and her two pilots had finally found enough clear dirt within the walls to come inside Deadline's palisade.

Now the dragons stood upright, each facing outward in a triangular formation while Americans formed a ring around them, gaping at their size and stealth.

This was also the first time Krazakowski had seen the creatures, and Waller glanced to Miller with a smile, looking forward to the American's reaction.

Immediately spotting Sass as the leader of the party, Krazakowski quickly marched in her direction, and as his men realized he was approaching, they made way. Noticing the crowd parting on her side of the ring of spectators, Sass watched Krazakowski arrive, determining that he was probably the commanding officer of this place — he'd returned with Waller and little old Miller, and his soldiers were standing aside for him.

Hissing that conclusion to her two pilots, she ordered them to face the newcomer, and straighten their tails.

Every American standing far below seemed surprised to see the dragons come to attention. Krazakowski reached the front rank of the audience in short order, and then with his typical earnestness, he saluted sharply.

"Madame, I am Major Krazakowski of the United States Army. May I present my men, of the 25th United States Infantry."

The black soldiers standing around their Major were surprised by the introduction. One Sergeant, though, realized that the 25th had just been formally presented, and he let instinct take over.

"Attention battalion!"

The order was repeated by NCOs around the ring, and suddenly the hundreds of American soldiers who had been gawking straightened up to attention.

Sass looked down with some surprise at the haste of that conversion, and then waited for the Major to lower his salute. But he didn't.

She hissed softly, hoping he'd take the noise as an indication that she'd accepted the respectful greeting, but his hand stayed up. Odd fellow. She glanced back to her pilots, then hissed them to their ease. Tails loosened, which would surely be a sign that the new soldiers could stop posing for her.

But the Major's hand stayed up.

Confused, Sass decided to go lower, so she dropped swiftly and silently down onto her hands, and brought her face very close to the Major's. His expression seemed not to change in the slightest as she came close to him — unlike many of the other humans she'd met, this man seemed entirely unimpressed by her size.

Strange.

Sass decided to try nodding: she stared at Krazakowski and nodded her head. Then a frown formed on his face and he nodded back, hand still up.

"I think that's supposed to be 'at ease'," Waller came up behind his American counterpart.

"Aha," Krazakowski said, then lowered his salute. "Thank you, ma'am."

As his salute came down, he nodded to the nearest Sergeant, and the men were put back at their ease as well. Completely fearless, Krazakowski then approached Sass' face and reached out with his right hand to lay his palm on her giant snout.

"Pleasure to make your acquaintance," he said, then withdrew his hand. Sass took that as a signal; she straightened up again with another nod.

Waller came up alongside Krazakowski, "They're very quiet."

"And she's in command of their contingent for this particular mission?" the American asked.

"Yes..." the Newfoundland Colonel paused. "You know Sass is a she?"

Krazakowski frowned at his Newfoundland counterpart, "Of course. Isn't it obvious?"

Waller stared at the American, wondering if that was supposed to be a joke. He didn't get a chance to find out, "Might I see the aircruiser now, Colonel?"

Without waiting another second, the American officer set off for the gate.

Strange man indeed.

CHAPTER XIX

Emily was endeavoring to sit up.

Annie, by now, had given up trying to stop the savage-born Lady from attempting such foolish things; the wife of Captain Devlin simply sat in the chair beside Emily's bed, reading a newspaper and occasionally looking around the broadsheet at the wincing woman who was too frustrated to convalesce like a sensible person.

As the latest attempt to get upright ended with a pained hiss, Emily flopped back onto her pillow and then had to tug on her hospital gown. The thing twisted too easily — every time she tried to force her way upward, it ended up in quite a state.

Of course, if she stopped trying to rise, it would stop twisting, but that sort of logic had no place in Emily's mind now. She had to get her strength back — she had to be out there. Tom had barely been gone for half a day and already she had a dread feeling that he'd need her.

"If you re-open your wound, you'll only be forced to stay here longer," Annie's words cut in just as Emily was mentally fortifying herself for another attempt, and the Lady shot a glare at her former maid.

Life as a Captain's wife had already made Annie somewhat immune to such assaults, and she simply went back to her paper. Emily let out a sigh and gave up tugging on her gown for the moment. It would just twist all over again when she next attempted to sit up, so she might as well leave it.

The pain was already dulling — her body was getting more accustomed to the discomfort that was necessary to get her upright. Eventually she might be numb to it altogether, and then she could rise.

Before she could think any more about that subject, the door to the hospital room opened, a nurse entering with a tray of dressings, "Time for a change, M'Lady."

Stopping beside the bed, the woman seemed to be staring solely at the materials she'd brought with her. When her eyes eventually moved to

Emily, a frown creased her brow, "M'Lady, your gown is very twisted. You haven't been attempting to sit up, have you?"

Emily started to turn red, and Annie looked up from her paper, managing to make eye contact with the woman before looking down again. The shared gaze was enough, and much to Emily's chagrin, the nurse started into a familiar lecture, "You have been told, and you will continue to be told, M'Lady. You cannot heal if you tear open your wound."

"I am familiar with the concept," Emily replied sharply, looking away in frustration.

The nurse shook her head and let out a slightly exasperated sigh, then pulled open Emily's gown and began to untie the bandages holding the dressing to her wound. There was no great flow of blood, at least — it seemed unlikely that harm had been done by the latest attempts.

Emily stared past Annie's paper at the window as the nurse's cold hands did their work. It was a strange feeling, having another person's fingers on her abdomen. Perhaps embarrassingly, it made her think of Tom — too much time apart from him now, and she was sufficiently recovered to realize exactly how much she did miss having him nearby.

But that was one of the current frustrations that she most certainly would not share with Annie or a nurse. She was trying to think about something else when she felt the dressing come off her stomach, and the nurse's hands pull away.

Nothing happened for a moment, and Emily assumed the nurse was simply preparing the next dressing for application... but more time passed without activity. Then the nurse stood and backed away from the bed very slightly before turning and leaving the room.

That was obviously not expected, and both Annie and Emily immediately frowned. As Missus Devlin folded her paper and laid it on the floor beside the chair, Emily tried to crane her neck to see what precisely was going on in her wounded flesh. Unfortunately, she couldn't sit up.

Annie came to her feet and rounded the bed, a little reluctant to view a wound that had only been recently stitched shut... but as it came into view, she stopped as well.

The scar was considerable — many cuts had been made to open up the wound for irrigation. But...

"What is it?" Emily's irritation was muted by concern.

Shaking her head, Annie tried to answer, but wasn't able to say anything before the door opened again.

"...like it's been knitting together for a few weeks," the nurse was saying, and behind her a frowning doctor followed, appearing frustrated that he'd been pulled from his normal duties. His expression changed as soon as he saw Emily's bare skin.

The nurse stood aside as the man bent down and gently began testing Emily's flesh with his fingers, "Lady Emily, is that uncomfortable?"

At first Emily wasn't sure what he was referring to, but then she realized he meant the soft feeling of his fingertips on her skin. She shook her head, "No, not at all."

Narrowing his eyes he leaned closer, studying her abdomen, "Well. I'd say we can take out the stitches."

Emily blinked, then decided she needed more information: "You can tell me what's going on now, doctor."

The man looked up to meet her gaze, then straightened up, pulling his hand away from her flesh, "M'Lady, your wound has completely closed. I've never seen anything quite like it. Very accelerated healing... weeks ahead of what I would have anticipated. If your muscles heal as quickly, you'll be well again in no time."

Needless to say, that was good news. Emily found herself smiling, and then she looked to Annie with a little immature glee, "See."

"How long is 'no time'," the Lady's former maid asked in a flat, almost maternal tone, and the doctor paused thoughtfully. "Perhaps a month. Maybe even three weeks."

Emily's smile faded, "What?"

The doctor nodded, "Remarkable. I would have thought you had a few months ahead of you. It will be vital that you don't try to move too fast, M'Lady, or you might undo some of the healing. But if you're patient and you don't fidget too much, you'll be the fastest recovery from such a gunshot that I've ever treated."

"A month," the words tasted bitter in Emily's mouth, but the doctor seemed not to notice.

"Exciting, indeed. We'll get those stitches out soon... and if you progress well, we might move you back to your house in a week or two."

That last part sounded more appealing, and Emily decided to draw some hope from it. She nodded, and then the doctor and nurse departed, muttering about scheduling the stitches to be removed.

As the door shut behind them, Annie shrugged slightly, "Well, at least then you can be frustrated in the privacy of your own home."

Emily glared at her former maid, but Annie Devlin simply smiled serenely before returning to her chair.

There was still much healing ahead.

The people of Deadline were being prepared for evacuation — whether the ambush went ahead or not, they'd need to be removed from harm's way by the aircruiser. Plans called for them to be flown to Pacifica City, and if the b'ys and the men of the 25th were to stay behind to fight, a messenger would go with them, to summon Skeen and his regiments to join the attack.

All of that was being arranged by Krazakowski, Tucker and Miller, to allow Waller a few moments for some personal business.

Well, he supposed it was personal. He wasn't really sure.

It was known to many that Tom Waller enjoyed no particular skill with horses. He had grown up in a merchant family in St. John's, knew his way around a schooner — more or less — and had a good sense for organization, but he'd never ridden a horse much at all.

Still, he had an affinity for the animals, or at least some of them... and one he knew to be a particularly fine ambassador for her kind was a painted brown Appaloosa mare. As far as Waller was aware, she had no name, but she'd been a faithful companion to a man who had been adopted as a Newfoundlander. Now it would be wrong to send her to Pacifica City with strangers.

When Waller stepped into the barn where Smith had last picketed his horse, a man from the 25th was already there, helping the local farrier get the townsfolk's mounts ready for transport. Neither man had touched the Appaloosa, though — perhaps they'd known special arrangements would be made for her.

Nodding to the black soldier and the civilian, Waller moved down the line until he found Smith's mare. He stopped short of her, and watched her eyes as she gazed at him. Perhaps she recognized him — they'd been around each other plenty of times in the past year. Hopefully he was a welcome familiar face.

"Sir, here's some oats for her. She's been sad since Mister Smith a-went without her," the soldier from the 25th was suddenly beside Waller, holding out a handful of the horse food.

Waller took it with a nod of thanks, but as the American moved off the Newfoundlander realized he didn't know quite how to offer it.

Nothing to do but try.

Leaning forward, Waller reached out to the horse with his empty hand, then rubbed between her eyes as he'd seen some men do. He offered her the oats from his other hand, and sure enough, she ate them comfortably. She seemed at peace, but perhaps that meant she was sad.

"I'm afraid I don't know what to say... erhm... Missus Mare. We've all suffered a loss, but you more than most," he offered feebly, immediately feeling absurd for talking to a horse.

For a moment, the Appaloosa seemed oblivious, but then she stepped forward in her stall, and nuzzled her face up against Waller's uniform. Surprised by the move, the Colonel nearly fell over, but managed to get a grip on her neck to keep upright.

He hoped it was a good sign that she was happy to have contact with him — were she a dog, he would have been more confident of the meaning of the sign.

"We're sending most of the horses to Pacifica City with their owners, but we're buying some and keeping them with us. And you'll be with us. Not going to send you away with strangers," Waller said, finding his footing again. "I'm no good at riding, but Lieutenant Kennedy is, and he'll be commanding our scouts. So if you don't mind, he'll partner with you."

The mare snorted at that, which was hopefully a good sign, and then Waller rubbed her nose again, "We'll figure out what we all do once we're back to civilization."

That was as much as any of them could do for now, and both the Colonel of the Royal Newfoundland Regiment and the horse of Smith knew it. After a few more minutes of visiting, Waller left the barn, and the American soldier got the Appaloosa saddled for her trip in an aircruiser.

She wouldn't be left behind.

CHAPTER XX

As the aircruiser floated over the difficult badlands terrain north of Deadline, Krazakowski and Waller puzzled over the moving picture screen in its cockpit. Devlin was standing nearby, and he listened as the American voiced his surprise at the nature of the intelligence guiding their flight.

"Just these blue markers, telling you there are lorries out there?"

Waller answered that query with a nod, "Don't know what sort of optics are behind them, but Sass has confirmed to us that there's something there."

To a skeptic, it might have sounded like a poor endorsement, but Krazakowski replied with satisfaction, "What excellent allies. Hopefully the blue men lack our dragon friends' visual acuity."

"She seems to believe they do," Waller confirmed.

Devlin tuned out after that — he knew the risks and the assumptions that had carried them this far. But there was no panic, because as he looked at the impassable ground beneath the aircruiser, he was repeatedly reminded of the impossible fights in Afghanistan.

Though Devlin had only been a Lieutenant on that Khyber campaign, Skeen had always advocated that junior officers be competent at all manner of jobs, and be party to higher-level decisions. It was pragmatic approach — with such bad terrain and such poor communications, it was necessary for every officer to be able to contribute to the success of a mission, even without orders.

That was how Jimmy had learned so much, so quickly... and why now he could be so confident in what he saw. This was a dangerous place — where a few savages could fall on a man from any peak... but where a column of infantry, no matter what it was composed of, could be vulnerable to attack.

It just depended on the ground.

There had been rough places in the Khyber — places where wrestling camels around the corners of narrow tracks had been dangerous enough, even without snipers nearby. Savages were deft creatures, but out here he had to believe they would be hard-pressed and disorganized.

And if they were down low, and the b'ys and Skeen and the Americans were up high with enough firepower...

It would be decided by the terrain. It all depended on the canyon.

They'd see it momentarily...

"That's it up there, I think..." George Tucker was also in the cockpit, and he was leaning over one of the boards of switches, face nearly pressed against the glass as he looked at the landforms cut into the ground ahead of the aircruiser.

Refocusing on the matters at hand, Devlin moved over to stand beside the Major, then leaned forward as well. In the midst of the uneven terrain — the many rises, falls and rock outcroppings — a strip was cut. Devlin wasn't sure if he'd have called it a canyon... it looked more like a narrow valley, because the slopes on either side didn't appear to be too steep, but it was deeper than the other depressions nearby.

Looking away from the window, the Captain scanned one of the moving picture maps with his eyes. It definitely appeared as though this canyon was the course the blue markers were following. The column looked to be about seven thumb-widths west of this place... so he guessed the blues were about seventy miles distant, since Deadline was about two thumbs away.

He tried not to think of how comforting it was to be making tactical decisions based on very scientific measurements, like thumb-widths...

"So there it is..." Krazakowski moved over beside Devlin, locking the canyon in his gaze as well. "Doesn't look too difficult to me."

Waller was frowning, "May appear easier from the air... but we'll need to look for a trickier spot if we're going to hit them here."

Turning back to Sass, whose face again filled the space at the rear of the cockpit, Waller gestured to one of the moving picture maps, and then dragged his finger eastward. He then pointed to his eyes, and pointed out the window.

Hopefully she would understand he wanted to have a look at the terrain, to find somewhere that suited their needs.

Sass followed the meaning quite easily — she knew she wasn't the best one to choose the ground for this ambush, since it was the Newfoundlanders who would have to do the fighting. She was just going to make sure she had something ready to explode in case their plan didn't succeed.

Hissing commands back to the pilot team, she had the aircruiser slow its flight, then start working over the canyon. From the cockpit, the Newfoundlanders and Major Krazakowski watched for a good landing spot. It didn't take them long to find the mesa.

Lieutenant Kennedy had his Webley in hand as the ramp at the front of the aircruiser began to lower. There had been no indication from the air that savages were nearby, but considering the many places a man-sized creature could lay low on ground this uneven, it would have been foolish to disembark unprepared for action.

Sergeant Halloran and his trusty section were beside Kennedy as the ramp descended, and once it touched the ground the men joined their officer in a move out onto the landing field.

From the air this place had stuck out like a sore thumb: a mesa with a sizable flat top, upon which there were actually patches of green grass. The vegetation added a little life to the desolation... but beyond those comforting oases, the place was stark and very red.

At least it wasn't as rife with dust as the Khyber...

Kennedy led his men cautiously away from the aircruiser's ramp, and as they emerged from behind the vessel the Newfoundlanders were greeted by a largely stunning sight: the mesa commanded the south side of the canyon the blue men were marching through. It had to be 500 feet above the bottom of the pass, and it was a sheer cliff face most of the way down, with only a slight ramp of loose rock at its bottom.

Basically, an impassable sheet of reddish-brown rock.

The only way up onto the mesa from the ground below was on the side opposite the canyon, where the loose-rock slope had a more gradual gradient. That was good; any attack launched from the canyon floor would either demand the scaling of a sheer rock face, or require the attacking savages to backtrack far enough to find a route out of the pass, then around behind — and all the while, they'd be under fire from men and machine guns.

This was clearly a strong position — easily secured, with a devastatingly clear line of sight and high enough up to deny savages or blue men much recourse when the ambush began.

"Perfect," Kennedy said quietly to himself.

Beside him, Sergeant Halloran nodded, "Bet that's what the Pathans said when they were getting ready for us too, sir."

That was a good point — what a strange role reversal — as well as a sound warning: the b'ys had been on the receiving end of fire from positions as perfect as this one, and they'd always found ways to survive... sometimes even to retaliate. Difficult or not, there *were* ways to get at this mesa. Caution would be essential.

For now, though, they needed to give the all clear.

"Let's get the Colonel out here," Kennedy said at last.

Halloran nodded, and turned back for the aircruiser.

"I think we might have found what we need, gentlemen," Krazakowski said as he neared the edge of the cliff that looked over the canyon, and Waller nodded.

Looking westward, the direction from which the blue column would be approaching, both commanding officers saw little but rocky, dry slopes and impassible rock faces. It did seem this place was treacherous... and a fine field for an ambush.

"Whatever they have coming up this canyon, we'll be in a good position to make trouble for them," Waller replied to Krazakowski without fully addressing his comment. He was already beginning to picture the engagement... ten lorries and however many savages marching down the canyon floor, hundreds of feet below... and suddenly they'd be set upon by intense rifle fire from above.

Such stories had played out in mountain passes all over the old world. The savages in the bottom would undoubtedly be dispatched to try to root out the snipers, but with 3,000 riflemen settled in amongst craggy heights, protected by steep slopes covered in sharp, loose rocks, it would be very difficult for even those beasts to respond. They could be picked to pieces as they came up... and even if they somehow hauled themselves up to the mesa faster than expected and surprised the Newfoundlanders and Americans, the aircruiser would be here — a means of escape.

All of that played out in Waller's mind's eye, and he knew this was the place Skeen had sought. Whatever force was moving up towards Pacifica, he could seek to destroy it, or at least to slow it down. Even if the Martians survived, they would have to be wary of other ambushes all the way to the foothills.

That sealed it: the blue men would meet the Indian Army's finest General in a desolate land where no civilians were at risk.

"Alright, I believe this is the place. Let's summon General Skeen," the Newfoundland Colonel said, and a few seconds of silence passed before Krazakowski nodded.

"Very well."

CHAPTER XXI

Smith was studying his hat intently, not expecting it to offer any particular answers, but figuring it was as good a thing to look at as any.

There had been no activity for hours, and he and the men of the 25th were left without much to fuel their determination to bring down the blue officer. There was no point planning something intricate, since they didn't know what opportunity might present itself, or when, or how. There was no way of escaping — they'd looked the cell over in detail, and had even tried yanking off the wall plates around the latrine trough. But the compartment was built to withstand savage strength, and there was nothing the Americans could do about it.

So they waited.

Soldiers knew how to wait, the black men of the 25th more than most. That had often been the fate of the regiment: they waited when others had duties, they walked while others took trains. They were second class soldiers, until the moment when there was a thankless mission, and then they were suddenly first into the fray.

The fact that waiting as prisoners of the blue men did not feel like an entirely alien experience to any of them was an indictment of their War Department, but it did make things easier as time ticked past within the silver cell.

Smith knew how to wait for other reasons. He was a drifter on the new world, and though he knew he'd changed a lot in recent months, his old patience hadn't gone away. Sometimes a body just had to wait, to take his time and let life move along to the point where he could join up with it again.

On the way out of Ambitia, he'd been thinking it was a good idea to give himself up. He'd been thinking that, sure as if the thoughts were his own... but the more he remembered, the more he wondered if it had happened that way.

Had the blue man, or the blue men, been in his head? He remembered shooting a bunch of the creatures down in the street at Ambitia, but for some reason their captors didn't seem to care. Wouldn't they mind if there were dead blue men lying in the street? So far they'd demonstrated plenty of concern over the fate of their fellows. Maybe those shot down were expendable, just soldiers.

Or maybe…

Smith's pondering had drawn a deep frown to his brow without him realizing. Sergeant Turner was sitting opposite the drifter, and as the veteran soldier took time to collect his own thoughts, he noticed the expression.

"Something important, Mister Smith?"

The drifter looked up, surprised that his musing had been spotted, though not offended by the question. He looked down at his hat, "Just thinking."

"Could tell that," Turner observed. "Not the kind to pry, sir. But we don't have much to talk about."

Smith looked up again, then glanced sideways to see the other men of the squad had also turned their eyes to him. It was these men who had saved Smith from bandits in Ambitia… the second time Preston and Marks had done that for him… so he reckoned he owed them enough not to stay quiet when they came asking.

Looking once again to his hat, the drifter started talking, "I think that blue officer got in my head back at Ambitia. I think he was making me think certain things, or think a certain way."

Turner frowned now, and glanced at his men, "Meaning?"

Smith shook his head, "Back at Promised Town, Lady Emily had a run-in with a blue who made her think she should surrender. Just after we all got off, remember when she had to swim out to us? Right before that, one had his psychic powers going in her head. She told us after. We reckoned it was because she was savage-born."

"They never got into our heads though, right?" Preston's question was a bit abrupt, and Smith didn't have a good answer.

"Don't know. Reckon when they got us at Ambitia, they might have been influencing our thinking a bit. I noticed my thoughts were different.

And they had more than just one blue man. All those we shot in the street...
maybe when a lot of them get together and focus, they can get through to
us as good as if we were savages," Smith reasoned out loud, and looked up
again at Turner.

"We know they can send the pictures to our minds, and see the pictures
we put in our brains," the Sergeant offered. "Suppose they could do it
without us noticing, at least to an extent."

That was a possibility, and a dangerous one. Or maybe not so dangerous.
Against nine men, they might have been able to work some tricks, but in
the field against dozens, hundreds or thousands, they'd been helpless so far.

Maybe it was about the numbers... maybe they could only sway one
man each, and figured there was no point trying when men had them
outnumbered and outgunned.

"I felt like I was seeing things in Ambitia, when all those Martians
came out in the open street," Marks pitched in. "They were really easy to
shoot. And that just didn't seem to be the smart thing, for a military bunch
especially."

Smith's eyes turned to the sharpshooter, and the thought occurred to
him then that if a blue could make a man think of surrendering, maybe it
was possible he could make a man believe he saw something that wasn't
there.

But if they had that talent, why not use it more? Why send hordes
when you could make men imagine the hordes? If the blue men weren't
actually in that street at Ambitia, and it was just this officer standing in
the woods somewhere, making all nine men think there were blues in the
street... that would mean he was awfully persuasive with his telepathy.

"Think we didn't actually shoot them down, Marks?" Turner asked
with a frown, and Preston joined in immediately.

"But we all saw them, and saw them drop. And the few who got away."

It was true, they all had seen the same thing. But what if it was made
up for them? These blue men could do a lot. They had so many machines,
they were waging a campaign against dragons... Hell, they'd even found a
way to build the tunnels from the old world to the new.

So what if they made nine men imagine things, and act accordingly?

The thought made Smith uneasy. His eyes went back to his hat, and he ran his fingers along the brim, then brushed off some dust. When else had the Martians been around so few men that they could have made those men imagine things?

Smith didn't know much about the expedition the Newfoundlanders had mounted to the dragon prison, but he figured there'd always have been enough b'ys together there to keep each other seeing reality.

Back on the grasslands the first time, the Newfoundlanders had always had been in large numbers when meeting blue men — and that had been in the beginning, before the fighting was serious. Same at Promised Town, except when Emily was running away. And then, during the blue man counterattack, there had been no chance for the creatures to isolate a small group of humans. They'd gotten a full belly from Byng and thousands of Canadians, and the same from Waller and the Voltigeurs at the end.

Only at Farfield, when Smith, Emily, Carstairs, and Caralynne...

Smith's hands stopped moving, and his finger clamped down on the brim of his hat. He stared at it intently and tried to keep his breathing regular. Blood was rushing to his face, so he kept looking down and tried to figure what he was thinking.

Smith and Caralynne had been alone on that street, and the blue man there had been some sort of officer too. A savage had put its hand through Caralynne's belly. Smith had seen it. He'd seen her die, and he'd shot savages and blue men after it was done.

How many had he shot? He couldn't remember. He was a man with a good memory for most things, but as he tried to picture Caralynne's death, it was starting to seem fuzzy. He wondered about that. He tried to force the pictures to come back into his head. It didn't help.

He knew that it was hardest to remember someone, or something, when you tried. Trying made a mess of memories... led to imagining. But maybe the fact that this moment, which he'd relived so many times, was foggy... had it been imagined by a blue man, so Caralynne could be dragged off that street still alive? The blue officer with this aircruiser knew who Smith was... had Caralynne been known as well? Had they taken her, as Emily believed?

Smith stared at his hat. Turner and the men of the squad all kept their gazes on the drifter, though none of them could tell his thoughts. Eventually, they decided to leave him be, resuming a few chats amongst themselves.

After everything that had happened, and all the certainty he'd gained, Smith found himself feeling wrong-footed. He didn't have his guns, or his horse, or his liberty.

And now he had to ask: did he have his mind? Or was Caralynne breathing out there somewhere, waiting for a rescue?

Smith didn't know.

CHAPTER XXII

"Sir Andrew?"

Skeen stepped out onto the platform at Pacifica Station and put his hat on his head to shield his eyes against the evening sun, then noted that American infantry were standing at attention in front of him, a General clearly at their head. The Indian Army officer had expected to be greeted at the station, but to be met by the commanding officer of the territory...

"Pershing?" Skeen asked, and stepping forward, the mustached military governor of Pacifica, known to many as Black Jack, nodded and extended his hand.

"Thank you for coming, Skeen," the American said gruffly. "Byng sends to me that you have some of the best men in the Empire. And recently arrived?"

Skeen wasn't prepared to have a conversation about the comparative merits of his men, but he nevertheless improvised, "Indian Army, General Pershing. Men who are excellent soldiers, able to fight in all conditions. Here to assist our friends and allies."

He elected not to add that he intended to take at least two regiments away from the defense of this place, if Tom Waller and the Newfoundlanders could find better ground for him. Byng had suggested it best to let Pershing find out about that possibility only if it came up.

But the American General seemed to detect that something was being left unsaid; his eyes narrowed very slightly at Skeen, and he considered a probing question... then decided against it.

"There's a field just off the station here, to the left," the American said instead. "Have your men and supplies unload and rally there. I'll take you to my headquarters and show you where to deploy, then we'll get you on your way immediately."

"Indeed," Skeen's reply was dry.

There might be some interesting conversations to come, if Pershing already had a clear expectation of the British troops joining his defense. Well, Skeen would deal with it.

As soon as Pershing turned from the train to lead the way to his headquarters, the doors of the cars flew open, and the men of the Indian Army began to disembark in fine style. There were plenty of white civilians on the platform when these men of various colors stepped off, and gasps could be heard from more than a few.

Skeen paused before following Pershing, those reactions catching him slightly off guard — there were few citizens of the British Empire who would have looked upon the arrival of disciplined Indian troops as little other than a blessing. These were renowned as some of the finest fighting men... but of course the Americans preferred not to allow their colored troops to fight.

Ditch-digging, Skeen had heard — clear enough evidence of the parochial nature of the United States Army...

But Sir Andrew stopped himself pursuing that line of thought. He was here to assist his American allies, and his expectations of their inferiority would not help matters.

As the audience on the platform grew more aghast, Pershing halted his march and turned back to see what was causing the commotion. Having been so preoccupied with the defense of his territory, the General hadn't realized that the Indian Army troops he was being sent were, in fact, colored men. Taking a step towards Skeen, he looked over the British officer's shoulder at a file of Sikhs wearing turbans, "Colored?"

Skeen heard the question, but wasn't entirely certain of how to answer — because it was plain enough that these men were not white. Pershing continued immediately, saving him the trouble: "They call me Black Jack because I rode with our colored cavalry, you know. Best damned men I fought with. Sent some of them out to Deadline before the Martians came... they're probably all dead now, and that's a waste."

Pershing offered those last observations with a shake of his head, and Skeen could hear genuine remorse beneath the words. Taking a step forward and linking his hands behind his back, he replied, "Well perhaps our Newfoundlanders will find them, General. We've sent an aircruiser out there to see what the blue men are about."

Pershing's eyes climbed to meet Skeen's, "What?"

Byng hadn't conveyed the entire plan to Pershing, as it had seemed all too likely the American would have been displeased to learn his British allies weren't sending every possible resource directly to his defense.

Perhaps Skeen shouldn't have let it slip so easily, but the Indian Army Officer didn't mind holding his ground.

"The Newfoundlanders," Skeen repeated. "I fought with them in Afghanistan, and understand they've done quite well here. They're out looking to see what the blue men are sending this way, so we'll be better prepared for them."

Pershing frowned, but didn't immediately say anything. As his thoughts collected, he eventually did reply: "That will help matters..."

"And if they find good ground for it, we might take a couple of regiments out to slow the bastards down," Skeen decided not to hold back.

"A couple of regiments..." the American muttered, clearly beginning to think through the implications of that on his defense — comparing the potential loss to the value of having them out causing mischief.

Skeen watched carefully as Pershing processed the possibilities. The Briton had no way to know whether the American would resist the idea, or embrace it; the position he took would speak volumes about his character, but would in no way alter the British plans. Pershing did not command the Indian Army — the Imperial troops were here under Skeen's orders, and though they would cooperate with any defense, the decision to ambush would belong to the Afghan veteran, not to Black Jack.

A gunshot interrupted both Pershing's deliberations and Skeen's musing.

Immediately the Indian Army officer knew the round fired had not been from one of his troops — the report was entirely different than that of a .303, or a .455 Webley. It had been a local caliber, and as he wheeled he feared that some racialist American might have taken a shot at his men.

But there were no signs of damage as Skeen faced the ranks of his soldiers, all of whom remained steadfastly at attention, even as their eyes darted around to look for signs of the shooter.

Then another shot sounded, and a woman screamed, followed by a man: "Martian air ship! Martian air ship!"

The voices were coming from beyond the station, and as he heard them, Skeen turned back to one of the nearest clusters of his men; a platoon of Sikh riflemen under the command of an Indian named Khattar, "Subedar Major, with me!"

Immediately that man barked orders in his own language, and as Pershing turned back to the squad that had accompanied him, Skeen jogged past, drawing his sidearm.

As he left the train station and emerged onto one of Pacifica City's streets, Skeen was greeted by signs of pure chaos. Townsfolk seemed to be scattering in every direction — some men drew their pistols, others had rifles, and others took women or children to shelter. Skeen didn't know if Pershing had informed his people of the potential danger coming their way, but whether they were expecting it or not, it seemed it might have arrived.

Black Jack surged past Skeen as the Indian Army General slowed in the street, and as he watched the chaos Pacifica's governor seemed to forget the arrival of the Imperial troops. He hurried away, undoubtedly to rally what defenses were available, but Skeen elected not to follow him. As Subedar Major Khattar formed his Sikhs into a protective ring around their General, Sir Andrew looked to the sky.

After just a few seconds, the General spotted the black shape of an aircruiser. Fishing out his field glasses, he raised them for a better look, hoping that he would recognize the craft approaching the city.

He did.

"Looks like Waller's craft to me," the General said as Khattar came to stand directly beside him. "But we can't assume. We'll return to the platform and hurry the disembarkation."

With that, Skeen and his men turned back toward the train station, then went to find his Brigadiers and Colonels.

Major Miller had been chosen as Waller's messenger to the capital of the American territory. Watching Pacifica City grow through the windows of the aircruiser cockpit, the Skipper now wondered what sort of defenses the Americans had for dealing with targets in the sky. He figured it would definitely be advisable to get a flag for the blue-built machine he was standing in, but for the moment he simply had to hope that the Yanks had nothing that would do it harm.

Sass was at the rear of the cockpit again, watching Miller as he stood with his hands linked behind his back. The Skipper was small and old, and she found him most interesting — he had to possess considerable wisdom to still be attached to a fighting unit filled with much younger, larger and stronger humans.

Presumably the fact that he alone was leading this mission meant he also bore sufficient authority to carry news to Waller's superiors... a fascinating little man, and Sass was staring at him when he turned back to her with a smile.

"Miss Sass, when we land, we'll be turning around right quick."

As usual, the words meant very little to her, and neither of them found this surprising. Miller chuckled softly, then shook his head, "Not to worry my dear."

He liked Sass — she was a giant lizard lady, and that was something he had never seen in his many years. Being near the dragons made him feel almost like a young man again — like there were magical things out in the universe that were worth seeing. The blue men had never filled him with that sort of wonder, but a being as incredible as Sass really did. Of course he would never see most of those things, but it was well to be reminded of their existence.

Miller moved to the aft stairway and then descended it carefully. His old bones and joints were actually quite accustomed to the motions of a ladder — he'd moved between decks on schooners for years in a similar fashion, and spent more time in warehouses besides. Once his boots hit the deck he hurried to the rear ramp, passing the evacuating people of Deadline along the way.

Many of those folk had kept their distance from the dragons, while others watched the massive lizards with great interest. The Skipper ignored them all, and Sass followed as the transport gently touched down in a field beside the Pacifica railway station.

The ramp began to lower as soon as Miller reached it, and holding up a quick hand to halt Sass behind him, the Major started down, reaching the bottom just as its metal lip dug into the soil. Trigger-happy Americans would hopefully see him and decide not to waste their lead...

But there were no Americans in sight: instead, companies from two Indian regiments — one of Sikhs, the other of Gurkhas — were arrayed before him in two ranks, the front rank kneeling and aiming their SMLEs at the Skipper's chest.

Skeen had obviously arrived, and true to form, he had his men in the right place to respond if savages were the aircruiser's cargo.

"Stand easy!" the General's familiar voice sounded as Miller was recognized, and then Sir Andrew stepped into view between the ranks of men he'd personally deployed.

Skipper Miller waved to the General, then looked back to the ramp and gestured for the civilians to begin disembarking. Sass remained aboard, and her pilots kept the engines humming. She expected this to be a short stop-over, and she was quite correct.

Skeen and Miller moved towards each other, wasting no time at all for pleasantries: "The absence of your b'ys mean Tom found our ground, Skipper?"

Miller nodded, "Yes sir, with the 25th United States Infantry, in the badlands about fifty miles west of the foothills. Sass has been able to spot the main blue man column with what we think is good accuracy. Ten lorries escorted by savages, though we don't know how many savages. No aircruisers... their only ones still seem to be in Destina and Ambitia. We're setting up on a mesa that dominates the pass they're using... should be exactly the spot we're looking for."

Skeen nodded at the news, simultaneously digesting a few different points. The fact that the main body of the attack force was still dozens of miles from the foothills, which placed them hundreds of miles from the capital city, was interesting — either a sign of poor coordination, or a mark of the respect the blue men now held for their foes. It was possible their attacks on Ambitia and Destina had been meant to keep that column's approach safe from discovery, so that no one would be able to ambush it...

Bad luck for them.

There were also Americans involved, and Skeen turned his eyes back to Miller with that question, "The 25th, you said? Would they be colored men posted to Deadline?"

Miller tilted his head a bit, "The very same."

Skeen nodded, though realizing his foreknowledge might seem unlikely, he explained himself: "Pershing was just lamenting their loss to me. Seems to believe they're good men."

"The b'ys think so," Miller agreed. He'd heard enough stories about Promised Town to think the same, though he didn't add that remark. It wasn't necessary, and Skeen was already descending into thought.

There was no question that if Waller said the ground was right, then an ambush could be successful. He could take two regiments into the field with him and join the Newfoundlanders... then could perhaps send the aircruiser back for more...

"How much time do we have?" he put that question to Miller, and a shake of the head started his answer.

"We think until the morning, but we can't be sure," the Skipper said, and then proved again that he was endlessly wise: "If you're thinking of packing up more that two regiments, I'd say no, sir. As it is, we can just cram two of yours into our big ship, along with the Americans and our b'ys. If we need to get out quick, then we can't have more than that many men around without leaving some behind."

Of course the dad of the Newfoundland Regiment would have a thoughtful answer to that question. The aircruiser could carry two full regiments and their supplies, or four regiments and no supplies. Should rapid escape be necessary, Skeen wouldn't mind leaving behind ammunition and victuals, but he'd be very displeased if he had to abandon any of his men. Multiple trips to bring out a stronger force would be a mistake, and as he reached that conclusion, he found himself smiling at the old Newfoundlander, "Yes sir."

It was an uncommonly warm acknowledgement, but one Miller quite deserved. And with it, Sir Andrew's decision was made: "Two regiments it is. We'll load up our ammunition and supplies for two days. Should be ready to depart in a few hours."

The ambush was on. But before Skeen could turn away, the Skipper frowned. Letting his eyes drift from his General to the many Indian soldiers formed up beside the Pacifica train station, the little Major asked, "Who will it be, sir?"

The Newfoundlanders had fought alongside many great regiments in Afghanistan, and now that a whole division was on the new world, it did seem as though Skeen was spoiled for choice. Who could best defeat savages in the badlands?

"These Sikhs here, the 15th Ludhianas..." Sir Andrew began, turning to the men who had been first off the train, and were often first into action when he'd led them through the Khyber. "And what do you think, Skipper? Would the savages enjoy a meeting with our Gurkhas?"

He smiled as he said that last bit, and so did Miller. Because if there were ever men born on Earth who could wrestle savages barehanded, it was the Nepalese soldiers with their kukri knives.

"I think the Gurkhas would enjoy the meeting more," the Major replied, and Skeen grinned.

"I do believe you're right, Skipper."

The blue men were in for trouble unlike anything they'd yet seen from humanity.

CHAPTER XXIII

"It's very tempting."

Waller lowered his field glasses and glanced at George Tucker. The two were crouched behind some boulders, a little over a mile to the west of the mesa, looking down into the canyon which was quickly being dubbed the 'low road'. These bigs rocks marked one of the last secure points either officer could see as they looked west: the further they went, the shallower the valley became, and the more passable its walls.

That fact confirmed the mesa as the correct place to position the main ambush force, but it also raised questions about how quickly a savage counterattack might find its way up onto higher ground. If all they had to do was retreat out of range, then scale the passable heights west of the mesa, they could be around the flank and very close to the b'ys in short order.

The aircruiser would of course provide a means of escape before the mesa could be overwhelmed... but it would be far better to hold the savages down low, where their strength and speed would do them no good at all.

"We can't keep them down forever..." Tucker continued his thinking aloud "... but if we wait to hit them until they're right under the mesa, then they start backing off and we've got men up here firing into them..."

"It might be enough to bottle them up while we do the job," Waller agreed.

As his Major had said, it was quite tempting — but a risk too. The idea was essentially to line men along the canyon ledge for a mile to the west of the mesa, then have them hold fire until the blue column was fully engaged. Any of the men not on the mesa would be terribly exposed, and very much at risk if the blue men had savages running across the heights as pickets ahead of their column, but if it worked, the blue men and their army would find themselves with no escape.

The avalanche of lead from the mesa would keep them from moving forward, and as they tried to withdraw, they'd face musketry to the rear.

If it worked. If the blue men didn't spot the farthest-west men and choose to withdraw before they were ever engaged.

"We'll have to talk it over with Skeen," Waller concluded. It was the sort of major decision the Colonel might make if no help were coming, but he knew Sir Andrew would be able to offer some clarity about what to do.

For now they knew the mesa was the center of their ambush, so the Newfoundland Colonel looked east again, and was pleased by how little he could see of the men working up on top of that high plateau, even from the higher vantage point he enjoyed amongst these rocks.

They'd be nearly invisible to the blues, just as the Pathans had been invisible to British columns so many times in the Khyber. Waller remembered once believing he would never wish such a deadly situation upon anyone, but now he would inflict it gladly on the Martians.

"Let's get back, George," he said, and together with the section of b'ys that had been following them, the Newfoundland officers started crossing the difficult terrain towards their base camp.

Jimmy Devlin crouched behind the Vickers gun and closed one eye as he peered down its sights. The low road below was fully visible from the sheltered position his b'ys had chosen, and as he turned the machine gun on its mount, he found he could traverse across quite a length of the pass without difficulty.

"Hellish spot," the Captain said approvingly, opening his closed eye and standing up before patting the gunner on the shoulder. "Now see if you can get some rocks or something to cover the position. Don't want them to see you!"

The men who'd set up the gun nodded, and then Devlin climbed out of their nest and back up the slope to the top of the heights just west of the mesa. B'ys were picking out good positions for Vickers and Lewis guns all around the high plateau — not just on top of it, but in whatever passable approaches they could find.

When the order was given, there'd be an avalanche of lead from the high ground, and if it was all as well-aimed as Devlin knew it could be, he reckoned the blues would be dead or running within ten minutes.

But then, if the savages managed to get up the slopes west of the mesa, and advance over the tops of those heights, things could get much more difficult. Looking in that direction, Devlin couldn't spot either Waller or Tucker, but he knew both men were out there considering options to control that flank... and he figured it might be a job for infantry. If Skeen had Gurkhas with him — the hardest-fighting men Devlin had ever served beside — then perhaps it would be their assignment.

Time would tell, and deciding he best not allow himself to be distracted by matters outside his control, he turned east and continued up the short track from the machine gun nest to the top of the mesa. It was alive with activity, as the b'ys made ready for action.

"We'll need to get someone down in the valley floor to pace off ranges for us. Shooting from the heights is unusual, remember," Captain Colbert was abruptly beside Devlin.

"Right. I'll send Halloran's section down. They could use the exercise," Devlin answer with a grin.

But as he turned and filled his lungs to bellow for his trusty Sergeant, his eyes swept past Colbert's shoulder. In the air there, he spotted something of greater interest.

"Aircruiser from the east!" one of the lookouts on the mesa called the warning before Devlin could. He stepped around Colbert and raised his hand to shield his eyes from the light, so he could get a good look at the approaching craft.

"Looks like ours," he said. "We should get the b'ys ready just in case, though."

Waller crouched down as the wind from the aircruiser cushioned the great machine's landing on the mesa. Fred Kearsey had 'D' Company lined up with rifles presented in case the machine turned out not to be the one the b'ys were expecting, but the fact that it was parking in the same spot as before suggested strongly that dragons were at its controls.

Holding his hat to his head and shutting his eyes against the gale being kicked up, Waller waited for a few moments as the craft settled down and quieted. The ramp began to descend immediately, and as soon as it was far enough down, Bert Miller came into sight, along with General Skeen, a regiment of Sikhs, and a regiment of Gurkhas.

"Interesting bloody place, Tom. Redder than the Northwest Frontier, I think," Sir Andrew called as he began his descent of the ramp.

Kearsey made an unnecessary gesture to have the b'ys of 'D' Company stand down from their defensive posture, and they eased off just as their General's boots hit the rocky badlands for the first time.

Waller moved to meet Skeen, taking the Briton's hand as it was offered. The Colonel then stepped aside so the General could get a better look at the terrain surrounding them.

"Incredible place. Looks hellish from the air... I can imagine why they'd be using this canyon to move through. Suppose we'd have done the same, but I'm rather glad to be on the high ground this time," he said as he began to fish his field glasses out of their pouch.

"Indeed, sir," Waller agreed. "George Tucker and I are just back in from the western approaches, though. We think we might need some strong outposts out there, to keep the savages contained down below."

As his glasses reached his eyes, Skeen directed them westward towards the high ground on both sides of the pass, "Want to make sure they can't get up here at us... or up the other side and under cover?"

"Yes sir," Waller answered, and Sir Andrew lowered his glasses and began to nod.

"Dangerous job for someone... but come, Tom, I'll need to see it up close before I can be certain," he said, then paused and nodded back towards the aircruiser, and the Indians stepping off. "I've brought the Ludhiana Sikhs, and the King's Own Gurkhas."

"A welcome addition," was all the Newfoundland Colonel managed to say, but it was a genuine statement.

All around the mesa, b'ys stopped their work and watched as their old comrades got themselves out of the aircruiser and into order, followed closely by Sass who seemed interested to see how much work had been done since they'd left the mesa hours before.

"We'll let them get established. I should meet the senior American officer, and then we need to sort out who gets posted where. I understand we may not have much time?" Skeen sounded enthusiastic to be in the field again, and it was that apparent eagerness which seemed to push Waller's mind forward again. He was back in the fray, just like Afghanistan...

"I'll take you to meet Krazakowski," the Newfoundland Colonel said with a smile, and then he turned to look for the unusual American.

Captain Adams had been helping his men position the crates of .30-06 ammunition they'd carried with them out of Deadline when work had been halted by the return of the aircruiser. As soon as it touched down, Adams ordered his men to return to their work, and as accustomed as they all were to getting hard tasks done, they didn't delay.

Until one of them stopped.

Adams was no blithe taskmaster, so when the soldier in question straightened up and his eyes went a little wider, the Captain turned to see what was drawing the reaction.

It was an orderly column of 2,000 colored men, crossing the top of the mesa towards the position the 25th had chosen for its own. There were some white officers, but Adams saw many colored men in command too... and then some of the white men started giving orders, in a language that the American didn't recognize.

Of course Adams had read of the Indian Army — it was well-known across the old world. But the stories were just words on a page, and the odd photos he'd seen were no great preview of these soldiers.

"By God they're proud," one of his men said reverently — but not critically. It was clear the Indian soldiers bore a great deal of dignity... and it was obvious as they passed by the Newfoundlanders working on the top of the mesa that there was much mutual respect.

Because orders were being given in a language other than English, Adams couldn't follow the directions from the Indian officers, or predict the movements of the newly-arrived troops... but he did recognize Colonel Waller approaching with a new officer — presumably General Skeen, the one the b'ys thought so highly of.

"Adams," Waller called as they neared the American Captain.

"Sir," he turned himself fully towards both approaching men and replied with a salute.

Skeen waved that down immediately, then smiled, "By God, a proper Captain? That's excellent."

"West Point, wasn't it, Adams?" Waller asked, and at first Adams didn't realize the question was referring to his own education. After a delay that was a few seconds too long, he nodded.

"Yes sir, I graduated West Point."

"Won't hold that against you, Captain," Skeen said. "I hear great things about your men. Glad to have you here. And Pershing sends his regards — he was happy to learn you weren't all dead."

Adams didn't know what to say, so he simply kept quiet.

Skeen's smile grew at the silence, and he shook his head, "Well damn me, wait until I tell Sir John French about this. So Captain, yours is a full commission. Same as any white Captain?"

"Yes sir," was the simple answer, and Skeen nodded. "That's excellent."

The comment meant little to Adams, and seeing as much, Waller offered some clarification: "In the Indian Army, colored officers are granted commissions by the Viceroy, instead of the King. Different strand of authority, so they can command their own men but not whites."

Adams blinked, then turned to look at some of the dignified colored officers who were walking past with their men. It hardly seemed as though they felt themselves to be lesser than the whites with them...

"I should hope we treat our Indian officers a bit differently than you've likely been treated, Captain. But I've been advocating for King's Commissions for Indians, and I daresay I might use you as one more argument towards that end," Skeen took another step forward as he spoke, then extended his hand to Adams.

Still surprised, the Captain slowly reached out and took the General's hand, then received a pat on the shoulder too.

"Excellent. Now, Captain, I hear you men are veteran jungle fighters. I have no bloody idea about fighting in jungles, thank God. Stayed the hell out of them. So help me find your Major, and tell me what it was like in the Philippines."

With that, Skeen turned Adams towards a denser collection of tan American uniforms some dozen yards away, and together they started walking. Waller hung back with a smile, entirely pleased that the General was taking properly to the men of the 25th United States Infantry.

Fine men would be in position to meet the blue column — fine men indeed.

CHAPTER XXIV

The sun was low as Skeen, Waller, and Krazakowski stood on the western edge of the mesa, squinting as they looked out towards the shallower parts of the canyon.

"I think you're right about the risk, Tom," Skeen repeated that opinion one more time, folding his arms as he did so. After a couple of hours studying the ground, the three officers had just heard reports from Kennedy and the riders who had carefully checked the bottom of the pass and routes up either side, and who had scouted the opposite heights.

It was quite evident that keeping the blue men and their savages in the bottom of the canyon gave the allied troops their best chance of success, no matter what their numbers.

But to do so would not be easy.

"We'll establish outposts starting a little over a mile out, with enough men and ammunition to drive any savages back off the opposite heights," Waller described his solution to that problem, and Skeen answered.

"I think so. Dangerous work."

It certainly was dangerous — the risks of being away from the mesa, away from the aircruiser, and near to the routes that savages might use to scale the heights were obvious.

"Colonel Mansfield will want the job for the Gurkhas, I suspect," Skeen looked back towards Waller with a smile as he spoke, and the Newfoundland Colonel matched the expression.

The Gurkhas were mythic, and always seemed to request the most dangerous work on the field. Or perhaps they were only perceived to request it, and were in fact sent into it as the b'ys often were, because they were victims of their own success.

Whichever was the case, Waller wouldn't mind letting the hard-fighting Nepalese warriors have this job. His b'ys would fight from the mesa, and secure the approaches to it against any assault.

"I'd say we have outposts the whole way along, on either side. I don't like the idea of a whole regiment being cut off that far out, so we need places of retreat between the farthest post, and this mesa. And a stockpile of ammunition out there. Give them options in case the savages come up faster than we expect."

Skeen was thinking aloud now, and Waller was nodding as he listened.

"Stretching them out a bit will also reduce the chance they're seen. And if the blue men have savages picketing the heights on either side of the advance, it'll keep them from seeing everything we have waiting for them," the Newfoundlander reasoned, drawing another nod from Skeen.

Discovery was one of the larger risks with this plan — if the blue men spotted one of the outposts long before getting into range of the mesa, the party could be off...

But if all they found was a small group of men waiting for them in the rocks, they might underestimate what they were facing, and continue. That was a slim hope, but then Waller and Skeen had both been a part of British columns that had followed the same practice in Afghanistan. Stopping for every sniper they found would have frozen those columns permanently, so on they'd pressed.

"It's not foolproof," Skeen concluded. "But I give it a damned good chance. As long as the right men are in those outposts, we'll crush whatever they bring."

The latter sentence was perhaps too optimistic — a statement of bravura much like those offered by Evelyn Hughes about the power of his trucks on the grasslands. But this was Sir Andrew, a proven man who was well aware of the dangers, and was willing to acknowledge them honestly.

With a nod, Waller turned away from the setting sun, and was about to offer his agreement when he saw Krazakowski's stoic face. The American Major was standing on Skeen's far side, arms folded and his brow deeply creased.

"Major?" was Waller's immediate question — perhaps prematurely assuming that this wasn't just one of the strange American's routine poses.

But Krazakowski's thoughts were anything but routine. The Major blinked when he heard the question, then he looked to Waller. Skeen turned his eyes to the commander of the 25th as well, and frowned, "Something wrong, Krazakowski?"

For all the positive things he'd heard, the Indian Army General did now wonder if the Americans might not have the appetite for a tough engagement, when the outcome wasn't absolutely certain.

"My men should be in the outposts, gentlemen. The 25th United States Infantry should hold your flanks."

Skeen hadn't been ready for that, and neither was Waller. Both men had been fairly set on the notion of the Gurkhas handling the close work, and the Americans holding the mesa with the Newfoundlanders and the Sikhs.

"On both sides, we will be the furthest-west regiment for this ambush. I'll divide my men accordingly."

Neither Imperial officer followed the thoughts behind those words, but Krazakowski didn't seem to notice until Waller voiced his confusion, "What?"

The Major from Baltimore turned fully towards his allied counterparts, his arms still tightly folded, "Gentlemen, I appreciate your willingness to deploy your men to the most dangerous posts in this engagement. But this is American territory, and it should be Americans who take those risks. Besides, if the blue men detect us at those early outposts, better they find American soldiers in them, than British. They knew about Ambitia and Destina, and so they might well have known our regiment was at Deadline. If they find us waiting in ambush for them, they might not think it unusual. If they find Imperial infantry, they would have to realize they face a more deliberate opponent."

Neither Skeen nor Waller said a word. Krazakowski's determination was as evident as it was unexpected. Sir Andrew was the first to frown and offer his counter, "Major, I'm not certain they'd know the difference between your men and ours..."

The General let his words trail off as he continued to study the American's face, which remained uncompromising.

Waller did the same, and then he took a couple of steps closer to the Major of the 25th, gently tilting his head, "Your men have nothing to prove to anyone, of course."

Krazakowski's eyes turned to the Newfoundlander, and then he shook his head, "We do, Colonel Waller. Not to you. Not to General Skeen either. But this is an opportunity for us to take on a role of significance, in an engagement that could truly save our territory. And it allows us to do so in the company of men who know what that means, and who will not be shy in telling others of what we have done."

That was the moment Waller pieced together the Major's reasoning. The job of holding those outposts was an important one — one the British were willing to hand to some of their hardest-fighting troops. The fact that those troops were colored soldiers from Nepal was evidence enough of the willingness of men from the Empire to recognize the abilities of those who weren't white... their readiness to commend them for their martial skills.

It was a sort of respect the 25th United States Infantry had never enjoyed. Expendable scouts, canaries in a mine shaft, or ditch diggers — those were the roles most often played by the black Americans. Or they were condemned to war in the Philippines, an Imperial conflict that the United States seemed determined to keep out of sight.

But here in the badlands, with the fate of the Pacifica Territory in the balance, only one United States Army regiment was present — only one American formation could be recognized for the deeds done when battle was joined. This was a real chance for the black men to prove to their country that they were fine soldiers — courageous, dedicated, and fit to fight alongside the most storied warriors of the British Empire.

Only the Gurkhas could hold those outposts — the Gurkhas, or the black soldiers of the United States.

Waller took a deep breath as it became all too clear to him. He honestly had no concept of how difficult it would be to lead men so despised by the people they often protected. He had no notion of what it would mean to have to prove oneself in quite this way. But if Krazakowski believed he needed the opportunity, then it was hardly his place to intervene.

Skeen shared that sentiment.

"Colonel Waller," he asked in formal tones, "are Major Krazakowski's men good enough to take the Gurkhas' place in our line?"

It was Waller's one chance to halt this notion — to spare the 25th a most dangerous duty. But to do so would have been wrong, so the Colonel of the Newfoundland regiment was honest.

"Sir, I believe they are."

Taking a deep breath, Skeen slowly shook his head, "Well dammit. Mansfield will be insufferable for the rest of this bloody mission."

It was a witty way to tell Krazakowski he would have his outposts, but no man laughed at Skeen's humor. He sobered immediately too, looking west for a moment as the sun touched the horizon, then turning his eyes back to the American Major.

"You want the outposts furthest west, on both sides?"

Krazakowski nodded, "Yes sir."

Skeen nodded slowly, then looked down, "Could be a death sentence for you and your men, Major. Or it could be the dullest position. They might never get out of the canyon, and you'll have no chance to prove your men."

"That is beyond our control, General. And I do hope it turns out to be the case. But if there is to be a hard day of fighting tomorrow, then my men must do more than is their rightful share."

Waller winced slightly at Krazakowski's earnest words, and then looked west as well. He shared his American counterpart's hope that the ambush would go smoothly — that neither blue men nor savages would ever get close to the infantry destroying them from on high.

But a dread feeling filled his stomach, and he feared it was with good reason.

"I'll have Mansfield provide you support on both sides, Krazakowski. Hell, with their slouch hats the Gurkhas might be mistaken for Americans. But you'll have your outposts, and your command. God bless you..." The General tapered off for a moment, but when Krazakowski began to nod, he interrupted the gesture: "And do not let us down."

In the end, the honor of a regiment was inconsequential compared to the success of the ambush, and Skeen was far enough away from sentiment to recognize that.

His cool order didn't seem to cause Krazakowski any discomfort; he nodded and then squared his shoulders, "Given this chance, Sir Andrew, we couldn't possibly."

So it was: the 25th United States Infantry would hold the flanks for the ambush.

The sun set over the low pass a few minutes later.

CHAPTER XXV

Under the light of two moons, men worked along both sides of the low road. The blue icons from the aircruiser moving picture screens had stopped at sunset, but there seemed little doubt that the column would arrive early the next day. That gave the ambush force all the time needed to finish preparations, and there were many.

Recognizing that the outposts on the side of the canyon opposite to the mesa would be at greatest risk, Krazakowski had decided to command them himself. Joining him were more than half of his men — 400 soldiers from the 25ᵗʰ, who would be accompanied by 500 Gurkhas. Together those companies set a string of positions along the tops of the steep slopes, and were working through the night to construct some partially-fortified ammunition depots that could serve as points for retreat if savages drove back their lines.

Similar preparations were made on the southern heights, as the 200 Americans assigned to the western-most outposts were joined by the other 500 Gurkhas, and the Newfoundlanders on the mesa were augmented by the Sikhs.

On both the north and south sides of the canyon, it was the Americans furthest west, and most exposed. The risk was plain to all those men, because they had faced savages before... though for the Indian troops who were so new to the world, it was not quite so evident. The b'ys meant to clarify the nature of their enemy.

"You just keep shooting," Sergeant Whealan explained to a Havildar — Sergeant — of the Ludhiana Sikhs, as they sat behind one of the mountain guns the Indians had brought with them. "They are faster than you'd believe, and stronger than oxes. But the thing is, they're used to fighting big dragons. Like a bunch of dogs taking down an elephant, that's what they're trained for. One to one, we can shoot them down. They haven't gotten used to that yet, so you just keep shooting."

The Havildar, whose English was very good, nodded at this explanation, and then translated it for a number of his men who were nearby. Whealan waited and contained a smile — he liked the chance to be giving a bit of wisdom back to the elite men of India.

Made him feel as though he was an elite man himself. What would his nan think?

Further down the line, Captain Sesk sat beside Captain Frost of the King's Own Gurkhas — a man with whom he'd once had a fist fight in India. They were happy enough to see each other now, as their fight had led to mutual respect in the strange way some fights do.

"Keep the ammunition coming, that's about all I can say, b'y," Sesk explained. "No need to be creative."

Frost was lighting his pipe, "Seems straightforward to me, Sesk. Not sure what the fuss is about. I realize you've come to respect these blackguard-blues, but I sorely doubt we'll have any trouble."

"I'll punch your nose again," Sesk shot back, then shook his head because he figured Frost wasn't entirely wrong. "You won't have a problem, b'y. If your sepoys weren't good men, and got uppity when they saw a bolt of lightning coming at them, then that'd be a problem. Or if they panicked when savages ran like horses at them, that'd be the death of you. But as long as your b'ys keep their discipline, and keep fuckin' shootin', then you'll be alive for me to beat you again."

Captain Frost puffed his pipe, "Beat me? Dear fellow, are you feverish or just mad?"

Captain Adams had been posted to the mesa-side of the canyon with Koster. While most of his men had deployed to their outposts far to the west by the time midnight arrived, and were struggling for scraps of sleep before the morning's fight, the black Captain had returned to the high plateau with a squad to collect the last of the .30-06 cases they'd stacked up the day before.

Every piece of lead might be needed for the battle, so Adams intended to have as much handy as possible.

Though most men on the mesa had bunked down, he found some still working to perfect their positions for the next day. Many of those b'ys nodded to him as he led his squad through their ranks, and he nodded back evenly. He liked the Newfoundlanders, and part of him wished he'd had the chance to meet them outside the context of impending action.

But action was his job as a soldier...

The job that had killed Sergeant Turner, and which might slaughter the rest of his men in the morning.

A great shadow seemed to loom over Adams as he thought of that possibility. As he reached the ammunition stacks and waved for his men to start collecting crates, he stood beneath that shadow and pulled his hat from his head. The dry wind that cut over the badlands was hardly as refreshing as those he'd felt further north, but it still cooled him a little.

That Krazakowski had volunteered the 25th for such a dangerous post in such a risky ambush was right. It was important that the black soldiers of America took this opportunity to prove their mettle, in front of men who would not allow the story to be twisted to exclude them.

But doing deeds worthy of story could well cost good soldiers their lives, and Adams wasn't blind to that. At Promised Town, Colonel Robinson had paid a similar bill... was the sacrifice worth it? Were the men of the 25th so proud that they were willing to die to prove a point?

Standing under the cloud of his own thoughts, Adams didn't have an answer. He also wasn't prepared when a man wearing a turban approached.

"Excuse me, Captain?"

The Indian man's English was flawless, and as he came to a stop a few yards from Adams, the American just managed to keep from frowning, "Yes?"

This soldier was a Sikh — a tribe or a religion Adams was entirely uninformed about — but his diction might as well have come from a British finishing school. The Empire was a fascinating conglomeration of cultures...

"I am Subedar Major Bahadar Khattar, of the 15th Ludhiana Sikh Regiment," the Indian officer continued.

The rank meant nothing to Adams, but based on the man's carriage, and the cut of his uniform, it marked him as important.

"Pleased to meet you, sir," was the American's reply.

Khattar smiled at the cordial words, then shook his head, "In fact, it is I who should call you 'sir', Captain. My rank is given to me by the Viceroy, not the King. Though they do not treat me as such, I am technically subordinate to my British Officers. I understand you are not?"

At first Adams didn't quite understand what the Sikh was saying, but pieces of Skeen's earlier comments returned to him with a few seconds of thought. He began to nod in reply, and that was enough to prompt Khattar.

"I just wished to say, Captain, that it is very well to see that in an army that is known to be as uneven as your own, a man of your color can serve as an officer equal to those who are white. This is something our people hope for soon, but which we have yet to achieve."

Even despite his recollection of Skeen's prior words, it was not a reaction Adams expected. The Indians were not posh-seeming soldiers — they appeared hard-fighting and tough. But every one of them appeared proud to be in uniform, and their colored officers had such dignity. They were not soldiers consigned to ditch-digging... and yet Khattar admired Adams? It was difficult to comprehend.

"I wish you and your men good fortune tomorrow," the Subedar Major extended his hand. "We will all be most pleased to say that we fought with one of the black officers of the United States Army."

Adams found himself at a loss for words. The Newfoundlanders' views towards colored men had obviously been shaped by soldiers of this sort; serving with the likes of Khattar in Afghanistan, the b'ys would have no reason to doubt the integrity of any man based on the tone of his skin.

"Thank you, Major," Adams took Khattar's hand. "It's an honor for us too."

It really was — an honor, and a chance to be seen as soldiers. The men of the 25th would not let their allies down.

A section of Sikhs followed Skeen and Waller as they made their way west, crossing the heights that led towards the enemy. Both men had been trained for war in country like this, so they knew not to cross the tops of the rises, but to traverse the lower slopes around them — otherwise they would be easily visible against the night sky.

They moved in relative quiet, covering the distance to the final outpost in half an hour. Strewn with boulders, this point was too narrow for a large body of men to be deployed upon, but Koster's sharpshooters would probably take their shots from it.

As they slipped in amongst the rocks and found a vantage point from which they could look west along the low road, Skeen and Waller finally came to a stop. The Sikh escort fanned out in silence, rifles ready and bayonets fixed in case savages happened to be nearby. It was a risk for two such senior officers to come out so far alone in the dark — the nearest support being a fifty-man company from the 25th, that was spending the night in a wash 400 yards behind.

But Skeen wanted one last look at the slopes the savages would have to climb, if they were to escape the inferno from the mesa.

"You picked good ground, Tom," the General spoke on that point, letting his eyes traverse the heights around him.

"Well taught," the Newfoundland Colonel answered.

Skeen laughed softly, "By who, man? Doesn't matter."

The two officers fell silent after that, letting the dim night fill their minds for a few moments — along with all the possibilities of what the next day might bring.

Perhaps there were only ten lorries in this column, and no savages would be present. In that case, it would end fast.

But it was equally possible that an army unlike anything yet seen was coming down the low road, and that it could overwhelm even the most thoughtful preparations. Still so many variables...

And Skeen knew it.

"My first fight against these blue men, Tom," Sir Andrew said. "If I make an error tomorrow, stop me. I will not lose men for my own ego, you know that. I want to outsmart these bastards, but I shan't have your American friends, or your b'ys, or my men pay the price for my hubris."

The sober words marked the first time Waller had seen any real doubt from Skeen since his arrival from Pacifica City — and they also reflected one of the truths about Skeen that set him apart from fools like Evelyn

Hughes. The man knew he could be wrong, and was willing to admit as much to a subordinate, under the proper circumstances.

But Waller believed he was right.

"Sir, I'll tell you. But I think we have this correct. I think you have outsmarted the blues, and they're going to regret this campaign in the morning," the Newfoundland Colonel replied evenly.

Certain words, and Skeen nodded slowly as he heard them, "Hope you're right. And due credit, Tom: if we outsmart them tomorrow, it wasn't just me. Good work. All that you've done since getting to this planet has been good work. My congratulations."

It might have seemed an oddly-timed compliment, but it was genuine and truly appreciated. Waller didn't quite know how to respond — how to convey to Skeen how much of the Newfoundlanders' success had been down to luck this far.

Fortunately, an interruption kept him from having to try. Some of the stars over the Colonel's head suddenly went missing, and when the light from one of the moons was abruptly eclipsed, he realized a dragon had joined them.

"Good evening, Sass," Waller offered his greeting as he twisted to gaze up at her.

Surprised, Skeen looked up as well, "Dear God, she's quiet."

When the two officers detected their guest, the Sikhs who had been standing watch realized they'd somehow missed her arrival. Skeen dismissed their concern with a simple order in their language, then looked back to the dragon, "Any idea what she wants, Tom?"

Waller came to his feet and moved closer to the dragon, as she gazed west with a rather intense expression. Devlin had spent an hour with her earlier, trying to gesture and draw his way through the battle plan. She'd seemed to understand the main points — ambush, with the possible need to retreat by aircruiser — but when it came to elaborating on particular points of tactical intent, there hadn't been any way to communicate.

"Probably just wants a closer look at the ground," the Newfoundland Colonel suggested in answer to Skeen, and as soon as the words left his mouth Sass was suddenly leaning down in front of him, holding up a dark box about the size of blue man lorry engine.

Sass then moved her free hand into position beside the box, closed it, rocked it up and down a few times — as if counting to three — and then flung open her fingers. It seemed an awful lot like a gesture for 'explosion', and Waller looked up at her eyes as he realized as much. Seeing the recognition in the Colonel's eyes, the dragon showed an upturned palm.

She'd made another bomb, like the one that had wiped out the horde at the camp? Nice of her to knock it together...

"What the devil is that?" Skeen came off his boulder and approached Sass' hands with a frown.

Waller glanced at the Briton, "If I'm not mistaken, sir, it's a devastating explosive. Sass converted a blue man lorry engine into a bomb in just seconds at the camp. I suppose she'd have the time to do the same again here... probably something unneeded from the aircruiser."

Skeen stopped beside Sass' hand and studied the dark crate in the moonlight. A massive bomb... that would certainly be useful if savages were hemmed in together.

"As long as she doesn't deploy it before we have them in range. Don't want to scare them off..." the General said thoughtfully, glancing to Waller.

The Colonel paused, then looked up to Sass, trying to figure out how he might confirm the timing of her throw. She was looking down at him, and though neither of them could swap words or thoughts, her intuition seemed to pick up on the concern.

Pointing to the box, she then pointed to Waller, and turned her palm up again.

He nodded, then glanced at Skeen, "I think she just said she'll do it when we tell her to."

That was precisely what Sass meant, though should circumstances warrant she would obviously take the initiative. She had faith in the Newfoundlanders, and extended that to the other soldiers present... but whatever happened, she and her pilots had to be ready to use the transport to evacuate the humans on either side of the valley, and to contribute some offensive power of their own.

And if this ambush worked... if the humans were able to destroy the main Hubrin assault force... then perhaps they could buy enough time for the Saa to learn to write the human language, and to develop a transmitter powerful enough to call for help.

A lot would depend on the outcome of the morning's engagement — perhaps more than any of the humans realized. She just wished she could explain all of that to them.

For now she simply nodded at Skeen, and that seemed to be enough for the Indian Army General, "My thanks, Sass. I expect you and I both look forward to tomorrow's outcome."

Waller believed his General had that right.

CHAPTER XXVI

The dust cloud was the first thing they saw.

Sitting in the rocks where Skeen, Waller and Sass had been the night before, Captains Koster and Adams had spent much of the following morning with their field glasses out, and their eyes panning the pass to the west.

The dragon pilots had remained in their aircruiser, and somehow that machine's optics had kept tabs on the approach of the blue men, but without the clearest sense of scale, it had still been impossible to know for certain exactly what time the column would be seen.

Mid-morning was the answer, and the first sign of it was the dust. Lorries and savages, all running along the bottom of the valley, sent up plumes of the stuff — evidence that there had to be many of them, because the rocky terrain did not give up dust easily.

Captain Koster detected it first, as he and his snipers were positioned at the outermost boulders. He passed a silent warning back to the commanding officers by way of a narrow white flag — actually one of Lieutenant Conway's bandages, dusted down to make it slightly less bright — that was tied to a stick and propped up between two rocks. It was the signal to get ready; the next message would be the sound of firing rifles, hopefully beginning at the mesa. If Koster's men fired first, it would mean savages had found them before the column passed.

After the warning was sent, Koster settled down beside Captain Adams, and both men watched the dust.

"That far out... probably another hour," Adams suggested.

Koster nodded, "Not long to wait."

Waller and the b'ys waited silently on the mesa. Movement was kept down to a bare minimum, for fear it would lead to them being spotted. For similar reasons, men were ordered to do everything they could to conceal the shinier pieces left on their kit — glass was covered, metals were scuffed or caked with dirt, and the aircruiser was parked far back enough from the rim as to be completely invisible from the ground below.

All was prepared by the time Jimmy Devlin lowered his glasses, raised them again, and then reported what he saw, "That's the streamer from the Americans. Can see it wiggling in the breeze."

Waller was standing near 'C' Company's Captain when the sighting was made, so the Colonel drew his own glasses and confirmed. The column was in sight.

Skeen crowded nearby, as did most of the senior officers left on the mesa. They all gathered with Waller and Devlin behind some boulders at the mesa's western edge, a few of them looking for themselves before turning to Sir Andrew.

The General had little to add: "Plan remains unchanged. Keep your men quiet until the time comes. We wait until they're in range below, then we hit them with everything. If they start cresting these heights before we're ready for them, we leave our equipment and withdraw to the aircruiser... then bomb them with Sass's weapon if there's a chance."

It really wasn't complex — at least not as outlined. Though Waller knew complications could come thick and fast as soon as the first shots were fired.

"Heads down, everyone," Waller said after Skeen finished, and then the officers began to part ways.

Krazakowski was at the western-most outpost on the northern heights, and after watching the dust grow for nearly forty minutes, he knew action was close at hand.

With him were Captain Insetta and the men of his company. Together they were hunkered down behind a series of boulders, probably 400 feet above the valley floor, rifles beside them and heads below cover.

Only Krazakowski was peeking out from behind concealment, his hat off and his glasses down so as not to reflect anything towards the approaching blues. Well-taught by experience, he was also leaning sideways around the boulder that was hiding him, so as not to present a perfect head-

and-shoulders silhouette that could be easily recognized as being human. Hopefully the blue men wouldn't be watching too closely... and hopefully there weren't going to be savages reaching the top of the slopes that were sheltering the ambushers.

The latter concern was Insetta's primary focus. Well back from the edge overlooking the pass, that Captain crouched in a depression and watched the heights to the west of the American position, waiting for any savage scouts who might be paralleling their column. Since the aircruiser was on the opposite side of the canyon, escape would be much more difficult for these men should they be discovered early. It made sense to direct rifles towards defense before offense, just in case.

The dust drew nearer, and switching sides of his boulder, Krazakowski looked across the valley to the opposite heights. Even with his trained eyes he could see no sign of the men of the 25th in the rocks facing his. Though not a perfect match for the red rock, the tan uniforms of the United States Infantry disappeared quite well, and now that the savages were so near, the streamer that signaled their approach had been taken in.

Soon they'd be able to get a good look at what they were dealing with. Glancing to Insetta, the Major then received an almost-frustrated shake of the head.

No scouts. No sign that the blue men were in any way concerned about ambush in this country. He began to wonder: was this some form of a trap?

It was too late to be concerned about that possibility — at least there were thousands of troops here in case of trouble... those Gurkhas with their slouch hats were waiting in posts just east of the ambush positions held by the 25th, and they would be a great help when the unexpected arrived.

Soon... very soon...

"Get ready, men," Krazakowski whispered.

"Streamer's in, not long now," Devlin was lying on his front in one of the grassy patches on the mesa's top, squinting because he refused to use his field glasses with the enemy so close.

Waller was lying beside Devlin, and he nodded, then rolled halfway and looked back towards Skeen, who was seated on a rock further to the rear, "Soon, sir!"

Nodding, the Indian Army General sipped a cup of tea, then handed it back to the sepoy who'd kindly provided it and began checking his revolver once more.

Waller then looked to the side of the mesa opposite the canyon, and saw the heads of three dragons poked up over its rim — Sass and her two pilots, each of them carrying a lightning cannon ripped from a blue man lorry, keeping their big bodies out of sight. Hopefully they would all stay out of the hottest fighting — they were the only ones who knew how to fly the aircruiser, and being many miles from any settlement, Waller had no interest in walking home.

Sass saw Waller was looking in her direction, and she nodded to him. He waved back, pointed west, and then made a slow downward gesture with his flat hand.

"Keep your head down..." the Colonel whispered, hoping Sass would get the message.

She stared at him for a moment, figuring and interpreting, then looked back at her two pilots and gave an order. The three dragon heads descended from visibility, completely concealed behind the lip of the mesa.

"This is going to be a bloody mess," Jimmy Devlin said after a time.

"It is indeed," Waller agreed.

Captain Koster crouched beside Captain Adams, and the two men watched the lead elements of the blue man column come into view in the valley to the west.

Four square formations of savages were running ahead, followed by a silver lorry with a lightning cannon in the back. Then came more savages — twelve squares of them — and a column of ten more lorries, then another ten squares of savages, then three more lorries, and a final four squares of savages.

More lorries than they had expected, though that was no great concern. But the savages... it was difficult to guess the number of beasts in each square, but it was at least 1,000. That meant 30,000 beasts, all marching — running, really — down the low road pass.

Koster felt his heart begin to pound as the numbers struck home — this was an army that, were it to reach the foothills, could do great harm. And yet it was moving without pickets flanking it on the heights?

That was good fortune for the ambushers — or a sign of the weakness of the blue commander — but in either case, it was only a small blessing in the midst of a greater problem. If there were 30,000 beasts, that was little better than ten-to-one odds. Keeping them all down in the canyon would be vital, and it would be all the more difficult for the men in the outposts.

"Hope we have enough ammo," Adams observed very quietly under his breath, and as the first square of savages leading the column began to pass beneath their position, Koster nodded in silence.

"Damn me, that's a whole division or more, wouldn't you say, Tom?" Skeen was crouching as he came up beside the prone Newfoundland Colonel, and Waller nodded slowly.

Without field glasses and a few quiet minutes to count, it was impossible to properly guess the number of savages per square, but the mass was considerable.

"Looks like there's no sign of pickets on the heights though," he said eventually.

Skeen frowned, then dropped down onto his belly as well, narrowing his eyes to try to get a look westward before offering a wry smile, "A column that size without pickets? We really should check to see if it's Baldwin commanding them. Be good to see the old fellow again."

Though dry humor seemed out of place under the circumstances, something about Skeen's confidence helped keep Waller's own anxiety well in check. The blue men were almost upon them... but no matter their numbers, they and their savages would be at the mercy of some of the British Empire's most experienced mountain fighters.

Soon...

Krazakowski had been part of more than a few ambushes in his time, particularly during the days in the Philippines, but never had he tried to assault a force of such size. He was beginning to realize how the partisans he'd once hunted must have felt, seeing such a seemingly overwhelming force out to destroy them.

But Krazakowski knew that the partisans could often win, when the column was poorly orchestrated. And here the blue men had foolishly sent out no flankers or advanced guards. Their final error.

The tail of the column was fast coming, and its head would be below the mesa quite soon. No one had fired — Skeen was to give that order when he thought the moment most opportune, unless the Americans were compelled to initiate the engagement early.

Either way, the fight was to begin in moments.

Major Krazakowski drew his Colt pistol — largely useless at this range — and stood up from behind his boulder. He almost expected a savage to leap from nowhere in that moment, and to tear him to pieces, but the heights continued to remain completely safe. Looking back to his men, Krazakowski decided to dwell no more on the foolishness of his foe; this was a nightmare of their own making.

"Twenty-fifth!" the Major called.

For the first time, savages below heard something that made them look up towards the high sides of their canyon. Too late: thunder began from the mesa.

Filling his lungs at the sound, Krazakowski bellowed his order: "Open *fire!*"

The avalanche began.

CHAPTER XXVII

The newspaper men would undoubtedly have a field day with metaphors when they reported on the 'Battle of the Badlands'. Tom Waller could just imagine their literary effusions — the statements that yes, indeed, the sky had rained lead down upon the blue men and their savages one afternoon in the red rocky wasteland.

And for once, the overdramatic phrasing so common in the papers would not be wrong. The valley thundered with the sound of rifles, machine guns, and mountain guns. All at once there was a deafening fusillade, with the shot pouring down from the heights into the blue formation.

It was devastating.

Savages were the first to fall. As Waller finally drew his field glasses and rose from his prone position — it didn't matter if he was seen now — his eyes found the carnage below, and he watched it with a grave feeling. Mangled savage bodies, so like those of men, were literally being blasted apart by the onslaught.

From the mesa it was the worst — the entire vanguard of the column was within range of the position, and it simply seemed to fold under the bombardment from the b'ys and the Sikhs, as well as the powerful machine gun emplacements.

There was nowhere for the beasts or their masters to run — the walls of the pass at the mesa were simply too steep. Some savages tried, either by blue order or by instinct, to start climbing the sheer rock faces, but with men shooting from either side of the canyon, there was no escape.

"Like a goddamned barrel," Jimmy Devlin was still beside Waller, and there was no joy in the words he called over the roar.

It was bloody slaughter, and while it was good that the men were not particularly imperiled, it was nevertheless a shocking sight.

Some 10,000 savages and half a dozen blue vehicles were almost instantly blasted to pieces.

**

From the opposite side of the valley, and the opposite end of the line, Krazakowski was witnessing a somewhat different picture.

The mesa was a veritable fortress — machine gun nests with endless supplies of ammunition, and two full regiments concentrated and firing straight down into a mass of savages. The further west the lines ran, however, the less concentrated the ambushers, and the less devastating the first fusillade.

Watching the rear squares of savages remaining essentially untouched by the assault, Krazakowski quickly realized how truly dangerous these western-most outposts were.

Seeing an opportunity, the blue survivors began sending beasts onto the west slopes at great speed, and they were coming in formation — like massive Napoleonic assault columns. Certainly they were slowed by the loose rock, but based on their sheer numbers the American Major knew his men, scattered between a handful of outposts, would not be sufficiently concentrated to throw them back.

They had to rally on the high ground, near an ammunition dump so they could get on line, and as Skipper Miller had described about Farpoint, destroy the savages with rifle fire.

Turning to Insetta, Krazakowski grasped the man's shoulder to get his attention, "We must fall back to the ammo dump and consolidate our lines quickly!"

At first the Captain didn't quite seem to hear the order — the thunder was tremendous — but then he nodded. The outpost had to be abandoned.

Captain Koster realized the danger just as he saw Krazakowski pulling back from the outpost opposite his own. With so much organization left at the rear of the blue column, it would be vital to consolidate the ambushing soldiers, or many could be cut off and overwhelmed.

"We must fall back towards the mesa, concentrate our forces before the beasts get up on us!" Koster called, his urgent tone catching Adams by surprise.

The black Captain hurried over to his superior, "Should we hold off a little longer — keep them down?"

Koster shook his head, then pointed north to the opposite side of the canyon. Adams followed the gesture, and his eyes settled on the base of the facing slopes just in time to see a full square of savages begin to climb.

"I bet there's one just like that coming up the bottom of our cliff," Koster added, though neither he nor Adams were inclined to go to the edge of the steep rise to look down and confirm.

"Back to the ammo depot, we'll pick up our men as we go and form new lines there," Koster concluded, and Adams could only nod.

There was no question of staying put — they'd be overrun, or run out of ammunition, or both. But hopefully allowing the beasts up onto the heights wouldn't spell the end of the entire ambush force.

Adams couldn't afford to worry; he barked for his men to get on their feet, and then led them east.

"Looks like we disabled most of the lorries," Major Miller had come up alongside Waller, and was looking down into the low road through his field glasses. "It's a killing down there."

The chaos below was kicking up large amounts of dust that obscured events further to the west of the engagement, but presumably the Americans and the Gurkhas were having success as well. So many creatures were being destroyed with such relative ease, it was sobering and somewhat sickening.

"Look there, lorry!" a voice called through the roar of musketry, and as soon as the warning ended, a lightning bolt soared up at the mesa. It was ten feet high off the ledge, but the sheer shock of it startled the men who'd been firing there. One fellow lost his balance and nearly plunged over the side; the men nearest caught him, and then every man pulled back from the edge.

Three more bolts followed almost immediately, hammering into the sides of the high plateau with breathtaking force, throwing up massive amounts of rock and crumbling some of the firing positions. Waller heard a shriek and knew that at least one man had fallen.

More lightning bolts came, raking the sides of the mesa, trying to drive the b'ys and the Sikhs away. Most of the machine gun pits along the targeted side were crewed by the Indian Army, and one suffered a direct hit — a bolt of lightning cut through the side of the rock and into the nest, burning the Sikhs within, and detonating the case of .303 ammunition that had been feeding their gun.

Waller half-ducked at the blast, then swept his glasses down to the killing zone again. At least five lorries still seemed to be actively returning fire…

"Mountain guns focus on the vehicles! Quickly men!" Skeen was still near the edge of the mesa, marching behind the Indian Army's mobile artillery pieces with his hands linked behind his back.

Sir Andrew was a man who held great disdain for anyone who tried to kill him. He was no fool — never one to be an easy target for a sniper unless it would gain him some advantage — but there were times like this when being at risk made him a better leader.

That was a principle Tom Waller understood very well, and as he stood tall on top of the mesa, he saw that none of the b'ys around him had wavered.

More lightning raked the red rock beneath their feet, but their musketry didn't stop, and then three mountain guns barked in succession.

A lorry blew up.

Adams didn't like running from the savages, and he thought leaving the outpost so quickly was an unwise move. Certainly there was a risk of being cut off, but letting the savages start their climbs without any harassment might allow them to come on faster.

But Koster had insisted, and Adams respected the Captain who had become the regiment's second-in-command after the death of Robinson.

Despite the terrain, the first seventy yards from the outcropping where they had been based were covered quickly, without any sign of savages. Fifty men of the 25th made that run with Koster and Adams — the remains of Adams' company, without Sergeant Turner among them.

Fifty more men were picked up at the next outpost, and then the last 100 were still engaging from the third outpost, which was only 400 yards from the place Adams had begun the day. His men were only halfway to that position and its ammo depot, but once they were there they would a least be more concentrated.

Adams was keeping his thoughts as hopeful as he could manage, but his quick scaling of the treacherous trail slowed as he looked ahead, past the his men and Koster. Savages began cresting the heights between them and their 100 comrades at the ammo depot.

They had been right to move after all... perhaps they'd waited too long.

"Let them have it, shoot on the run!" Koster barked those orders, leveling his pistol as he did so.

Firing began, and savages fell, but more were coming. They'd found a way up the southern slope in no time at all, and there were thousands poised to exploit it.

Krazakowski had nearly 300 men with him when he looked across the valley and saw a long line of savages making their way up what might have been called a goat path. There had been no savages up his side of the canyon so far, though surely now they had to be coming. No matter: the lack of immediate adversaries gave him an opportunity to help the 200 men in trouble... and indeed, to disrupt a large force of savages that would otherwise threaten the mesa's flank.

The Gurkhas were too far to the east to assist — on both sides of the pass, they were still pouring fire down into the savages with great discipline, and shooting away any savages attempting to climb the slopes opposite. But this far west it remained in the hands of the 25th, and with his men concentrated, Krazakowski knew they could succeed.

"Captain Insetta!" the Major called over the roar of the fusillade, and the company commander looked back.

"Sir?"

"Take your company to the depot, collect Captain Vogel's men and all the ammo your men can carry, then return to us. We will form here to try to keep the savages in check!"

Insetta heard the orders, looked to the opposite side of the canyon, then back to Krazakowski, "Yes sir!"

The Captain set off to collect the rest of the regiment, and Krazakowski hurried to a promontory a dozen yards from the nearest cliff edge, "Here, men, join me!"

As Sergeants and officers saw the move, the black American soldiers followed quickly. With a wave the order was given for them to form a firing line.

"Quickly, men: drive those savages back from our comrades on the opposite slopes. Long range, now, fire!"

Adams heard a new thunder, and as he look northward he saw a line of khaki-clad men along the opposite side of the pass. Savages were climbing up the cliff beneath them, and surely they'd soon find their way to the top, but for the moment Krazakowski's men were unaccosted, and their .30-06 bullets would help staunch the flow of savages that were trying to cut Koster's force off from the mesa. Long range fire couldn't stop all of the beasts, but even slowing the flow would make a mighty difference.

Thanks to hard lessons from jungle warfare in the Philippines, the men of the 25th were very skilled at simultaneously moving and shooting. Now Adams' company demonstrated a mastery of the practice once again, as savages reached the top of the heights and were cut down immediately by hot fire.

"Get past them — hurry!" Koster was pointing in the direction of the nearby ammo dump with his Colt pistol, and wheeling his other arm to spur on his men. They had to get around the savages who had made it to the top — had to link up with the other 100 men from their regiment, then likely fall back towards the Gurkhas.

Adams guided his company in the necessary direction, looking back towards the rock outcropping they'd left behind as he hurried them along. Savages were cresting the heights there too now as well — and were chasing after the Americans.

It seemed they were climbing everywhere.

"Hurry, come on men, hurry!" Adams called to his soldiers, and then followed as they continued their race around the savages who trickled into their path.

"We'll need to link up with the Gurkhas, then hold this flank!" Koster called loudly as he followed his men.

It would be close, but as the khaki soldiers continued to move past fallen savages and close the last few yards to the ammunition dump, Adams allowed himself to believe it would be possible.

Krazakowski watched with relief as his men on the opposite side of the valley seemed to pick their way around the savage incursion. The beasts were still racing up the narrow goat path and onto the high ground, but good volleys from across the canyon were keeping the flow manageable for Koster's men.

Unfortunately, the volleys couldn't continue forever — ammunition was running low, and Insetta and Vogel had yet to return with more. Staying too long in this position and waiting for more rounds to reach them could be a mistake — considering their success scaling cliffs on the opposite side of the pass, Krazakowski knew savages had to be close to joining him on these heights.

No, he couldn't afford to cover Koster any longer without jeopardizing his own flank. Turning his eyes east, the American Major found too much dust billowing out of the chaotic canyon for him to get a clear look at the mesa. He could only hope the Newfoundlanders' firepower would reach further west, and soon.

Until then, his men needed to move.

"Displace — to the ammunition dump, double quick!"

Lightning cannon shots were coming fast and thick. The weapons were not terribly accurate — they were certainly making some lucky hits, but weren't as useful as a focused artillery barrage. Still, they were disruptive, and as Waller watched one destroy another Sikh machine gun nest, he gritted his teeth.

There were thousands of savages below, but because of the unexpected volume of dust kicked up both by their feet and the lightning shots, none of the b'ys could avoid wasting shots on those already dead. All the soldiers could do was keep up consistent, hot musketry, and hope live savages weren't finding ways to evade it.

Hope wasn't a good thing to rely on in battle.

Turning his glasses from the immediate killing zone and looking west, he found too much dust in the way for him to get a clear sense of what was happening. Was the situation as bad out there, or worse? The Americans hadn't enjoyed nearly as much firepower or natural fortification as the b'ys on the mesa...

Such a dangerous job, and in spite of the chaos, Waller paused for just long enough to regret the death the men of the 25th might be suffering to carry it out.

But it was only a fleeting second of regret. Skeen appeared at Waller's side, his face dusty but his eyes active, "We need to get rid of those lorries!"

Waller nodded his understanding — the lightning shots from the vehicles were the only real danger the blues were posing just now... but getting rid of them with only mountain guns would be difficult, especially because of the poor visibility.

The solution swept over the Newfoundland Colonel and the Indian Army General in a silent shadow; Sass had come to the conclusion that her overload-ready power cell was going to be needed. She was a large target — exactly the sort of target Hubrin pulse cannons had been design to kill — so as she approached Waller at the rim of the mesa, she moved speedily and kept low. Catching his eye, she saw a look of realization on his face, and then an urgent nod followed by a gesture towards the canyon below.

Without even stopping to nod in reply, she crushed the power cell's regulator with her thumb and threw it into the fray.

Unfortunately this jury-rigged bomb wasn't as robust as the main engine she'd taken out of a Hubrin roller back at the camp — she couldn't afford to sacrifice her transport's main power systems. Still, it would be potent.

As Sass went low, Waller roared: "Cover! All men down now!"

With that he grabbed Skeen and dragged him to the ground, just in time to avoid the blast.

The shockwave knocked flat any man who'd been standing.

CHAPTER XXVIII

Adams picked himself up unsteadily and tried to figure out what precisely had knocked him down. Some sort of explosion? He didn't know, but whatever it had been seemed to have taken all his men off their feet, and now swirling dust was keeping him from seeing any more than a few yards in front of him.

The savages had been chasing... had they been knocked flat too?

"Up... come on, up!" he started to call, and as men struggled to get their rifles and find their footing, the order to get moving again was repeated by other officers and NCOs. Men started to make way, and order was restored — at least partially.

But through the reddish dust, Adams couldn't see any of the slopes to the west — savages could be anywhere.

Looking to his men, he began waving: "Keep moving."

Koster was suddenly to the right, and he was giving similar orders, "Come on men, hurry! We need to link up with the Gurkhas!"

As the Captain spoke, he turned to look west once more, and a savage landed on him. Koster tried to shoot the beast, but it didn't matter: Adams watched it drag him over the nearest ledge, and they plunged down into the pass. If the Captain survived the fall, the beasts would finish him.

"Savages!" one man cried a warning before another beast dropped on him from the dust cloud. The monsters were upon them.

"Bayonets!" Adams roared, and then two more of his men were dragged away. He couldn't see the enemy — the dust wouldn't clear — and he felt certain that every second they stood still gave the beasts more time to get into range. But how could they try to escape when they couldn't see? They'd be as likely to run off a damned cliff as to find safety.

Maybe the Gurkhas were near enough to provide support.

"On the left there!" that call, from one of the Lieutenants on the flank, led to rapid shots. For all the chaos, the men of the 25th were still excellent soldiers, and savages fell.

"Fall back by company," Adams turned away from the cloud. "My company will stand, everyone else fall back right now. Get to the Gurkhas, establish a defensive position!"

It was all they could manage under the circumstances. Nearly 150 men processed those orders, then turned and climbed onto the eastward trail as best they could, watching their steps and hoping that the fifty — or less than fifty now — men who were staying behind could keep the savages occupied for just long enough.

"Dammit," Adams muttered to himself, then moved to join the rough line his men had formed behind him. "Keep a clear eye!"

Savages came from the dust again, and they were met by bullets from the soldiers of Adams' company.

"What a mess…" Devlin struggled to his feet and tried to look over the edge of the mesa. All he saw was dust — the blast had stirred up more than he thought existed in these rocky badlands. Now every man within range of the initial explosion was covered in fine reddish particles.

But the lightning cannons had stopped blazing at the mesa, and given the choice, insidious dust was probably preferable to direct fire.

Except that they couldn't see whether savages remained.

Waller managed to reach Devlin a moment later, and the Colonel coughed before giving his next order, "They might all be dead down below, but there might have been some out of range to the west. Someone should go make sure the Americans have it under control."

Devlin nodded, still trying to dust himself off, "My company?"

"Take Fred's too. If there are any savages up on the heights, don't let yourselves get cut off," Waller replied, and without another word, Devlin hurried away to gather his b'ys.

Four hundred men would have to descend from the mesa and make their way west until they determined whether there were savage survivors to be wary of. Hopefully the Americans and the Gurkhas had them handled, but it was best never to assume.

Skeen found Waller shortly after Devlin departed, and the Briton was coughing, "Damn me, Tom, I thought it was dusty at Jalalabad."

"I wouldn't have argued, sir," Waller agreed. "Need the dust to clear before we see what's left of them, but I've sent two companies west off the mesa, to make sure the Americans have held."

"Would be a shame if they weren't able to," Skeen replied, then tried dusting off his sleeves. It only kicked up more of a mess.

When would a breeze come along to clear this air?

Sass was not pleased with the amount of debris the explosion had kicked into the atmosphere — it made for difficult combat, even with her robust senses. She couldn't imagine how the humans were coping, so she turned to her pilots and hissed orders for them to return to the transport. It was unlikely they'd have to worry about more direct Hubrin fire now — the vehicles would have been destroyed outright — so the transport could safely get into action.

Once the pilots were assigned, Sass turned west and followed the terrain she'd covered the night before. She was looking over these treacherous slopes for the attackers who would inevitably be using the dust shroud to cover their advance. There was no way the blast had been large enough to get them all.

Quickly and silently, the Saa engineer passed the lines of the new troops — the ones with the same uniforms but different skin colors from the Newfoundlanders. Continuing on, she saw the other soldiers, the local ones with the darkest hides and different weapons, flee past her as well. The dust was too thick to identity what they were fleeing from, though, and deciding not to over-commit herself without human support, she stopped and prepared to turn back.

It would do no good at all for her to stumble into a horde, and risk falling down one of the steep slopes as she fought them blind.

Gunshots sounded from the dust cloud — many projectile weapons firing in a fast sequence. An organized unit must have stayed behind as a rearguard. Engineer though she was, Sass came from a fighting clan, and it was not in her nature to casually abandon other warriors. She considered her chances of aiding the men, then decided the odds were good enough. She surged silently into the dust.

Adams shot a savage in the face, and then another in the chest. More were coming, but the man he'd been covering finished reloading his Springfield, and was ready to kill the next few.

Moving on, the Captain fired the last shot from his magazine, then quickly replaced it. He had only two more left in his webbing... they couldn't stand as rearguard much longer.

More savages were coming, too — thick and fierce they lunged from the dust, some landing on bayonets, others landing on his soldiers. He couldn't keep track of how many of his men had fallen — the damned dirty dust cloaked them, like a fog of war from the black powder era of human conflict.

Cursing, Adams looked back to those he could see, "Keep tight, watch out for each other!"

The men nodded, but already were doing as he asked — these men always looked after each other, even in the direst of times.

And this, Adams imagined, was about as dire as a time could become.

He was right, and what confirmed his assessment was the snarling rush of beasts from the dust cloud ahead. Two dozen came straight at him, and though the first dozen fell instantly in a .30-06 hail, the rest surged ahead lightning quick.

Adams shot one, and another, but knew the survivors would tear him apart.

Except that a giant foot came from the heavens, and landed upon them. The shattering sound was pronounced as Sass collapsed the skeletons of the attackers, and then her tail swung and batted a dozen more right off the heights, down to the gruesome canyon below.

Adams staggered in surprise, and then backed off a few steps when Sass let fly with a lightning bolt from the cannon she'd brought with her as a sidearm.

More savages destroyed.

It took no more than a few seconds for the American to realize his good fortune, and to give them the appropriate order: "Fall back, hurry!"

Then, as the men of the 25th turned to leave, there was a great wind.

"Jesus, that's the aircruiser!" George Tucker, lost in the dust, exclaimed that for anyone to hear as he recognized the droning engines of the big vessel. Dropping to one knee, the Major wondered what was going on — had one of the officers gotten aboard and ordered a retreat?

It was impossible to see...

The massive wind caused by the aircruiser suddenly hit Tucker, and he just managed to plant his hand on his head in time to save his hat from blowing off. Across the mesa, surprised men again dropped from their feet, and the dust whipped past them in vicious currents, stinging their eyes.

But when eyes opened again, the dust had been blown away.

"Jesus," George Tucker staggered to his feet as the sound of the engines began to wind down. "Why wait for the good Lord to provide a wind, when you have dragons to make one."

Shaking his head, he staggered to his feet and looked westward. The American outposts seemed to be gone, and the situation was chaotic... but one sight was impossible to miss.

"Sass, God help me."

Sass appreciated the help her pilots had granted her; a quick blast from the landing thrusters had done wonders in clearing the air over the canyon. As the dust was blown away from the engineer, she was at last able to see what she was facing: at least 600 attackers had made their way up onto the heights so far, and more were on their way. She needed to withdraw quickly.

The local soldiers she'd come to assist had picked themselves up and were already hurrying away, so after giving them a short head start, she began to follow. Attackers continued to come for her, but she was faster and stronger. Her tail batted dozens away, throwing them over the side and down to the canyon below. As she ran eastward, the projectiles of the soldiers on the heights began whipping past her in a flurry, protecting her withdrawal.

When she reached a line that was rapidly organizing itself in the absence of the cloud, she saw both the local troops and the new Imperial ones joining together in a hastily-drawn formation, and every one of the humans was shooting with speed.

Sass quite literally stepped over these lines, then turned back to the west with her acquired lightning cannon and let off a shot. There were perhaps a thousand attackers on the heights now — more coming from below every minute. The Hubrin column had been spread out when she dropped the overloading power cell; a significant number had survived.

Fortunately, the humans had many rifles, and were quite capable of dealing with the attackers, given time and clear lines of sight.

"Looks like we've got a line forming out there," Fred Kearsey pointed to a mixed formation of Gurkhas and buffalo soldiers as he and Devlin led their companies — 'C' and 'D', the first two Companies of Newfoundlanders to reach the new world — down from the mesa and onto the adjoining heights.

Devlin nodded at the point made by his elder counterpart, then noticed that Sass was adding to the fusillade with her lightning bolts. After all the carnage from the mesa, it seemed somehow astounding that there were still thousands of savages coming up from the pass.

But there was nothing but sloping, rocky ground between those beasts, the Gurkhas and Yanks. The savages would all be killed, unless the line ran out of ammunition.

"We better relieve them before their ammo runs out," Devlin said, keeping his feet moving as quickly as he could manage over loose red rock. "Who knows if they even got near the depot in all this confusion."

Kearsey nodded, then looked back over his shoulder to Lieutenant Conway, "Make sure we have plenty of cases of ammunition up close to the line, we're going to need to keep the fire going."

Conway saluted and headed back up the trail towards the mesa, and then Devlin took his turn to assign a job. Looking to Kennedy, who was also near, the Captain gestured towards some of the nearby firing positions that were peering down into the valley, "See if you can borrow a Vickers for us. Looks like we'll stand them up right here."

With another salute, Kennedy barked for Halloran's section, then went machine-gun-hunting.

The Newfoundlanders hurried towards the Gurkha-American line.

Adams was out of ammunition, and half his men were nearly in the same condition. He looked to the nearest Gurkha officer — a Nepalese man he'd never met, and who clearly commanded authority, no matter who granted his commission — but the Lieutenant had nothing to offer either. Not only did the SMLE fire a different caliber round, but his hard-fighting Indian troops were nearly out as well.

"We will fight them with our knives if we must," the Lieutenant said, smiling fiercely as he pulled a mean-looking bent blade out of his belt.

Adams didn't share such enthusiasm, but fortunately he didn't need to order his men to stand with bayonets before a new voice entered the fray.

"Adams, withdraw to the Mesa!"

James Devlin stepped almost heroically into Adams' line of sight, his hat sitting at a jaunty angle on his head.

"You Yanks have done enough and we don't have any ammo for your Springfields," the Newfoundlander continued. "But we have plenty for the Enfields!"

That last comment was directed towards the knife-wielding Gurkha officer Adams didn't know, who sheathed his blade and answered with enthusiasm, "Excellent."

Men from Fred Kearsey's company quickly hurried forward with cases of .303 ammunition, and distributed those boxes with desperate speed — no one wanted to be left empty as the savages came close.

As the ammo was rolled out, Adams realized that he and his men were now, if anything, in the way — occupying a part of the line that needed to be filled by men who were ready to shoot.

"The 25th will withdraw twenty paces and form ranks!" Adams yelled, and with a parting look at Devlin, he followed his men as they backed away from the fight.

Men from 'C' Company hurried past the Americans, and then with practiced ease the Newfoundlanders oriented themselves into a line of two ranks, the front rank kneeling.

Half of 'D' Company formed on 'C' Company's flank, but the bulging hill they were atop dropped off too dramatically there for the line to be lengthened any further. Fred Kearsey's last two platoons thus fixed bayonets and fell in alongside the 165 surviving Americans — they were the flying platoons, in case the savages broke through somewhere and needed to be driven back.

Sass waited behind all of them, observing with interest as the humans draped themselves in a formation perpendicular to the canyon. The ground from one side of the line to the other sloped at nearly thirty degrees, but the Imperial troops settled in and stared down the attackers scrambling towards them.

Finally, as ammunition was distributed, the Gurkhas ceased their fire long enough to dress their ranks — neaten their firing lines to match the more precise ones drawn up by the Newfoundlanders adjacent to them — and then their fire resumed.

Getting into position just behind his men, Devlin found Fred Kearsey, and the two veterans of many savage fights gave the orders together.

"Right b'ys, you remember how this goes," Kearsey called.

"Rapid *fire!*" Devlin bellowed.

The savages were advancing in their usual style — their tight marching ranks seemingly forgotten, perhaps because their officers were dead — but because of the terrain they were on, they couldn't cover ground nearly as quickly as they were accustomed to. A disorganized mob, they advanced under the muzzles of a line of Imperial infantry, all of whom were firing in the old style — many mad minutes, sheet after sheet of solid lead.

Tom Waller watched the shooting through his field glasses from the mesa, and as he did, three of the Sikh Vickers guns that had been directed towards the pass below repositioned in the dirt beside him.

They had the advantage of height, and Devlin's line was only 500 yards away; it was possible to shoot over the b'ys heads at the beasts further to the west.

"Careful lads, don't plunge any fire into our own," Skeen was behind

Waller, giving the Sikhs a little reminder to err on the side of overshooting. A machine gun burst into the backs of the b'ys would not be well-received.

A Vickers gun started roaring before any of the Sikhs were set up, and Waller swept his field glasses across Devlin's line, until he came to a small gap where a Vickers had been hastily deployed. Probably one of the Gurkhas' weapons, moved into position with all possible speed.

It had a pronounced effect on the savages.

As had been the case in the pass before the lightning cannons had begun firing, here again the prodigious amount of lead being laid through the air proved devastating. Though savages continued to arrive on the heights from the canyon below, their front line seemed to push further and further back — not because they weren't coming, but because they were falling sooner to bullets once they reached the top.

It was gruesome slaughter... and then, quite suddenly, it ended.

Savages ceased appearing atop the heights, and the firing subsided after scant seconds. A carpet of dead, sometime five or six deep, remained on the ground... but the enemy seemed to be gone. As gravity and loose rock combined mercilessly, some of the corpses began to slide towards the cliffs, and plunge down to the canyon floor.

"That's done them in," Skeen said sharply — neither too proudly, nor too sadly. This was victory, though in the face of such carnage no man could be too keen...

"Jesus, Mary and Joseph."

George Tucker had just returned to Waller's side when he released those words. At first both Waller and Skeen thought the Major was referring to the horrific scene on the southern heights. But then the Newfoundland Colonel looked to the opposite side of the canyon, and realized the savages hadn't stopped coming because all were dead. Most of them were — Pacifica had probably been saved by Sass' bomb and the brutal musketry of the Newfoundlanders, the Americans, and the Indian Army...

But there were enough savages left to exact some retribution. And on the other side of the canyon, a smaller force of riflemen seemed a more realistic target for their wrath.

Somehow, the savages had realized this, and had found their way up a path not far to the east of the promontory from which Krazakowski and his men had fired across the canyon to stop the savages racing up to attack Adams. There had to be a few thousand of the beasts remaining — perhaps the last of the column's rearguard — but only 500 Gurkhas and 400 Americans were left there to receive them, each unit waiting around a small, barely-fortified ammo depot.

Too far to the west for any of the machine guns from the mesa to safely engage.

"Mountain guns, try to disperse them!" Skeen ordered.

Waller was already wheeling towards the aircruiser, "George, get whatever men you can find — we must get over there and take them off!"

CHAPTER XXIX

When the savages crested the heights near the makeshift ammo depot to which the men of the 25ᵗʰ had retreated, Krazakowski realized they were too close to his lines.

The first volley from the black soldiers immediately cut down every savage that came into view save for one, and that beast didn't survive long. But there wasn't enough distance — barely sixty yards of basically flat, passable ground — between the depot and the edge from which the beasts could leap.

The depot was in the wrong place — there was ammunition, but not enough room to use it. When more beasts came over the ledge than could be gunned down before his men reloaded, all would be lost.

Looking to his left, Krazakowski could see the Gurkha post 400 yards away, similarly near the edge of the heights. The savages didn't seem to have a way up to that position, so perhaps retreating there with as much ammunition as possible would make the most sense.

But there was no time.

As soon as Krazakowski opened his mouth to give the order, another hundred savages popped up, and it took too many seconds for his men to bring them down. Unless no more of the beasts were coming, this would not end well...

The nearby sound of screaming artillery rounds surprised the American Major, and then the ground shook slightly as the shells impacted the face of the cliff on which he stood. They were probably killing savages on their way up... but that wasn't enough either.

By Krazakowski's estimation, the day had gone relatively well — from the perspective of the bigger picture, the column of savages and blue men had been finished. Even if he and all the men here with him died, they would have accomplished their mission. The Pacifica Territory was safe, the threat to it destroyed in the badlands.

But so many of his men were soon to fall.

Another hundred savages came, and a hundred more right behind them. With each wave they got a little further along before his men were able to shoot them down. Then there was movement from the right — the westerly direction — as beasts who reached the top the heights near Krazakowski's initial position now charged at the depot.

Captain Insetta was over there, and he ordered his fifty men to give those beasts their fill. The shooting was smart and fast, but again, the numbers were too great and the beasts kept coming.

And now fifty rifles that had been defending the nearer ledge were shooting in another direction...

More sounds of rifle fire came from the left. Krazakowski looked to the east, and saw that the Gurkhas had emerged from their post and formed a line, to provide fire support to the American position. At least a company — a 200-man, Imperial company — was dedicated to that duty.

But as soon as they emerged a third fountain of savages appeared, closer to their post. They were suddenly shooting in their own defense, which meant that as Krazakowski watched, the beasts were drawing closer on two sides.

Standing amongst his men, behind boulders and in front of stacked crates of .30-06 ammunition, Krazakowski took a solemn breath. Captain Vogel was nearby, and he took his hat from his head, and wiped his brow.

Men all around looked back at their Major as they reloaded and shot again. They kept firing, never stopped, but somehow managed to look at him too. For all their desperation, there was no anger or contempt. Perhaps there was no point to such feelings now, or perhaps there was no cause.

Krazakowski had been with these black Americans for years, and in the field with them for many hard fights. He had insisted they have this job — this thankless, deadly mission — because it was their chance to make a mark that could not be erased by color, politics, or hate.

Now they would die for their chance.

And he would fall as their leader.

"Men," the Major called as savages poured onto the heights around them. "You are credits to your nation. May God and America remember you all for what you have done today. May the glory you won resound in the halls of power, in schoolrooms, and in homes across the United States, and the world. May you be remembered for your courage, your skill, your gallantry, and what you did today to save Pacifica. I have been proud to be with you all these years, and I am proud to be with you now. God bless, and thank you for your hard fighting..."

Pausing, the Major took a breath. Raising his Colt to the sky, he then called out: "Ready and forward!"

At his bellow, the men with him yelled out those familiar words of the regiment: "Ready and forward!"

Perhaps, Krazakowski realized, he should not have spoken, because his words distracted his fine soldiers from their shooting. But it wouldn't have made any difference. Major Ernest Krazakowski was an unusual sort of man, and he could be forgiven his tears of profound sadness as savages leapt into his position.

The men of the 25th all around him had their bayonets fixed, and they fought fierce and hard. Many were big and strong soldiers, but none so powerful as the savages. Only one civilized human was that strong, and she was in New World City.

So their bayonets sometimes found flesh, but not often enough. Savages tore men — the brave men of the 25th United States Infantry — limb from limb.

In their midst, Krazakowski repeatedly fired his Colt. Vogel and a dozen men fought with him, backs together as they made their final stand amongst the crates of ammunition. Krazakowski thought of trying to blow up the stockpile, but he didn't have the opportunity.

He didn't see the savage who finally hit him — that often seemed to be the way with the beasts. One minute Krazakowski was shooting, and the next his head was no longer with the rest of his person. His body fell to the dirt.

None of the men who'd joined him that day survived.

***

They didn't even bother raising the ramp as the aircruiser blasted off the mesa; Waller and the 600 men who'd been hurriedly loaded into the craft simply hung on for dear life as it hopped across the pass.

Two Vickers guns were in the door of the aircruiser, both crewed by Sikhs. As the craft crossed the canyon and slowed to touch down near the Gurkha outpost — the one nearest the mesa — those Indian machine guns cut loose, spraying the growing horde of savages with streams of lead. This fire provided cover as 'A' and 'B' Companies of the Newfoundland Regiment, and 'A' Company of the Sikhs descended the craft's ramp at a run, bayonets fixed and lines forming immediately.

The beasts were well-focused on the Gurkha position by now, and closing in fast, but the fire from the aircruiser and its reinforcements bought time.

Not that Gurkhas seemed to need it. The fire from the Nepalese men never let up, even as seething currents of beasts collided with their lines. With orders that Waller couldn't possibly hear, the officers of the Indian Army regiment formed their men into a square, as though they were facing Napoleonic cavalry on the peninsula. As the formation came together — admittedly somewhat haggard, since the men took more care in shooting than dressing ranks — the Gurkhas began their withdrawal.

"Fire to clear their flanks, Billy," Waller turned to Captain Sesk with that order, and in seconds there was thunder, the Newfoundlanders and Sikhs carefully directing their intense fire to parts of the swelling horde not in line with the Gurkha square. There would be no losses to friendly fire this late in the day.

The combined fire of the Newfoundlanders, the Sikhs and the Nepalese men was predictably devastating. Lead in .303 caliber came from all sides, and the savages didn't seem to know which way to turn.

As they began to fall in great carnage, the pressure on the sides of the square let off... and then Tom Waller saw something he had never thought he would witness. Without any obvious fear, the dark men from Nepal drew their kukris and charged into the confused horde.

"Jesus Christ," Bill Sesk was close enough to Waller for the Colonel to hear his oath over the sound of riflery. "What's their motto... better to die than live a coward?"

As far as Waller could remember, that was indeed the motto of the Gurkha regiments. And as he watched, savages learned that a visit to Nepal might not be in their best interests.

The kukri was like a machete that bent forward at its top half. It swung like an axe, could cut throats, could destroy trees...

And savages.

Waller and Sesk watched as one Havildar — a wiry Nepalese Sergeant who could not have stood more than five feet and four inches — clutched a savage by the hair on its head, wrenched it off its feet and separated it from its limbs.

And then did the same to another.

The destruction was quite unbelievable — confused savages, perhaps unprepared to defend themselves, and certainly not ready for knife fighting, began to come apart... and then turn away... and then run from their stone-faced attackers.

But running simply brought them before the muzzles of sharpshooting Imperial infantry. The beasts had nowhere to go, and slowly, painfully, they were all destroyed.

"Jesus, I guess the Gurkhas had something to prove after they didn't get the western outposts," Sesk shook his head as firing slowed down.

It had been an incredible display of prowess, and as the Gurkhas reformed their ranks and wiped clean their iconic blades — seemingly without the loss of a single man — Waller could only shake his head.

"I'm sure the Americans made their mark too. They probably weren't so casual about it."

He was right. He was terribly, brutally right.

CHAPTER XXX

There was a commotion outside the cell, and Smith came to his feet when he heard the sounds of hurried boarding and of aircruiser engines beginning to warm up.

It had been more than a day since any of the blue men had checked on their prisoners — no food, no attention of any sort — and that had left the captives plenty of time to begin feeling disconnected within their metallic cell. The circumstances allowed for plenty of wondering what the blue men were trying to make them believe, where they might end up, and whether they would ever again breathe fresh air.

Perhaps now they were set to find out.

"Sounds like the blues are getting ready to move," Turner rose beside Smith, and the drifter nodded, putting his hat on his head.

"It does."

Which direction would these creatures be heading — towards their next target, or back to their home? The former seemed more likely, since they'd been sitting out near Ambitia all this time, presumably waiting for their next mission. They could have gone home any time.

But if another attack was to be mounted, it would make sense for Smith, Turner and the men to try to disrupt it... give the defenders a chance.

But how could they get out of this cell?

Approaching the doorway that had been shut for more than a day, Smith pressed his hands against it, then studied its simple silver surface one more time. There were barely even seams where the door slid into the wall when it opened... the chances of prying it were nil.

No, they needed the blue men to open the hatch.

"Think they'd fall for it if one of us pretends we're sick, and we need a doctor?" Turner asked, and Smith shook his head.

The Sergeant wasn't surprised by the answer, "Yeah, how would they even know if we were sick…"

Smith stepped back from the door and turned to the men within, head continuing to shake, "There must be something we have that they're paying attention to…"

That could indeed be the case, but the drifter had no idea what it might be. He only knew he needed a way out.

Occasional shots sounded from the valley below as the 15th Ludhiana Sikhs swept the low road, executing any surviving savages, and ready to make prisoners of any blue men they found alive. So far, that number was zero — the musketry had been quite destructive — but the orders still stood. Any survivors were to be kept for interrogation.

That was all terribly important, but Waller paid it very little attention.

On the mesa, 165 men of the 25th United States Infantry were sitting together, still in shock at the utter destruction of more than two-thirds of their regiment. Krazakowski, Koster, Vogel and Insetta were all dead. Adams seemed to be the senior man left alive, and like the rest of his men, he appeared rudderless.

Waller could think of no words that might help. Had it been the b'ys who'd been wiped out in such a wholesale fashion, he wasn't sure what he'd have done to cope with the trauma… except, of course, died with them.

As it was, only a handful of the Newfoundlanders had been wounded on the day — based at the mesa, they'd only been subject to harm from blue man lightning cannons. A couple of b'ys had been injured during their rescue of the Gurkhas, but ultimately all were well.

Waller wasn't sure whether to count his lucky stars for the lack of casualties, or fear for the day of reckoning when fate balanced the tables. Not a thought he wanted to dwell on, but as he looked over the shocked men he'd been with in Promised Town, the Newfoundland Colonel had a difficult time shaking the anxiety.

Fortunately, a veteran General was also on the mesa.

"You men, may I speak with you?"

By any measure used in the military history of the British Empire, Sir Andrew Skeen had won a massive victory on this day. A column of 30,000 savages and fourteen blue man lorries had been devastated by fewer than 4,000 infantry, with the loss of barely more than 600 men. Certainly the losses had been great for the Americans, but it had been their own territory saved by the action. As such, British historians would likely thump their chests, toast the brave Negroes, and call the day a success to match those of Garnet Wolseley, or Wellington himself.

Skeen knew his business well enough to understand he would be lauded as a hero, and he was honestly pleased with his success. But he was also the sort of officer who won the respect of his men because he led them well, and actually did care for their well-being.

Now the Indian Army General passed Waller as he addressed the black soldiers sitting on the rock of the mesa. Being senior amongst them, Adams was the first to process the arrival of the General, and slowly he forced himself to his feet, "Sir."

Coming to a stop beside Adams, Skeen fell silent for a moment as he studied the American's face. Then his eyes turned towards the black men sitting all around, many of whom looked up at him now with grave stares.

"None of us here are new to war. I will not tire you with brave words about our fallen friends on the other side of the pass... about how men die in our business, or about how your fellows fell to save this territory. You men are all aware of that, and knowing you for only this short time, I can hardly profess to offer new wisdom." As ever, Skeen knew how to avoid traps — be they in the field, or in the world of easy rhetoric.

Folding his arms, Waller listened as his General continued: "Looking at you men as an outsider, I see two great sadnesses in this moment. The first is obvious: that more than 400 of your friends have perished. Your Major, many of your officers, have fallen."

So numb were the survivors that none of them seemed to visibly react to those words — which was perhaps just as well.

"The second is that those friends of yours will not be here to witness the changes to come. When Major Krazakowski asked that you men be posted to the west, to the most dangerous positions on the field, I asked him why. He explained to me that this was an opportunity, unlike any your regiment has yet enjoyed, to be noticed in action doing a job that really matters. You men did that job. Up came those savages, faster and stronger than any foe I've ever faced in my decades of soldiering, and you kept them at bay long enough for us to finish the job. You men did that, and as I promised your Major, I pledge to you: this will not be forgotten."

Skeen was taking a very positive interpretation of day's events, but as he listened, Waller knew no one would object.

"Our histories, and I do hope your own, will tell what you have done today. It will not be forgotten. And I hope that your War Department will learn here what our Indian Army has always known: that a good fighting man will be so, no matter what the color of his skin. I am not a General of any importance, but I promise to you that I will tell them. You have proved it, and now your country must know."

Perhaps that was some comfort to the men of the 25th United States Infantry, but as Waller turned his gaze to the black soldiers, he found few expressions suggesting any positive response to Skeen's pledge. Many had spoken to these men before, promising that the next action would bring glory. None had, because the problems in American society ran too deep for one story to turn them all.

"But while I cannot speak for your country, I can speak in part for mine. I must thank you, all of you, for what your fighting here has proven. And specifically, I must thank Captain Adams," Skeen turned slightly and gestured to the black officer. "In India, our colored officers are not commissioned equally to our white officers. Captain Adams here has proved that we are foolish in this. So with the story of what has happened here, and how Captain Adams and his men fought today, I think we can at last bring about change. Men, it might not mean anything to you, but your example will be seen around the world. And many Indian officers, like the men who fought with you today, will one day credit your stand here as a moment that helped change their history."

That was an ambitious boast, and Waller wasn't certain how genuine it would prove. Skeen had been determined to have Indian officers granted King's commissions for as long as the Newfoundlander had known him. Perhaps it was true that Adams' presence at the battle could help convince the War Office to finally begin initiating change... though the Indian officers made a powerful case for change all on their own.

"Men, rest for now. We'll have you back to civilization soon, and then our trials will continue. But this will be the start of a new era in your history. It may take time to fully arrive, but it is a beginning. For that, thank your Major, and thank your fallen friends. Make sure that, in the years to come, when children ask you what happened today, you remember those men well."

That was where Skeen finished, and after reaching out and shaking Adams' hand, the General turned away from the still-shocked American soldiers, who all watched him go in silence.

Sir Andrew spotted Waller as he moved away, and altered course to join the Newfoundland Colonel. As he stopped with his back to the 25th, the General asked quietly: "Was that too much?"

Waller blinked, "Um. It was a warm sentiment, sir..."

"It's not for today. Today they'll only feel misery. But I want to make sure they have something to hold to when they look back and try to rationalize the slaughter. Hope it's enough."

Again, Skeen was outsmarting his enemy — in this case the foe just happened to be grief. Now every survivor of the 25th had something to draw on in hindsight... a cause their friends died for, and something to take pride in.

When they were ready, which could be months or years hence.

"And by God if I won't use this to my advantage about the Viceroy's commissions," Skeen continued. "About bloody time we... we..."

He trailed off, and after a second's pause, Waller glanced sideways at him. Skeen still had his back to the Americans, which meant he was looking past the shoulder of the Newfoundland Colonel, and he was frowning.

"Sass seems in an awful hurry..."

As he heard that comment, Waller turned quickly. The great dragon lady was racing across the mesa behind him, deftly stepping around men and equipment.

There was no mistaking the look of concern on her face. Something was happening...

***

Smith was fairly certain the aircruiser in which he stood was flying. He'd noticed a jerking sensation as it took off, and though he felt none of the sensations that he'd experienced when riding with Carstairs, his instincts told him he was in the sky — and moving fast.

Still, he was trapped in a room with no obvious way out, and unless he could figure something...

The door opened.

Turning in surprise, the drifter watched as the blue man with four bands stepped in, a squad of savages entering behind him. Before any man could think to make a foolish attack, the beasts swept forward, one taking each of the Americans in its grip and dragging them out.

Smith didn't struggle against the one that grabbed him. As he passed the blue man, he glared at the creature, and it glared back.

The men were taken through the corridors of the aircruiser to a room with two chairs, each with bindings on them. Several blue men were standing around, and though the only controls Smith could see were flat switches on the wall, he got the sense that this place was used for some sort of science. He'd seen similar setups at Fort Martian... places where savages were probably poked and prodded.

No sooner did Smith make that connection than did the blue officer point to two of the youngest soldiers in the squad. They were dragged immediately to the chairs and strapped down by the savages who had taken them from the cell.

Seeing their comrades being hauled to some sort of torture implements, the men of the squad began to struggle against the savages holding them, but the beasts had them well in hand.

"Sarge?" one of the boys being strapped down was wide-eyed.

"Keep calm..." Turner answered immediately, though he realized that was probably the most hopeless order.

"What are you doing?" Smith turned that question against the blue officer, but it was ignored.

Without any further delay, the blue officer and his two fellow creatures stepped in front of the restrained men, then remained still. Though the blues had their backs to the rest of the Americans, Smith could only guess they were starting a form of psychic interrogation.

But why start with two junior men, not him?

The drifter didn't know, but he reckoned he better make the most of the fact that he was free to think.

Sass urgently led Waller and Skeen into the aircruiser and pointed them up the ladder into the cockpit. As the officers arrived they found the moving picture screens showing activity; the blue markers from Destina and Ambitia were both flying... and not westward, as though they were coming to relieve the column that had been destroyed.

One was headed towards New World City, the other towards Pacifica City. And they were moving fast.

"Dammit, suppose they have to try something," Skeen shook his head, then turned to Waller, "We have to try to warn home..."

Waller began to nod, but without really processing the commands his General had given him. There was no way to tell what sort of strength either of those vessels truly possessed but it didn't matter much how strong or weak they were: if they got over the two new world capital cities, they'd be close to the tunnels back home, and anything could happen...

What if they tried to get through to Earth in their flying vehicles? Would it be possible to stop them short? Both cities needed to be warned, and far behind though it was, the aircruiser they were standing in had to go after them.

"Tom, tell Sass we need to get airborne. I'll pull together what men I can," the General ordered immediately, knowing he'd be no good at the pantomime communications with their dragon ally.

As Skeen turned and hurried down the ladder, Waller turned to Sass, prepared to make gestures to the effect of 'get us to New World City' — because his own territory was, perhaps unfairly, foremost on his mind — but the dragon was ready with gestures of her own.

Pointing to the aircruiser she was standing in, she gestured to her eyes, then indicated the screen.

Waller frowned at that message. This ship had seen the blue vessels moving... he understood that. Not sure why she'd brought it up, he simply pointed to the aircruiser deck beneath his feet, then pointed to New World City on the moving picture map.

Sass showed a downturned palm, which deepened Waller's frown — why now, at the most critical moment, was she disagreeing with him? She herself had warned them of this attack.

Then she repeated the gestures from before — she pointed to the aircruiser, then to her eyes, then pointed again to the moving picture map.

This aircruiser could see the blue ships moving...

And the aircruiser in New World City could too.

Of course. Pacifica had no air defenses, but there was an aircruiser and a huge defensive establishment in New World City. And Sass was saying Sask and the dragons left behind could see the same thing she could. This ship needed to go after the craft that was heading for Pacifica City.

Waller nodded as soon as he understood, and Sass seemed relieved as she turned her palm up. Immediately she swung away from the flight deck and hissed to her pilots; the drone of the engines began seconds later.

Captain Adams was still standing as Skeen descended the ramp from the aircruiser, and began calling to any men close enough, "To arms immediately! Get aboard the ship — we must counter a move against the capitals by blue aircruisers!"

Adams was still deep in darkness, but he was not divorced from reality: it sounded as though a crisis was at hand, and if nothing else, action would give him and his men less time to dwell on those left dead in the badlands.

"Sergeant Philips!" he turned to his men and bellowed, and as a new electricity seemed to overtake the mesa, the men of the 25th rose quickly, collecting their rifles as they did.

As they rose and hurried without much organization towards the ramp of the flying machine, Jimmy Devlin appeared at Skeen's side, "Sir?"

"Get your men aboard... I'm going to find Mansfield. Tell Tom to hold the flight as long as Sass will allow," the General's answer was entirely out of context, but before Devlin could even consider asking for clarification, Skeen moved off in a hurry.

As he went, the engines began to drone — a precursor to the great wind Devlin knew the aircruiser could kick out.

"Shit, Sergeant Halloran!" Jimmy turned to find his veteran Sergeant was nearby, and at the wave of his Captain, the NCO was on his feet. "Get as many b'ys aboard as you can."

Americans started climbing the ramp just as Halloran stepped on, and then the wind began, shooting out across the mesa with a huge blast of dust. Pinning his hat to his head with his hand, Devlin struggled to the ramp beside Halloran, and together with whatever men were close enough, the Newfoundlanders dragged themselves aboard — out of the way of the gale.

Through the dust, it was the hard-worn men of the 25th who were near enough to follow, and with Adams leading, most of the survivors of that regiment dragged themselves aboard...

Until suddenly the aircruiser was up, leaving behind Skeen and most of the brigade.

"What the hell is going on?" Adams staggered to a stop beside Devlin as both men looked out through the open ramp door, and saw the badlands falling away beneath them.

Jimmy had no real idea, so he shook his head, "I think we volunteered ourselves for trouble. Better see how many men we have. And if we have any ammunition."

That was prudent, and with a nod Adams moved off to check on his men. Looking back to Halloran and the same old section that seemed to follow Devlin and Waller everywhere, the Captain managed a wry smile.

"Don't do that," was Halloran's immediate response to the expression, and taking that scolding seriously, Jimmy sobered.

"Sorry."

With barely 200 men aboard, Sass, Waller and the haggard survivors of the battle in the badlands meant to warn Pacifica City.

God only knew if they'd be in time.

CHAPTER XXXI

Emily was sitting up in bed, reading the newspaper with a slightly smug expression. Sitting in the chair beside her bed, Annie Devlin was reading another copy of the same paper, and every now and then the savage-born Lady would shift around in an effort to draw the former-maid's gaze.

After this happened for the dozenth time, Annie lowered her own paper, "Yes, I see that you're sitting up."

"Just checking that you saw," Emily replied, a bit too sweetly.

She was very pleased to have her back vertical again, though she wouldn't admit how painful the process of sitting up was. Frankly, it was worth it just to show the doctors that she was mending quickly enough to be allowed to leave *soon*. She was going to lose her sanity in this hospital, if she hadn't done so already.

Annie raised her paper again, and the two women continued to read for a few moments... but then Emily heard something. Sounds of commotion. Lowering her paper slowly, she looked towards the window. The positive feelings that came with being able to sit upright rapidly melted away as she realized what she was hearing.

"Sounds like an aircruiser is coming," she said.

Annie looked to the window, "Think the b'ys are coming back?"

A frown creased Emily's brow, and she shook her head, "No. This is different."

Colonel Currie arrived at the park just as Colonel Alain Lapointe descended the ramp of the aircruiser situated there. In the absence of the Newfoundlanders, the Quebecker and his Voltigeurs had taken up most of the liaising duties with Sask and the remaining dragons, so he got the news first.

"There is an aircruiser coming to our position, and another going to Pacifica City. I do not know exactly how the dragons have seen it... I think

Waller's aircruiser might have signaled… but we have very little time to prepare," Lapointe reported as soon as he reached Currie.

Nodding, the Canadian Colonel looked up and scowled, "Damn. Prepare your men… we'll deploy you as soon as we see where they land."

As Lapointe saluted and turned to head down to the parade ground where his regiment was being formed up, Currie caught sight of Sask and the rest of the dragons coming out of their craft, wielding a variety of devices that he didn't recognize. For a moment he considered going over to the large creature and trying to ask what precisely they had in mind, but there was no time — Byng had to be informed immediately, and communication with the large lizards still took too long.

Blue men were on their way.

Captain Carstairs was in his favorite place in either world — his plane — and as he finished another patrol loop of New World City, he banked and looked down at the airfield to check for signals from the ground below.

On most days, messages posted by flag were mundane — the occasional green streamer would fly, denoting a need to land and take on new orders, or a blue one to indicate an incoming train that he might fly over. This time, as his Avro 504 banked and he looked down its wing, the Captain received a surprise.

Red flag, along with a white one: enemy attack coming from the sky.

Leveling out immediately, Carstairs looked back over his shoulder and saw Hennessy was right there on his wing. The Flight Lieutenant had clearly seen the same message, as his eyes were slightly wide. The afternoon would be more interesting than either had expected.

Air attack meant an aircruiser… one must have been spotted crossing the foothills, and warning wired in to headquarters. The advance notice was good; it would let the pilots of the Royal Air Corps get some altitude. If they were above the thing when it arrived, perhaps that would give them an edge, at least for a little while.

Pulling back on his stick, Carstairs led his wing higher, then yanked the charging handle on his Lewis Gun as he climbed. There'd be shooting soon enough.

* * *

Byng was at his window with field glasses in hand when Currie returned. "Seems the dragons got a message from Waller's aircruiser... I suppose they must have wireless between the two... there are aircruisers heading here and to Pacifica City. I've sent a cable to Pershing to warn him as well."

Byng lowered his glasses at Currie's report, then nodded, "Good man... I suppose it's about time the blue bastards realized we were here."

Currie didn't seem ready to editorialize; he moved straight on to tactics: "We have 4,000 men ready for the field, rallying with the Voltigeurs at the parade ground. All our air defense QF guns are crewed, Carstairs is airborne and the dragons seem to be ready with something of their own."

Byng raised his glasses again, still wondering which direction the craft might come from. He'd have to move from his office to get a wider view.

"Good," the General finally answered. "The field telephone hookup to the parade ground is working soundly?"

Currie nodded, "Yes sir."

"Alright. This fellow is likely going to land somewhere... unless he's different than anything we've seen and is going to try to shoot us from the sky. As he comes in to land, you keep an eye on him, then make sure we have at least 2,000 men in place to meet him. The rest stay in reserve in case there's an overland attack."

The General's plan seemed sound to Currie, and the Colonel agreed immediately, "Yes sir."

"If we're lucky, our QFs will shoot that thing from the sky before it can deliver its troops," Sir Julian continued, then lowered his glasses again. "But I don't know if we're quite so lucky."

Sask led his splinter through the streets of the human settlement in silence. The dwellers were running between their structures, some verbal with their panic, others silent. All were surprised to see five warriors of Saa outside the park, but none seemed to question their presence.

That was good. Sask knew that, were the defense of this settlement his responsibility, he would have been frustrated to have unfamiliar creatures intervening in a way that had not previously been agreed to... but until they found a way to properly communicate, it would be impossible for him to explain to Byng the nature of his combat experience.

The Hubrin were sending a single light transport this way. Based on the readings from the passive scans, it wasn't even armed. Shocking how poorly equipped the frontier force on this world was — the planet was truly far from the front lines. It was still inconceivable to him that the Hubrin had not seeded its orbital space with planet-facing defensive satellites... it would have been very useful for them to be able to irradiate the surface if they faced this uprising, but perhaps they had never foreseen such an occurrence — their attackers becoming free, and building up into such a potent adversary as these humans clearly were.

Or perhaps the artificially-created ecosystem of this world was too valuable for them — as the Saa had discovered in their prison camp, the attackers seemed to thrive on these grasslands. This place was a valuable training ground, and given their mounting losses to the scourge Queen, it seemed possible the Hubrin couldn't afford to part with it.

Sask expected the involvement of his warriors would soon change the Hubrin reaction, though. An uprising of freed attackers might be dangerous, but having Saa active on the planet was a strategic threat. A warship was probably on its way.

But for now there was just a light transport to deal with.

Sask was not an overly aggressive officer by Saa standards, but he'd seen his share of combat. Knocking a transport out of the sky was hardly difficult, if you had the tools and the will... and while the humans lacked any real concept of the technology they were facing, or even how fortunate they were to be confronted by such an embarrassing collection of non-military resources, their weapons could undoubtedly do the job.

Still, the stolen and jury-rigged arsenal at the disposal of the Saa survivors could do it more quickly, with less chance of non-combatants being killed.

The four dragons with Sask therefore moved southwest, until they reached the edge of the settlement. Coming to a stop beside the air defense gun position that had been dug there, they surprised several Canadian officers and men who had been quietly trying to contain their nerves as they waited to be attacked.

Sask looked down at one of the little creatures, and it saluted to him. A brave thing, the freed-attacker human. Sask straightened his tail in return, then looked skyward and waited.

Overhead he saw the tiny aircraft of the freed attackers circling — that would be Carstairs, the very strange man who had spent the night with them at the camp. Sask didn't pretend to know much about the day-to-day living of these beings, but it was obvious to just about everyone that Carstairs was odd. The fact that he was willing to fly such a crude machine into combat was sign enough of that.

So the local force was ready; just a matter of welcoming the Hubrin...

At that moment, Sask heard the first hint of an engine in the distant sky. Looking back to his splinter of warriors, he waved them forward, and they went down onto four feet and pushed their way into the forest.

"Call from one of the QF posts... southwest number three. Five dragons just arrived, then slipped out of town into the woods," Currie lowered the phone from his ear as he made that report, and Byng frowned.

"They're not running, surely," the General said.

"No idea, sir... they also think they hear the engines of an aircruiser."

Whatever the dragons were up to didn't matter — the enemy was coming.

"Send up the warning flare, order all batteries to engage when they have the range," Sir Julian ordered. "I'm going to the roof."

Carstairs saw the aircruiser before anyone on the ground could, and expected the craft would have seen him long before he saw it. Clearly undaunted, it came on, and as it drew nearer it looked smaller to the Captain than any he had seen before.

Perhaps it was a military craft — like one of the single-seated fighter planes the Air Corps had delivered to the new world. Those machines would be climbing off the field even now, but they'd be too late to get to altitude before this fight.

Instead, two veteran Avro 504s would just have to engage the enemy alone... if they could get close to it before it shot them down. Indeed, it almost surprised Carstairs that both his machine and Hennessy's hadn't yet been assaulted. Perhaps the blue men knew them to be no threat, and were looking for more powerful ground targets... like the dragons...

If they were, that preoccupation would give Carstairs a chance to at least make some noise. Looking over to his right, he saw that Hennessy was with him, same formation as always. He waved to his wingman, then pointed towards the oncoming craft and nodded.

Hennessy returned the nod, and the two banked in towards the attack.

The aircruiser was coming in fast and low over the treetops, perhaps hoping to remain unseen from the ground. Carstairs' flight would certainly have the advantage of altitude... but God only knew if that would mean anything. Together, the two biplanes raced down from their vantage point, each topping 100 miles per hour as they charged. The blue ship continued its course straight for the city, completely ignoring the impending attack, and Carstairs narrowed his eyes behind his goggles.

His finger floated over the trigger on his control stick, and he tried to line up for the best shot he could...

The explosion came before he squeezed off a single burst.

Byng had just reached the roof when he saw lightning lance out of the woods. Raising his field glasses as quickly as he could, he spotted three or four bolts, all of them connecting with and slicing through one side of the flying machine's metal hull.

There was an immediate explosion, and the small aircruiser heeled over before driving straight down into the forest. Seconds later, a much larger explosion sent flames up from behind the trees.

Then two aero planes soared right over the scene and began waggling their wings at the sight.

Lowering his glasses, Byng frowned — those dragons had been in the woods with lightning cannon?

Must have been.

When Sask and his splinter of Saa warriors emerged from the trees and passed the QF battery they had seen on their way out, they were greeted by verbal sounds from the humans. The noise seemed celebratory, and the mood both joyful and relieved.

Trudging back towards the park where they were sequestered, Sask and those who had joined him for the simple shoot-down of an unarmed and unarmored transport did start to feel the slightest bit proud of their work. It was nice to be appreciated.

Nevertheless, another transport was making an attack... hopefully Sass and their Newfoundland friends would have that one under control.

CHAPTER XXXII

When the straps were released, the two soldiers of the 25th United States Infantry who had been interrogated psychically by the blue officer were both pushed from their seats, and fell forward onto the metal floor without any apparent control over their bodies.

The fact that they could not control themselves was no surprise to Smith — it had been a bad sign when their faces had contorted, and blood had started running from their ears. Turner was furious, as were the rest of his men, but struggle though they did to reach their friends, they were kept well in hand by the savages.

Smith didn't bother fighting — he knew now wasn't the time to spend strength, though he thought the moment might come soon. The engines of the aircruiser were changing pitch, and the drifter figured that meant something. Maybe they were close to their target.

He needed information, so as the blue man with the four bands turned back towards the rest of the captives, Smith caught his eye, and pushed a picture of the machine landing into the front of his mind.

The blue man stopped, appearing surprised that Smith knew what the craft was doing. But the surprise cleared quickly — Smith was, after all, one of the leaders who had done great harm during previous encounters between the blue men and the humans of this world. It made sense that he'd have some insight into what was going on.

Beginning to turn away, the blue man gestured for the soldiers to be taken back to their cell, but before savages could move to carry out the orders, Smith raised another inflammatory picture — one he hoped would get attention. It did.

Hundreds of soldiers firing at the small craft they were in, as well as artillery and machine guns... lead hitting the aircruiser repeatedly until finally it burned.

It was an embellishment of the infantry's abilities, at least based on what Smith had seen when the Newfoundlanders and the Voltigeurs had faced an aircruiser like this one back at Fort Martian... but if it made the blue man think the drifter had more knowledge than he did...

The blue officer turned back to Smith, and this time responded with sharp pictures. Smith gritted his teeth as those images pierced his mind... but he recognized them. A place... a city... a big city that was right at the foot of a mountain, had a tunnel, and no defenses to speak of.

Pacifica City.

Smith could see this aircruiser landing beside the train station in that city... near the tunnel... and could see that there were a couple of machine guns already firing ineffectually.

Was this where the craft had just touched down? There were no sounds that suggested a machine gun rattling shots off the hull, but maybe the aircruiser's armor was too thick to let such noise through.

The blue officer let go of Smith's mind and turned away, gesturing for the other blues in the room with him to follow. The savages remained where they were, restraining the standing soldiers, as well as Smith...

Then, suddenly, the one holding Smith started dragging him after the blue men. They went through the corridors of the aircruiser almost faster than the drifter could keep his feet moving, and emerged into the late afternoon sunshine seconds later.

As the blue leader had shown him, they were beside the Pacifica City railway station, and there seemed to be no defenders around at all. That didn't make sense — Smith had seen at least two machine gun nests here in past years when he'd ridden through...

The savage dragged him across the ground, stopping beside the four-ringed officer. After a second, Smith realized that man was looking at the defenses — or where the defenses had been, before lightning guns had gone to work on them.

As the drifter at last noticed the destroyed emplacements, sounds of gunfire reached his ears. It was close, but not right on them — probably a few streets over. The savages from the aircruiser were likely out there now, attacking, killing, destroying... but to what end?

Smith was taking in all sorts of information, but it wasn't fitting together neatly in his head. Why land exactly here... was it the town's weakest point? Had the American defenses been set up at the edge of the city, forgetting the ability of the aircruiser to soar over their lines?

Controlling the tunnel — the most important connector between new world and old — was probably a valuable strategic objective, but there was no way the aircruiser held enough savages to subdue the whole city garrison. They could only stay here a while... so what were they up to?

Smith turned as best he could back towards the tunnel, and then he saw for the first time a silver cylinder, about the size of a lorry, that was being rolled out the back of the aircruiser. It was a simple-looking thing, but large. And heavy. A half dozen savages were trying to move it and were having a difficult time.

The blue officer noticed that Smith had seen the cylinder, and he forced a new picture into the drifter's mind: the cylinder rolling into the tunnel, and then at a point far along, exploding.

Bring down the tunnel. Cut Pacifica off from the United States. Smith blinked at the prospect, and realized immediately how wise a move it would be — without the manufacturing power of the States and the British Empire, the armies defending both the Selkirk Mandate and the Pacifica Territory would be helpless.

The blue men had that ability... why hadn't they used it already?

Gritting his teeth, Smith put pictures into his mind: he recalled the attack at Farfield, and Fort Martian, and then replaced them with the image of the cylinder exploding. He didn't know if the blue man would understand the images were meant as a question...

But it did. Damned thing was wise enough to.

Drawing on visuals that it must have pulled from various human minds, it pictured blue men standing on the steps of the United States Capitol Building, and presiding over crowds on the lawn of Canada's Parliament Buildings. He then plucked one of the blue men standing in these places, and put him in the midst of a battlefield... no, not just in the midst of it, but dead amongst many others.

Smith tried to interpret, but couldn't quite, so the blue man tried again.

He showed the same image as before — the blue administrator sitting behind a desk, as opposed to soldiering. Then he showed that same fellow standing over the people of America from the steps of the Capitol Building. Then he showed him dead in a pass in the badlands.

The blue administrator commanding their army... he'd believed he could conquer the Earth? Maybe take the people there as an army of his own? It seemed to Smith like a familiar madness — the sort of ambition held by someone like Custer, or Colonel Robinson of the 25th. An ambition not shared by this officer... a blue man who had seen war, and probably figured all the benefits of trying to conquer the Earth (were that even possible) paled compared to the risks of allowing the humans on the new world the support of the British Empire and the United States.

Better to protect what you had, instead of risking it to get something that might be out of reach.

But now, whatever blue General had thought to take the Earth was lying dead in the badlands, presumably killed by the men of the 25th near Deadline. This blue officer in front of Smith was thus free to follow his own plan... or perhaps this plan had been the backup all along.

As Smith put the pieces together, he watched the last twenty savages who'd been aboard the aircruiser join the effort to push the cylinder into the tunnel. With that many beasts, the thing started to roll pretty steadily, but the tunnel was long.

Somehow, someone had to stop it before it got to a place where they could detonate it.

Smith didn't have many options. There was one savage left that he could see, and it was holding his arm. He had no weapon, but the blue officer was very close...

With no time to figure a plan, Smith did the only thing he could: he fell.

The savage let him drop, as that didn't seem the act of a man trying to escape — at least not to the beast's instinctive brain. Only paying partial attention, the blue officer turned with some surprise, perhaps wondering if the American had fainted.

Smith watched the creature's feet, gauged how close he was, and then launched himself upward.

This was something the savage noticed, and would have been fast enough to stop if he hadn't been so slow to realize what was happening. As understanding dawned in the blue officer's brain, the drifter got his arm around its long neck from behind, then used his other arm to lock the grip in place.

The blue officer knew as well as Smith did that this was a good method for snapping a neck — particularly a narrow, Martian one — so a psychic order went out instantly, freezing the savage and compelling the dozen blue men nearby to keep their weapons down.

It was a nice gesture, but Smith figured keeping the blues from shooting him was only the solution to one part of his problem — if any of them got into his mind, they could compel him to let their officer go. As warning not to try, the drifter pictured the Martians causing his mind pain, as they'd done to Emily... and him snapping the officer's neck.

Hoping that would hold them at bay, he moved fast to demands. He thought of telling them to stop the cylinder, but knew they wouldn't. Instead he asked for something easier: the men of the 25th to be brought out — hopefully too many minds for the blues to control — and their savage guards sent to join the attack that was happening in the town.

It was a strange demand, because it didn't go against the plan the blue men were carrying out. The blue officer was somewhat confused by this, but encouraged by the pressure against his throat, he acceded. After just a few seconds, Turner and the five men still standing from his squad emerged into the afternoon sun, and then the savages who had dragged them out sprinted away.

"What the hell?" Turner didn't understand what was happening — he hadn't seen the cylinder — but that was irrelevant.

"Just a minute," Smith called back to the Sergeant, then he pictured something else in his mind... something he hoped would buy some time.

He would let the officer go, as long as he and the five men from the 25th were allowed to run off and ride away from this place on their own. Save themselves. Smith wanted the blue man to believe that he had no interest in what came next for the Pacifica Territory — for the bigger picture.

But it was a tough case to make. The officer pushed back, in spite of the pressure on his neck. He dove into Smith's mind, looking for pictures that reflected his true motive.

Fortunately, the drifter's life was there for the creature to see. Riding on his own for years, with no ties to anyone. Why would a man with so few connections to organized society change his priorities now?

A picture of Caralynne was suddenly dragged before Smith's mind's eye, and he tensed sharply at the sight of her. The blue officer seized on the picture and twisted it... showed her fall in the street in Farfield, showed her sitting in a chair in a glass building, with a mighty spire standing outside the window behind her.

The pictures didn't make sense to Smith, so he struggled against them and then pictured his grief. He remembered being beaten in the streets of Ambitia, and hoped that would be enough proof that he was a broken man — a man who cared no more for the world, because he'd always been alone, and his interlude with a loving woman had ended in blood.

The officer considered the entire case... the loss of a mate, the loss of commitment... and eventually seemed to give in. Perhaps a half-dozen Americans who wanted to run away weren't dangerous enough to worry about. His bomb was being rolled into position anyway — there was nothing these few could do about that. So the blue man repeated Smith's original mental image: that of the drifter and the five American soldiers fleeing into the woods, unaccosted.

That was it. They were free to run.

Smith then pictured his guns, and the Americans' rifles. To explain himself, he showed the escapees shooting at their fellow American soldiers... using the weapons to escape the army who was chasing them for betrayal and desertion.

The blue officer seemed more reluctant at the idea of arming these humans, but between the pressure on his neck and the case Smith had made, he seemed willing to comply. His savages would be back soon enough anyway... so he pictured the room within the aircruiser that held the weapons.

As Smith saw it, he called out to Turner: "Our guns... just inside and to the right. There's a locker... press the flat switch furthest to the left."

Turner was understandably surprised that the drifter had such information, but under the circumstances there was no time to waste. Nodding to his remaining men, he led them back into the craft to collect their guns.

Smith stayed where he was, arm around the officer's neck while the rest of the blue soldiers watching him kept their lightning rays handy. They were probably seeing the thought exchange he and the blue officer were sharing, but that didn't mean they trusted it. The drifter would have to be very careful if he was going to manage any sort of retrieval of this situation.

Could he and Turner's men shoot all the blues here, then get into the dark tunnel and kill all the savages, then find a way to stop the explosion? It was a long shot — a two-mile shot — but he was going to try...

He shouldn't have thought that.

The blue officer tensed as some of those thoughts edged close enough to the top of Smith's mind to be detected. Wrenching to try to get free, the creature summoned back the savages who had run from the field, and ordered his blue men to level their lightning guns on the drifter.

Smith saw it happening just before his mind filled with pain — not just inflicted by the officer, he realized, but from every blue man staring at him. Together, they were all beaming thoughts into his brain, and that was enough to make him as susceptible as Emily would have been.

But the drifter knew pain — he'd felt his share. He'd watched Caralynne dragged away by the savages. No, wait, killed by the savages...

Smith screwed his eyes shut at the painful thought. He could see Caralynne now, being dragged away from the street in Farfield City, and him doing nothing because he was seeing her dead. Because the blue men were putting thoughts in his head...

But did that really happen? Or were these blue men now trying to torture him with a memory that wasn't real? Dammit, he didn't know... how could a body know if a memory was real or not when faced with monsters who could make him see things, or think he was seeing things?

Smith felt like he was caught in a raging blizzard. It felt as though wind was pounding his face, his ears roared and his heart pounded. The whole world seemed to be screaming at him, or trying to blast open his mind from the inside out... but he held on. The blue officer wasn't going to get free of his grip, and if a savage tried to pull him off, the thing's neck would break. The drifter didn't know what was real beyond that. He didn't know if Caralynne was dead or alive. All he knew was that he wouldn't let go.

And as that certainty settled in, the pressure on his mind seemed to ebb a little. The whipping wind that was slamming him all over stopped, his blood pounded less angrily in his veins and the roaring diminished, replaced by louder sounds of rifle shots from the city behind him.

Maybe certainty was all it took to put the Martians out of a man's mind.

Taking a deep breath, Smith opened his eyes again, and found the blues facing him with lightning guns to be looking back and forth, as if anxious. Perhaps they realized he was serious.

The officer struggled under his grip one more time, and then Smith tightened his arms. Snapping the creature's neck was as easy as it was cold, and as Smith let the thing drop, he prepared himself to be blasted or torn to pieces.

"Dammit, was hoping we could interrogate that one," Jimmy Devlin shook his head as he came to a stop beside the drifter. "Was going to threaten to shoot him in the brain."

Sergeant Halloran pointed to the half dozen blues who were now laying down their lightning guns, "Well we have them."

Smith watched the two Newfoundlanders with no sense of confusion whatsoever. He watched tan-clad men of the 25th United States Infantry approach the surrendering blue men and roughly take them into custody at bayonet-point. He saw Adams reunited with Sergeant Turner at the exit of the smaller aircruiser.

He turned around and saw a much larger Martian air machine had landed on the ground behind him, and Waller and Devlin both trying to say something to him, smiling and then patting him on the shoulder in greeting.

There was even a dragon.

The drifter looked down at the dirt, adjusted his hat, and then his legs promptly buckled beneath him. As he fell, Devlin and Waller both saw blood trickling from his right ear.

CHAPTER XXXIII

"Need to get him to a doctor," Devlin crouched beside Smith as the drifter crumpled to the dirt, and Waller nodded.

"We'll see if we can find one as soon as we figure out what the hell they're doing here..." the Newfoundland Colonel was already looking from the smaller aircruiser to the surviving blue men and back.

Why land in front of the tunnel and then send savages into town... unless you were trying to keep the defending forces away from the tunnel while you got up to something.

Captain Adams and Sergeant Turner — both men clearly very happy to see each other still alive — approached Smith's fallen form as Waller was having those thoughts. Turner's bright expression dropped into a frown at the sight of the fallen drifter.

"They interrogated a couple of my men, and that's how they were after," Turner said, pointing to the blood running from Smith's ear.

Waller blinked, looked down at the drifter, and then up again, "God willing he'll be alright. Sergeant, I'm sorry to be short: what the hell is going on here?"

Turner looked up at Waller and shook his head, "Don't know, sir... they landed here and took Smith. I think he was having a psychic fight with their officer, and then he managed to get the thing to tell us where our rifles were. We were coming out to help when you showed up."

It was certainly good timing, Waller decided... but there had to be more to this than just Smith's killing of an enemy officer. Why were they *here*?

"Holy Jesus," Turner let out that exclamation, and as Waller looked to the Sergeant again, he realized the man's eyes were aimed at a point above the Newfoundland Colonel's head.

Sass. Of course she knew.

Turning, he saw that the dragon engineer had a lightning cannon in hand, and was pointing to the tunnel. They'd sent savages through…

"Captain Adams, leave a man with Smith, then your company with Sass and us!" Waller barked that order as he began to run for the tunnel. Running was probably the worst way to try to catch savages, but there was no time for anything else.

Devlin looked after his Colonel with surprise, then glanced at Smith with a frown. Leaving the drifter down in the dust seemed wrong… but then Sass charged after Waller, and the Americans started running too. It was impossible for Jimmy Devlin not to follow, so with Halloran and the old section in tow, he made a run for the tunnel.

Staying behind with Smith were two men who had twice saved his life: Privates Preston and Marks.

The tunnel was dark indeed, and Waller had not thought to look for hand torches before entering. Instead, he waited for a man to catch up with him — one who turned out to be American — and quickly pulled out a handkerchief, lit it with a match, and stuck the burning rag on the tip of his fixed bayonet.

It was precious little light, but it was enough to keep them moving.

Sass was ahead of them all, her long legs granting her great speed. The feeble light of a burning rag couldn't catch up to her, so the men chasing simply trusted that she was somewhere ahead and could see in the dark.

As more men caught up to Waller, a few better light sources were arranged. Men with alcohol — no one asked what kind or where from — soaked their own kerchiefs, and lit more effective temporary torches. The massive width of the five-track tunnel was barely revealed… but still, there was no sign of Sass ahead.

"How long would it take to walk to the other side?" Captain Adams arrived next to Waller with the question, and the Newfoundlander shook his head.

"No idea… thinking we should go back for a train?"

Given all the chaos, it might take an hour for a train to be made ready to take men to the old world. In that time there could be great trouble on the other side of the tunnel… but it would give them a chance to organize.

More troops would be at the tunnel soon — they had to be.

So the knee-jerk response was not the best one. Waller took a breath and stopped his advance into the darkness, then shook his head at his own over-enthusiasm.

"Alright, we go back," the Newfoundland Colonel said.

As he turned back towards the entrance, the tunnel behind him lit up. Devlin was just catching up to his Colonel when that white light cut through the darkness, and he was looking the right way to see its origin.

"Lightning cannon shot... about 300 yards!" the Captain barked, then waved for Halloran's section to follow.

They burst past Waller, and as the Colonel turned another cannon bolt fired off in the dark. Sass had found the savages and she was fighting. No need for a train after all.

Hurrying after Devlin and the b'ys, Waller led more than 100 black American troops to the attack.

Sass didn't see many attackers in the tunnel — fewer than forty. A couple of shots from her acquired pulse cannon swatted most of them away, and she crushed the rest with tail or claw. What they were doing here, though, was a mystery. Perhaps the rearguard for a main force?

Continuing on up the tunnel, Sass kept her cannon ready in case more were ahead. Her vision in the dark was generally quite good, but its range was limited. She'd keep going, fast as she could, until...

Abruptly, she stopped.

Sass was a Saa starship engineer. She'd been involved in the war with the Hubrin for a long time, had served on a variety of ships and in all sorts of battles. She knew very well what a Hubrin warhead looked like, and the sort of blast it could deliver.

Why did they have a ship-to-ship weapon down here?

At first questioning her own recognition, Sass slowly approached the large cylinder. The nearer she drew, the clearer it became: a real warhead. It was armed, too — she could feel the vibrations of the energy field it was emitting.

Like most Hubrin projectile weapons, this one was largely inert until it was armed... but now that it was active, Sass wasn't entirely certain she could disarm it. It was something that didn't often come up — typically these things detonated on impact with hull or shields... they were relatively powerful, though not so potent as she figured the Hubrin expected them to be.

Still, down on a planet, in a rock tunnel with no shielding, the blast could be catastrophic.

Arriving beside the cylinder, Sass dropped her lightning cannon so she could look for an access panel. Would the Hubrin who prepared it for this work have had time to rig it to explode if someone tampered with it? Probably not — and they wouldn't have anticipated the presence of anyone who'd know what the thing was, let alone how it *might* be deactivated.

Steadying herself, Sass found a seam, then slid her claw in and pried it open. The glowing power source was revealed, along with the programming board. As usual, the controls to all the internal functions were built at Hubrin size — virtually impossible for her to manipulate with any precision. Without being able to safely get into the computer controlling the bomb, she'd have to look for a simpler mechanical solution...

Perhaps she could separate the detonator from the main warhead.

Digging her claw in, she wrenched the alloys, and was surprised by how easily they gave way. Perhaps it shouldn't have been a shock — the Hubrin built everything delicately, even their primary weapons — but as she pulled aside irrelevant conduits and essentially crushed the guidance system that was still present, she found the small glowing detonator.

Carefully she slid her claws around all sides of the box-shaped explosive, and then began to pry it loose.

Again because of the Hubrin's delicate engineering preferences, the thing come out easily.

Sass felt an instant of relief at the successful removal... but she halted that feeling as she examined the detonator in her hand. On its own, it was still a powerful explosive — it could easily collapse the tunnel she was in, it just wouldn't be able to crater the mountain above her without the reactive material it was now disconnected from...

And it was still glowing.

A detonator with its own power source... and based on the energy she could feel as she turned it over in her hand, it was close to going off.

She needed to move... and just as she realized as much, she found an audience had arrived: panting but determined, Jimmy Devlin came to a stop beside her feet.

"What's this?" he gasped the question.

As more men arrived behind him, Sass held up the glowing detonator, then covered it with her hand and made the explosion gesture. Devlin was doubled over, hands on his knees as he caught his breath — he'd run at least a mile — but he still looked up in time to catch that.

"Bastards," he muttered.

Waller was less out of breath as he appeared from the darkness, "Did she make the explosive gesture? We need to get that out of here."

Sass didn't know the words, but she guessed they were expressing a sentiment to match her own. She sniffed the air, found it was fresher ahead than behind, and decided to continue the way she'd been travelling. She'd have to get out the other side of this tunnel, then find a place to let the detonator go off safely.

Plan clear in her mind, she started to walk, then paused and looked back. If there were human defenses on the other side of the tunnel, she might need someone to speak for her, and none of the humans could possibly keep up with her sprint. Motioning to Waller and Devlin, then, she pointed to her tail.

It was easily the oddest gesture she'd made in her time communicating with the Newfoundlanders, and both officers looked at each other before Devlin went ahead and said it, "Think she wants us... to climb on... for a ride."

"Yes, steady there, Jimmy," Waller grimaced, then hurried over to Sass' massive tail and climbed up. Jimmy Devlin followed, as did Halloran and the b'ys for good measure.

Adams arrived, Turner at his side, just in time to see the dragon and her passengers race away, visible only because the bomb in her hand continued to glow.

The Americans stood still for a moment, and then one man with a torch saw the light glint off something metallic to his left, "What's that?" It was a massive cylinder, and no one knew what it did.

Waller was no good on a horse, and that being the case, he was even worse travelling by dragon. He held onto Sass' tail for all he was worth, and the tunnel flew past. It was probably for the best that it was so dark — if he'd been able to see how fast they were moving, it doubtless would have added to his discomfort.

Some of the b'ys were having more fun, though.

"Sure, you don't need me for a runner no more, sir! Look at her fly!" Private King was nearest the end of Sass' tail, and he clearly had a greater affinity for speed than his Colonel.

The pace continued a minute, but as the air grew noticeably different, Sass slowed her progress. When she could actually make out the end of the tunnel ahead, she stopped completely. It looked to be dark beyond the exit — shaded, or perhaps overcast — but that was irrelevant for the moment.

As she halted, Waller and the b'ys slid off, then found their feet and moved up around to her front.

"Thanks," the Colonel offered awkwardly, then saw that the tunnel mouth was just a few hundred yards away. "We'll go let them know, I'll wave when it's clear."

Sass didn't understand the words, but there was no time for gestures, and she figured he'd make it obvious when the way was clear. She nodded.

"Right b'ys, another jog!" Devlin called, and his old section seemed enthusiastic.

"Shit, Captain, so nice that you've come back to keep us fit," Connolly jibed.

Devlin grinned and then they all ran, Waller at their head.

It didn't take long to get close to the entrance, and as they neared, the Newfoundland Colonel drew his Webley. Depending on what news had been wired back to the old world from Pacifica City, the men here could be ready to fight, or completely at ease.

Either way, he needed their attention.

Gesturing for the b'ys to get up against the tunnel wall — hopefully out of the way if someone overreacted and opened fire with a machine gun — the Colonel advanced to the middle of the tunnel, then approached the exit with even strides. As soon as he felt he was near enough to the open night beyond, he fired off his revolver three times, then three times again. The shots were particularly deafening as they echoed back down the tunnel, and the b'ys all cringed just a little, their ears ringing.

"I am Colonel Waller of the Royal Newfoundland Regiment, we have friendly men coming through to report immediately!"

Silence greeted his words for a few seconds, and then a few more. Each second felt altogether too long. He waited, the b'ys waited, and Sass waited — keeping a nervous eye on the detonator.

"Hello?" Waller called again after that delay.

"Yeah. Come out!"

An answer at last. Waller hurried out into the night, his b'ys coming off the tunnel wall and following quickly. Together, the Newfoundlanders found themselves facing a field battery of artillery and three regiments in line, all ready for a volley. The single moon of Earth — one that Waller hadn't seen in nearly a year — was illuminating the scene, as were some electric spotlights from towers on either side of the tracks.

The Americans had been ready to repel invaders, but the fortifications didn't appear to be terribly deep. Recalling how well-protected the station in the Rockies was, Waller couldn't help but wonder whether these few thousand men and some field guns would actually be enough to stop a blue incursion, if one ever got this far.

More American unpreparedness...

He cut off that thought as a General approached him.

"I'm Liggett, what's the situation?"

"Attack on Pacifica is being controlled, but the blue men managed to slip an explosive into the tunnel. Our... comrade is about to come out with it, but it's essential you don't shoot her."

It was difficult to read the General's expression in the moonlight — night was so much darker on Earth than on the new world — but his next question revealed his thoughts.

"She? Is that Lady Emily?"

Obviously General Liggett had been reading the papers... perhaps he thought Emily was recovered.

But Waller shook his head and then clarified, "She's called Sass. Big dragon, might be mistaken for a monster in bad light. Be sure your men don't open fire."

Liggett blinked, then nodded and turned back to his lines, "Colonel Marshall, men to stand down. Friendly dragon coming through, no firing!"

With that declaration — probably the most unusual order these Americans had ever received — Waller nodded back to Devlin, and the Captain hurriedly turned back towards the darkness and gave a great wave.

That done, Waller looked back to Liggett, "If you had to dispose of a bomb somewhere where it would do no harm, where around here would it go, sir?"

Liggett was frowning at the tunnel, clearly interested to get a look at the dragon, so his answer sounded rather distracted, "How big a bomb?"

Waller answered honestly, "No idea."

"Ah. Hm," Liggett paused, then looked to the left. The train station sat there, but behind it appeared to be thick trees. "Just woods out there. Drops off into a lake."

"Thank you, sir," Waller nodded, and just as he did, Sass emerged tentatively from the tunnel. The men in the American ranks literally hushed, their eyes wide as they saw the creature stand up in front of the mountain, a shadowy monster in the night.

Any of them who were nervous might have been overcome by the circumstances — fearful of the great monster from the new world — so Sergeant Halloran decided to break the spell of the scene with his powerful lungs: "She's a lady, so any man thinking poor thoughts be mindful of his conduct!"

Sass paid no attention to the human reactions. Coming up to Waller and Liggett, she looked at the glowing box, then all around. She hoped that Waller had found a place the damned thing could explode without doing harm...

The Newfoundland Colonel pointed to the left, then made an arching gesture with his hand. Sass looked in the direction he'd indicated, saw structures were nearby, and then decided he meant she should lob the detonator far over those. Taking a few steps in that direction, she gave a mighty throw, and the glowing box disappeared into the night.

It didn't explode, though — it was still on a timer. She'd have to wait to make sure it went off before leaving. She supposed it couldn't take too long — the Hubrin wouldn't have wanted to have to hold the tunnel mouth forever — but still, she'd have to be patient.

There was no point standing, either. Uncommonly, Sass found her legs were a bit tired... perhaps evidence of how poorly she'd been eating lately, and how little proper exercise she'd gotten while a captive of the Hubrin. Sitting herself down on the dirt, the Saa engineer ignored looks of surprise from the defenders of the tunnel mouth, and took a deep breath of the night air.

Sass actually found the air on this side of the mountain tasted different, and clearly the—

She stopped thinking for a moment, as her eyes turned up to the sky.

When had the sun set? The tunnel through the mountain had not been long enough to allow for night on one side, and day on another. Not even the Hubrin's artificial environment technology could shift a planet's rotation to change night into day over such a limited time.

But it was night.

And as she craned her neck to look up past the single moon at the constellations in the sky, she realized something was entirely wrong.

Where was she?

Waller didn't notice the dragon's confusion; he simply turned back to Liggett, "Sir, I'm sorry we don't have more time for pleasantries, but we'll need to return to Pacifica immediately. There's still a savage attack underway, though I expect it's being handled. A request may come to you for support, but that's not my decision. For now... I think, Sass is just waiting for the thing to explode. If you could clear out your men, we'll be returning soon."

Liggett was staring at Sass, but he seemed to hear Waller's words anyway, "Thank you, Colonel."

Eventually the General moved off, and turning back toward the tunnel,

Waller found Jimmy Devlin and the b'ys were waiting for him.

"Worked out pretty well," Devlin observed, and just as he said it, there was a mighty explosion from the woods behind the station. The ground trembled, and flames lanced high into the sky. Everyone ducked, but there was no shockwave this time — not like the one in the pass.

Private King let out a laugh as he straightened up, "Holy jumpin' Moses, hang around with the dragons if you like explosions!"

His enthusiasm drew some chuckles from the b'ys, and Waller allowed himself a smile — the day had been long, and good men were lying lifeless on the rock of the badlands, but at least the blue plan had been thwarted.

Then Waller realized he didn't know if a similar tunnel attack had been successful at New World City. They really did have to get back, so information about this bomb could be relayed to Byng and Sask.

"Start back, I'll get Sass and we'll pick you up," Waller said to Devlin, gesturing towards the tunnel.

The Captain nodded, "Come on, b'ys. No rest for the wicked."

They started off, and Waller moved over to Sass, who was staring at the heavens. She didn't even seem to have noticed that the bomb had gone off at all... and as Waller arrived alongside her, she seemed equally oblivious to his presence.

"Sass," he called up to her, but that didn't work either. "Sass?"

She was fixated on something... did she perhaps recognize the stars constellations that could be seen in the night sky of the old world? It stood to reason that...

Wait. A question came to Waller's mind.

For some reason — for some fool reason — he'd just assumed that Sass and the dragons knew the tunnels in New World City and Pacifica City led to another planet.

But how could they know?

Stepping up to Sass' huge leg, Waller knocked on her skin the way he might have knocked on door. Finally she looked down, but something about the expression on her face reflected serious turmoil.

Seeking to answer her questions without forcing her to find a way to ask them, Waller pointed to himself, and then held up his hand to indicate the land all around him.

Sass stared at him, and then changed her position on the ground so she could draw in the soft Earth with her claw.

She drew a circle, with two smaller circles looping around it. She then pointed back to the tunnel, and Waller nodded in understanding — that was the new world, with its two moons. Then, a few yards away from that planet, she drew another, this with only one moon around it. Pointing at the dirt, she then tapped that second circle, and Waller nodded again.

"Earth," he said, though he doubted the name would be of any use to her.

Next Sass drew a line between the two planets, and then she pointed again at the tunnel. Waller nodded, then kicked one of the rail lines that was close to where Sass was sitting. Sass looked at that, then tapped the line she'd drawn, and Waller nodded again.

Sass sat back. It made no sense at all: a tunnel that included some sort of space-time singularity... a wormhole... something that allowed instant travel between different planets in different spiral arms of the galaxy?

A singularity so subtle that Sass had just run through it without even realizing it was there? A singularity that humans had been able to run *fixed ground transport* lines through?

It was impossible.

And importantly, it was well beyond the science of the Saa...

And certainly beyond the Hubrin.

But who could have created it, and for what reason?

An uncomfortable feeling crept into the back of Sass' mind. Out of the corner of her eye, she thought she saw something move in the woods, so she looked. It was just an animal of some sort, gray with pointed ears and a snout, watching her.

This place had animals. It was a naturally-occurring environment... not the artificial construct of the other world. The Hubrin... or something... had shaped the other planet to resemble this one. Perhaps the humans were native to this place.

That was one question among hundreds that appeared in Sass's mind, and she knew there was no point even trying to ask them with gestures. She would report to Sask, and they would have to redouble their efforts to learn the human written language. Much had to be explained.

For now, they needed to return to the other side of the tunnel... to the other world. Sass finally came to her feet, and gestured for Waller to get on her tail again. The Newfoundland Colonel did so, and she started back for Pacifica.

Only as she was entering that dark mountain again did she realize another, rather more helpful implication of her discovery: if the humans' world was in a different part of space to the Hubrin training world, her transmitter might have enough range to reach Saa command from there.

Many possibilities, and soon there would be answers.

Sass and the b'ys returned to the new world.

CHAPTER XXXIV

Many explanations were owed to many people, but after wasting as little time as he could with Pershing in Pacifica City, Waller and the men who'd come with him returned to the badlands. The small aircruiser that had landed for the tunnel raid was left behind — no one knew how to fly it except for the dragons, but unlike the much larger vessels from the prison camp, it wasn't big enough for any of them to get inside.

The Americans could study it to their hearts' content, as far as Waller was concerned.

Smith had been sitting up, albeit dazed, by the time the b'ys got back to the new world, so he'd been loaded into the aircruiser as well, and together with the men of the 25th United States Infantry, he was making the trip to the badlands.

The sun was hanging low in the west when the aircruiser touched down on the mesa again, and the situation was far more organized when the ramp lowered to the rocky red ground. Skeen and Miller were there waiting as Waller descended, and immediately the Colonel went off with the officers to explain all that had happened.

As a single force, the men of the 25th stepped down to the mesa together, and then went on their own private mission. They had no orders, no place to be, and plenty of grieving to do. At least Turner and some of their lost comrades had come back to them.

Finally, Jimmy Devlin and Sergeant Halloran helped Smith down the ramp. When some of the b'ys recognized the drifter, word spread like a wave. Well-wishers crowded around the American, and as the familiar faces closed in, his mind continued to clear.

He was back with the Newfoundlanders. He was able to see that much.

They took him over to a rock beside a fire and sat him down, then they all closed in around him, mercilessly happy and welcoming.

"Easy b'ys, he broke the neck of a blue man General right in front of us... but that blue bastard was trying to break his brain at the same time. He's still brain-sore," Halloran said, and word passed quickly again.

From eager men, excited to see the American who'd become an honorary Newfoundlander, they turned into a quieter bunch, wondering if their old drifter friend would be himself again soon.

Eventually they broke up, to get some supper for themselves and set up camp. Smith needed time to get his brain sorted, and that was fair enough. The man was most welcome back in their ranks, and they'd hear stories from him when the time came. They hoped, anyway.

Devlin stayed with Smith as he sat by the fire. The Captain checked the drifter's guns, which Turner had recovered from the other aircruiser, and gave them a quick cleaning to make sure they'd be ready when they were needed.

But time dragged on, and the sun began to set, and Smith showed no signs of talking. He was able to sit up, able to take the food and drink offered to him, but not to speak. It was like he was in a trance, and he wasn't coming out of it.

Time, Devlin decided, would sort him out... or maybe an even more familiar face could help.

The Captain got up and left the fire.

"I don't think Sass had realized we're from another planet," Waller was finishing up his recounting of events from Pacifica City for Skeen and Miller, and both men were interested in that last conclusion.

"Of course, I suppose we might have assumed they would know, but why would they?" Skeen nodded, sipping coffee as he quieted.

"Think that'll change the way they see us?" Miller asked softly. It was fair to wonder, though impossible to guess at the answer.

Waller shrugged and then sipped from his own cup, "No way to know. But they took us back here without any trouble. I'm sure they'll have more questions for us... whenever they can actually ask them... but for now, they'll have to speculate amongst themselves."

As good as the partnership between men and dragons had been in recent days, perhaps the limitations would soon be tested. A common enemy was a great binding force, but what would the giant lizards really think when they learned of another world covered by humans? Would they see an ally, or a source for food, or something else entirely? Waller didn't want to wager a guess.

"Well, Tom, for all the questions, I think this place proves one thing for certain," Skeen said eventually, waving his cup over the moonlit badlands. "When we cooperate, we can do a hell of a lot of damage. If the blue men doubted that before, they can't now. I expect whatever they send us next will be a lot more powerful... and I don't know whether we'll be equal to it."

It was a stark but very wise conclusion — though Waller had to admit, he'd expected the blue military to have learned more from its previous experiences than it already had. They'd failed at Promised Town, and Farpoint, and had suffered raids in the beginning at Fort Martian, and again later at the prison camp...

Was the column that had died in the pass below really the most wrath they had to offer as retribution? Somehow Waller doubted it... again. But only time would tell.

For now, they had to rest for the night, and then get their men home.

"You get some sleep," Sir Andrew said at last, directing his words to both Waller and Miller. Then he smiled: "I'm going to go try to complain to Sass for leaving me behind when you flew to Pacifica."

With that, the Indian Army General moved off into the night, and the Newfoundlanders watched him go. One of them probably should have made a joke, but neither the Wall nor the Skipper found they had enough energy to manage one.

It took until after sunset for the men of the 25th United States Infantry to bury their dead. The b'ys of 'A' and 'D' Companies, who had been posted along with the Gurkhas to watch the northern heights for the night, helped where they could... but for the pride of their regiment, the black men did most of the work on their own.

There was bitter irony there — men who had been wasted for years digging ditches were, on this day, using their hard-laboring skills to put their own friends and comrades to rest.

Major Tucker and Captain Kearsey watched in silence. Like their men, the Newfoundland officers prayed for the Americans, but mostly they stayed out of the way.

The last man to be buried was Krazakowski. It was gruesome that he was not all together as a man when he was placed carefully into the ground, but the survivors of the 25th didn't concern themselves with his state. They simply put him back together as best they could so that he would rest whole.

As the men of Adams' company covered the Major with red rocks and dirt, that Captain stood back with his personal bible, speaking quietly as the moons hung over his shoulder: "We lost our Major today, and too many of our men."

The surviving buffalo soldiers had all crowded around, and behind them, keeping a respectful distance, the b'ys listened too.

"Today we fought as men, which we always do. But tomorrow our brothers will be remembered as men, which is something new. May the good Lord God take them all up into heaven. May they look down on us with pride, and watch us carry forward their honor, their deeds, into a new age. May God protect their families, and ours. And may we see our brothers again, one day when our time comes to pass."

In that vein, the prayers continued for an hour, with any man amongst the survivors who wanted to speak having the chance to do so.

As they watched, George Tucker glanced at Fred Kearsey, "There but for the grace of God we go."

"Aye," 'D' Company's Captain agreed. "There but for the grace of God."

They said goodbye to Krazakowski and so many good men.

It had taken Devlin longer to find Kennedy than he'd expected. By the time he started back for the fire where Smith sat, the moons were high, the Americans had made their way back across the valley to the mesa, and the music had begun.

Like Newfoundlanders, the black men of the 25th United States Infantry knew that the best answer to sorrow was joy — a song driven by Private Gellately's accordion and Sergeant Whealan's fiddle was beginning to fill the gloomy night. As they had at Promised Town, Americans and Newfoundlanders were sharing a tune.

But that didn't matter to Smith. He was staring into the fire when Devlin returned, and the Captain could only imagine what the drifter was seeing within the flames. That was some spell he was under, one that no man might know how to break.

So Devlin had something better than a man.

Smith's mare nudged him in the back with her nose, and at first the drifter didn't respond. Unimpressed with his lack of reaction, she nudged him again, and snorted. That made Smith look over his shoulder, and then turn around on the rock. He started to rub her as soon as he realized who it was, and she stepped a little closer to provide him easier access.

The man still didn't say anything, but that was fine. It was better that he get his wits back, and if anyone had wits to spare, it was that Appaloosa mare.

Standing back from the fire with Kennedy and Halloran, Devlin folded his arms and smiled, "Well how's that for a reunion?"

Neither Kennedy nor Halloran said anything for a moment, and then the Sergeant spoke up, "So, Captain, you going to admit to your wife that Sass got you to climb on her for a ride?"

James Devlin nearly shot his Sergeant — he got his Webley out of its holster and everything — but Kennedy talked him down.

CHAPTER XXXV

Emily was able to argue her way out of the hospital five days after the assaults on Pacifica City and New World City were stopped. By the time Annie Devlin, James Devlin, and a section of men from 'C' Company escorted the savage-born lady down the hospital steps and into a motor car for the short trip to her rented house, the crowds were relatively small.

Certainly the people of New World City wanted to know that the popular heroine of those adventures against the blue men and savages was well again, but there were new distractions in town — and indeed, a new heroine for them to admire.

Sass' role in the victory at the newspaper-named 'Battle of the Badlands' had quickly made her the talk of the town; her ride to the rescue of the Pacifica tunnel had made her a proper heroine. Of course, having been involved in both actions had again made the b'ys the most talked-about soldiers in Selkirk, so there were many free drinks bought, and enthusiastic young potential brides presented.

But the Newfoundlanders had seen such treatment before, and they were growing weary of it. They were polite, but they steered clear of trouble, more inclined to think about what was in store for them next.

While the attention was more than they might have wanted, the stories of both the 'Battle of the Badlands' and the Pacifica tunnel attack had at least done a great deal of good for the reputation of one well-deserving unit.

Major Krazakowski and his fallen soldiers of the 25th United States Infantry were already surpassing David Crockett as heroic legends of America — the black men who fought the savages, and saved the States.

Captain Adams had rapidly been promoted to Lieutenant Colonel, and under his charge, a rebuilt regiment of black men would soon be ready to defend the Pacifica Territory against whatever dangers awaited.

It was a political stunt, of course — a chance to cash in on the vibrant press coverage of the attacks, to create new heroes who would raise American interest in the new world, and to justify any taxes levied in its defense.

At least these heroes were men who actually deserved the title, and while many difficult days were undoubtedly ahead for the 25th — particularly once their fickle fame faded, and their notoriety earned them disdain from white units in their own army — at least they would have gained a good leader from the trade.

And a piece of history. As Skeen had promised, they would be remembered, not ignored. That truly mattered, and in time those words he'd spoken to the survivors of the unit would take hold.

For New World City, though, the story really was the dragons. Sass had been integral to the defense of Pacifica, while Sask and his warriors had turned a similar attack on the Selkirk capital into a complete non-event. And all of this had been done without the creatures asking for so much as a pat on the back.

The fact that the dragons wouldn't have had the words to ask for that pat was irrelevant as far as the press was concerned; they had demonstrated their quintessential Britishness by selflessly doing a difficult job, and doing it in a decidedly modest fashion.

They were heroes, and would continue to be so until a more complex reality was revealed. That time was coming, Emily knew, because the linguists from Britain had arrived during the week, and now they were working quickly, using the latest techniques to teach the dragons their letters.

What would the great lizards have to say for themselves, once they could convey more than simple thoughts?

Emily looked forward to that answer, but it wasn't top of mind for her. The motor car that was carrying her home made its final turn, and then continued down the street to her rented house. Tom was supposed to meet her there — she'd wanted to see him immediately upon her return — but he had been needed by Skeen to assist with some planning thing or another.

As she carefully climbed out of the car, Emily moved with slow and deliberate focus. She climbed the stairs to the porch one at a time, and then slowly approached the front door. She refused to be seen as weak, even though every step was painful.

She was not recovered — not really — but she had to get out of that hospital. To get out meant being mainly better, and no one knew how quickly a savage could heal. So as long as she acted the part, she would be free.

Alice Waller opened the door for Emily as she approached, and then stood aside as the savage-born Lady entered. It was good to be back in the simple rented house — a great relief to breathe the air again, after so long stuck in the hospital atmosphere.

Annie and Jimmy came in behind Emily, and the former maid asked the obvious question, "Do you need help with anything?"

Shaking her head, Emily turned partway to look back at her escorts, "Just some privacy, if you don't mind. Thanks for getting me here."

She tried not to sound too cold, but she failed. Still, in spite of that chill, Annie and Jimmy smiled. The Captain then tugged the brim of his hat: "Take care, Lady Emily."

They departed, but Alice still waited at the door.

"Do you want me to stay or go?" her question matched Emily's cooler tone, and the wounded Lady just managed to avoid a wince. She did want to be entirely alone, but somehow she didn't want to be so bluntly rude as to cast Alice out.

"Alain was hoping we could meet for tea," Tom's sister added after a second, and Emily accepted that excuse.

"Well give Colonel Lapointe my best, thank you," the Lady replied.

Alice nodded, then promptly collected her hat and stepped out, closing the door behind her.

As soon as the audience was gone, Emily let out a long breath and grimaced with the pain in her stomach. Finding the rail to the stairs with her hand, she held on and gritted her teeth. Each step was a campaign all its own... one by one, step by step, she carried herself upwards.

The pain was quite remarkable. She supposed that was mainly a matter of her muscles — the powerful savage muscles that gave her such ability — knitting back together. But she was no doctor. She was through with doctors, in fact.

And it didn't matter. She came to the top of the stairs, and that was a relief. Bracing herself on the railing, she stood upright for a few moments, then trudged towards her room, one hand gliding along the wall, a support in case she needed it.

By the time she turned into the bedroom, she found her energy flagging. She barely made it to the bed and then sat down fully dressed. She would need to get her boots off at least, and her tunic too... but it was too much for right now. Her own fault for insisting on being fully dressed when she walked out of that damned hospital.

Catching her breath, and letting her muscles relax against the pain, she just sat there. For ten minutes she didn't shift, and then another ten. It was more comfortable to just be still than to try to move, so she didn't force herself.

Then she heard Tom coming down the street. Her hearing, at least, was still sharp. She detected his boots on the porch, and then on the stairs, and then in the upstairs hallway.

"Emily?" he called for her just short of the door, and as he stepped into the room she looked up.

Her shoulders were slumped, her hands planted on the bed beside her hips, and she looked most uncomfortable.

"Finished with your beloved General, Tom?" her opening question was sharper than she meant it to be, and he stopped in surprise. She looked down at the floor again as he digested her words, but then before he could offer any response, she shook her head, "I'm glad you're here now. I need you here."

Deciding not to fixate on his Lady's frustration, Waller moved towards the bed, "Was it wise to leave hospital?"

She nodded slowly, "I had to get out."

He let out a slightly disapproving breath and crouched in front of her, his hands landing on her knees, "You need to lie back."

"Not when I'm fully dressed, thank you very much."

Waller frowned at her, but then went to work on her boots. They came off without much difficulty, and as they did Emily started unbuttoning her tunic as well. His fingers interdicted and took over that duty.

"Just sit back," he insisted.

"Sitting back isn't comfortable," she countered, and when the buttons came undone, she started to shrug off the tunic. It wasn't easy, and as Waller realized she was having difficulty, he slid his hands in to render assistance. One arm came free, and then the other, and then his hands came to rest on Emily's shoulders.

Her blouse was short-sleeved, and that put his fingers on her skin — a feeling she had missed. She began undoing the buttons of the blouse, and that caught the Newfoundland Colonel by surprise.

When he didn't offer assistance, Emily took one of his hands in hers, and guided his fingers to the buttons, "I think you owe me some release, after leaving me so casually to campaign with your General."

She guided his fingers under her blouse, and as his hand settled on her collar bone, she let out a long breath, then pressed her forehead against his.

Entirely unprepared for the quiet demand, Waller stammered out an answer:"I... you're recovering."

"There are more buttons for you to undo," Emily ignored the protest, her words disconcertingly certain. "You're back with me, and I must feel that in case you leave me again. We must be together... it's the most important thing in this world. Please do as I say."

Waller didn't see Emily's point. Perhaps it was rational, perhaps it wasn't... but he still loved her, and deciding his comprehension wasn't necessarily important, he eventually — very carefully — did his best to comply.

Because of the obvious discomforts, the sounds that resulted were hardly loud enough to break through the modesty of the house's walls. Indeed, only one creature seemed to notice anything at all.

Sass stopped for a second to look at the structure, then decided she wouldn't be able to find out what some human verbal cues meant — at least not without the assistance of the written language.

And even then, she probably wouldn't ask, because according to the press, dragons were eminently British in nature, and that meant such things were not discussed. The dragon lady went on about her business, and left the Colonel and the savage-born Lady to theirs.

EPILOGUE

To say Smith was a different man than when he'd last been in New World City would have been an understatement. He had regained speech after a few days, and had spent time with the b'ys again, telling them where he had gone and what he'd been up to.

He'd talked about the Shylocks, and Cameron Kard. About the Murdos and about how the men of the 25th had saved him. About being a prisoner of the blue officer, about fighting him and snapping his neck.

In a few days, he'd said more than he figured he might have said in a whole month during his drifting years. Smith wasn't sure if this meant he was turning into a more talkative person, or if he just had a lot to say because he had been gone for a while. Time would tell.

For now, though, he was taking the chance to do what was best for him: he was riding a trail west of town, not because he was going anywhere, but because it was a peaceful way to get closer to his thoughts.

Much of the fight he'd had with the blue officer was playing back through his head, like a nightmare that wouldn't go away. And one part of that exchange interested him more than any other: the thing had dwelled on Caralynne.

Everything those Martians had forced into his head... every picture of her living through that encounter at Farfield City... what did it mean? Had the blue officer fixed on her face because he realized she was significant to the drifter, or because maybe he'd seen her before?

The blue men had to have been getting their information about Pacifica and Selkirk from somewhere — how else would they have known that attacking further south would be easier? Why couldn't that information be coming from her?

Smith let himself think that for a minute, and then he dismissed the case. Caralynne wouldn't have known to take Ambitia and Destina. She wouldn't have known much more than the general facts about Pacifica.

There was no reason to think she was their prisoner.

But the thought kept recurring, planted in his head by those blue men. In its way, it was a kind of torture — hope when there was none.

Closing his eyes against his thoughts, Smith slowed his mare on the trail and took a deep breath. Here in the north the air was fresher again, and it helped.

But the questions wouldn't stop. Was she out there after all? Had Emily been right? Or was this just a cruel last revenge by a blue man Smith had killed?

Whatever the answers, at least the drifter was where he needed to be. Time and action would probably reveal more of the truth about what had happened, and what was to come. Now that he was back with the Newfoundlanders, the drifter would have a better chance to find out more, and then eventually, perhaps, he could be released from this questioning.

In the meantime, he'd keep riding, keep clearing his head, and get himself back into a state that would be useful in the field. The blue men had to be beaten, and the b'ys had to survive, so that was all he would think about.

Smith adjusted his hat, nudged his mare forward, and headed towards the horizon for a while longer.

He was leaving behind thoughts of Caralynne.

For now.

HISTORICAL NOTES

These notes contain spoilers — it is recommended that you do not read them until you have finished the book!

With the blue men, the dragons, and the humans all clashing on the new world, it's time to take a look at the real history that has influenced the *The Badlands*.

Races In War

I wrote in the Historical Notes to *The Frontier* that I'd been unprepared for the importance race played in the texture of the story. You might expect me to have remembered the lesson, and been ready for all the questions of racialism that emerge with the reunion of the Newfoundlanders and the men of the 25th United States Infantry.

Obviously, though, I'm not that bright.

The sad truth remains that the experience of black Americans during this period was consistently grim. The months between Promised Town and the 'Battle of the Badlands' could hardly change it, and one would be wise to wonder whether the months and years after this book's events will see lasting evolution.

Don't hold your breath.

Since writing *The Frontier*, I've been fortunate enough to have been contacted by readers, and exposed to historical vignettes I'd never known. One, ironically, pays off my lengthy defense of the b'ys' positive treatment of the men of the 25th in the Historical Notes to that book. If you'll recall, I spent many words telling of my grandfather, and his openness to people of other races (including my own father). I spoke of common experiences between people who must work without privilege... I even included a picture of myself with my great-grandfather, who was black.

While history might produce anecdotes that refute my reasoning, the story of Lanier Phillips does more to prove me right than any argument I could hit you with.

One night during the Second World War, the American destroyer USS *Truxtun*, in company with USS *Pollux*, ran aground in heavy seas. The ship was near enough to shore for the men to jump into frigid waters and swim for their lives... but the black cooks aboard the ship contemplated whether they should bother, because they were on the North Atlantic run and knew that colored men weren't allowed ashore in Iceland.

They truly did have this debate amongst themselves — better to risk a lynching, as they were accustomed to fearing, or to die at sea?

Eventually one of these men, Lanier Phillips, decided to chance it. He hit the North Atlantic waters and damned near froze, but he clawed his way ashore, onto the brutal rocks beneath an Iceland cliff. Like most of the men who swam for it, Lanier came out of the water covered in fuel oil — *Truxtun's* bunkers had ruptured.

Local rescuers had hurried to the coast when the first survivor staggered into a nearby mining camp. No man or woman was left out of the effort to save people from the ship; it was a rural area, and the custom of the North Atlantic is to save any who fall victim to the machinations of the sea.

Soon Lanier found himself being carried into a triage area, where local women were stripping down stricken sailors, and trying to scrub the oil off their skin. This was a horror to the black seaman: in his native Georgia, were he to be stripped down and bathed by a white woman, he'd have faced a lynching.

Now he was surrounded by white women, and they were scrubbing him raw because the oil wouldn't come off his skin. Finally he found enough courage to inform the women that the color wouldn't come off — he was born with it. They did keep trying for a while, as none of them had seen a black man, and they probably thought he was delirious. Once they realized he was right... he discovered he hadn't swum ashore to Iceland.

Those of you familiar with this story will know that the USS *Truxtun* ran aground off St. Lawrence, in southern Newfoundland. And because no shipwrecked man is any different than any other shipwrecked man to a Newfoundlander, Lanier was not lynched; he was dressed by the ladies, fed a good Newfoundland supper at the table with a local family, and spent the night in a warm bed, with a missus looking in on him from time to time to make sure he was alright.

For decades later, he would tell the story of how that experience changed his life — how he discovered that the rules of race relations he learned growing up in Jim Crow-era Georgia were not universal.

Lanier got involved in the civil rights movement, and became the United States Navy's first black sonar technician. He always credited this experience with Newfoundlanders for reshaping his worldview, and making him believe a world without racism was possible. Indeed, just a few weeks before his death in 2012, he had returned to St. Lawrence. His story has been publicized by the likes of Bill Cosby, but it needs to be told more often, because these days, it's mostly known as a joke.

Have you heard the one about the Newfoundland missus who'd never seen a black man? Who knew jokes like that could have happy endings.

As much as I am a proud Newfoundlander, and I would love to tell you that this sort of thing would only happen on the Rock, I imagine most small communities along the North Atlantic would have been the same. These places are filled with people who know the awesome power of nature, and the fragility of humanity. The law of the sea is to save those in distress, and by extension, to fundamentally see those working upon the sea as humans like yourself.

I'll not take that case too far, but nevertheless, I hold Lanier's story as more evidence that the racism the fictional men of the 25th faced from their own was a construct forced upon them by a society that had spent centuries dependant on segregation. The b'ys lived outside this structure, and so their continued respect of the black soldiers from the US was based on their common experiences.

However, the arrival of the Indian Army on the new world opens another set of questions about the structure of race relations.

The Martial Races

I've discussed before how the African-American experience was one of purposeful, systematic subjugation, for sake of a slave-driven economy.

Undoing the dehumanization that came with such a system remains a problem faced in the United States to this day... and it is an experience quite different to the Indian one.

Make no mistake: British colonialism in India was brutal, unsympathetic, and culturally insensitive. The Empire arrived to 'civilize' its prized possession, and it did so by whatever means it felt were appropriate at a given time. But — and this is a key point — this was not the subjugation of a minority, but *by* a minority. That meant that, unlike in the United States, the British needed a lot of local help.

The British in India relied on their integration with (and you can argue, manipulation of) local political and social systems, as well as their superior military technology. Right back to the time of Wellington, there was a definite need for Britons in India to depend on local notables and their armies for control. I obviously can't recount this whole process here — there are many fine books on it — but the bottom line is that the British had long come to appreciate the quality the systems already in place in India... and for our purposes, to respect the soldiers native to that part of the world. Indeed, in classic Darwinist fashion, they began to classify them into a hierarchy based on perceived military prowess.

Over the course of the new Imperialism, the British came to believe that their territories held certain 'Martial Races' — tribes in which men were, due to culture and experience, simply better warriors than most. It was not unusual for ethnic groups branded with this designation to wear it with some pride — even begin to perpetuate it — because it set them apart from their peers.

The Zulus were considered a martial race after their successes against other African tribes, against the Boers and then the British. The Nepalese Gurkhas remain almost a mythical force, renowned for their courage and feared for their skill. Many of the peoples of India's Northwest Frontier were similarly respected, because they fought regularly in the difficult terrain around Afghanistan, and did so most effectively. Wherever they came from, martial races were often recruited heavily, and over time they built reputations that earned them profound respect, both in spite of and because of their race.

Whether these soldiers were intrinsically superior to any others, I hesitate to say. The case can certainly be made that men with certain social and economic backgrounds might make for more effective soldiers (a polite way of saying that hard-living men, be they from the Scottish Highlands or the mountains of Nepal, might be raised tough), but whether that's correct is irrelevant for our purposes, because everyone believed these men to be better fighters... and often, these men believed themselves to be better too. Such confidence can be a powerful tool, provided it is not blind.

But here's a question: in the presence of such purportedly powerful martial races, who should command?

The Viceroy's Commission

It's worth pointing out that the various peoples of the Indian subcontinent had been warring for centuries before the British Empire arrived. Within this context, British military successes in India were significant; the ability of a European power to move in and successfully (if gradually) defeat long-victorious armies drew attention.

Imagine it from the point of view of indigenous warriors: a new fighting system with its associated technology allowed not just white Britons, but the Indian troops they armed and trained, to defeat armies that had previously been dominant. It would be too simplistic to say that these British-Indian military successes made all the peoples of India want to become a part of the military machine that was so successful against them... but I think it's fair to say there was a certain meeting of military minds.

While the British came to admire the martial qualities of certain conquered peoples, many of those colonized groups came to respect the 'modern' scientific ways of war. Any European powers who possessed the ability to fight industrialized wars came to be seen, by some, as patently superior. Broadly speaking, white officers for indigenous regiments were thus not seen as an imposition, but a necessity to make the most of the martial abilities of those troops. It was in some respects a symbiotic relationship.

Except when it completely broke down, as with the Indian Mutiny in the 1850s. But for our purposes, let's just recognize the fact that it wasn't a situation where white 'owners' were driving ethnic 'fodder' to their deaths in the field. There was a mutual respect, and real efforts by both sides to learn from each other. But there were divisions, and one came with the treatment of Indian officers.

From the beginning, having Indian leadership within regiments of the Indian Army was vital... but because they were more 'primitive', the British could not imagine allowing Indian troops to command white soldiers. A separate officer class needed to be created to fill this need — to provide leaders who spoke the language, and understood the ground. Thus began the Viceroy's Commissioned Indian Officers (as opposed to British King's Commissioned Officers).

In practice these men were well-respected by British officers. Accounts differ as to how this respect played out in the field... and realistically, it undoubtedly changed and evolved regularly. The bottom line, though, was no matter how experienced or respected, these Indian Officers were not equal to the white officers they fought beside. Ironically, then, an American Captain like Adams would have held more relative authority than did these Viceroy's Commissioned Officers... he just would not have received the same respect that they did.

In our real history, it was the First World War that changed the situation for Indian officers; the myth of absolute European military superiority died a million deaths on the western front, and by 1920, a move began towards 'Indianization'. Indian officers started training at Sandhurst, with eventual authority over white troops, and Skeen was involved in increasing the number of Indians involved. By the time of the Second World War, while black men like Lanier Phillips were still expected to serve as cooks in the US Navy, Indian officers were helping lead the war against the Japanese in the Pacific.

I suppose you could conclude that the British-Indian relationship was more advanced than the relationship between black American fighting men and their armed forces... but whatever you decide, the most important thing to recognize is that, during these decades, the politics of race were complicated no matter where you happened to go.

In our alternate timeline, we can simply hope that the exploits of the

25th United States Infantry, and the role of Indian troops in the defense of Pacifica, will have a positive impact on their position. And while no First World War has occurred to prompt the Indianization of the British Indian Army, our Skeen will undoubtedly work hard to use Adams as an example that prompts the process in the years after our alternate 1920.

Of course, that point raises another question: who was Sir Andrew?

Sir Andrew Skeen

The real Third Afghan War (not the fictional one we've included in our timeline) was a complete mess on many fronts, but one British officer who proved himself most adept during the conflict was Sir Andrew Skeen. Given a relatively inexperienced Indian force (made up of regiments raised late in the First World War, when most of the Indian Army had been used up in Europe), he managed to outsmart his Afghan opponents, and turn back the invasion of India very effectively.

Later in life, he would write a book called *Passing It On*, about his experiences fighting on the frontier. I was fortunate to acquire a reprinted copy of this book some years ago, and though much of its advice is rooted in its time (apparently getting camels around a sharp bend on a mountain track is *very* tricky), the fundamentals seem universal.

Skeen was a man determined to be smarter than his foe. He sought to understand the way his Afghan opponents fought, to predict their ambushes and observations, and to find ways to trap them. He was a stickler for professionalism and discipline, but not in the stereotypical 'do up your top button' way. He wanted his men to always be on guard, and to never be lax or ignorant of their surroundings. Any unit that revealed itself to be sloppy in the field would be identified as an easy target for ambush, and he wasn't about to lose his men to those sorts of attacks.

Needless to say, I came to have a great appreciation of Skeen. The version of Sir Andrew presented here is not necessarily a true reflection of his personality — unfortunately I haven't had the opportunity to review his personal papers, or find too many impressions of him from those he served with... but given his intelligence and his priorities, I did my best to cast him as the mentor the Newfoundlanders had learned so much from during their time in Afghanistan.

I hope that my portrayal has done the real man no injustice — I've been governed by the simple principle of making him into the true leader the b'ys would want to follow... the genuine article, who men like Evelyn Hughes aspire (or pretend) to be, but who exceeds them in every way.

Waller, Byng and Currie are lucky to have him on the new world.

Dragons' Stars

At last, Sass is beginning to fill in the picture of the new world — and its human occupants. Though humans and dragons have managed a great deal of communication so far, the ability to exchange more complex thoughts is still in the offing — unfortunately, unlike in many stories of interactions between humanity and an alien race, universal translators aren't readily available. And everyone doesn't speak English.

(If you think that I'm taking a shot at other writers with that remark, just go read the *Equations* Novels. We've all done it.)

But not this time; Sass has been doing her very best to integrate into the relatively primitive 'freed attacker' society she's found, and to assist them against the blue men (or 'Hubrin'). Her technical abilities and her good military sense have undoubtedly made a huge difference in keeping those enemies at bay... but what will the implications be, now that she knows the tunnels exist?

While the men and women of the British Empire and the United States might not have realized how unlikely it was for an alien race still reliant on technologies like wheeled vehicles (no matter how spectacular) to be able to create the gateways, it is entirely obvious to a starship engineer that the tunnels connecting the new and old worlds are well beyond the science of those supposed Martians.

Who could have constructed such portals, and to what end? Why did the Hubrin take credit for their creation when they first encountered Waller? Was it indeed their technology from a long-lost time, and if so, would they be able to utilize it again in future?

Beyond that, what are the implications of an entire planet filled with freed attackers, all of them presumably at a similar technological level to those the Saa survivors have partnered with since their rescue?

The possibilities are numerous and daunting, and Sass will have to work with her fellow Saa survivors to determine how best to move forward. In the midst of these many considerations, though, one common problem remains: the Hubrin blue men are still on the new world, and though another of their assaults has been thwarted, in no small part thanks to their suspect leadership, a real challenge must be soon at hand.

How long can this backwater planet — a footnote in a much wider war between Saa and Hubrin, and the Hubrin and the scourge Queen — remain toothless in the face of such a powerful uprising? With the dragons actively working with the humans, and potentially creating a forward base of operations for their armadas, the Hubrin need to take serious action.

The time for local tinpot Generals is over; the main event is at hand. A true test of survival is soon to come on the new world — one that will shake both the United States... and *The Empire...*

HIS MAJESTY'S NEW WORLD

by Kenneth Tam

1919. The British Empire and the United States have been colonizing a new planet for nearly 40 years. But there are secrets yet to be uncovered on His Majesty's New World...

His Majesty's New World novels by Kenneth Tam

Book One: **THE GRASSLANDS** (April 2008)
Book Two: **THE FRONTIER** (April 2009)
Book Three: **THE REPRISAL** (May 2010)
Book Four: **THE EXPEDITION** (July 2011)
Book Five: **THE BADLANDS** (July 2012)
Book Six: **THE EMPIRE** (July 2012)

For more information, please visit

www.newworldempire.com

THE
EQUATIONS NOVELS

The Earthers evolved after humans were driven from the Earth by an intelligent bio-weapon dubbed 'Omega'. They are faster, stronger, smarter, wiser, *better* than humans, and they are the only hope for the survivors of the human race as an interstellar war between two great alien powers absorbs the galaxy. But all is not as it seems, and the humans and the Earthers face challenges that overshadow the wars of alien empires and threaten to destroy their civilizations...

The Equations Novels by Kenneth Tam

Book One: THE HUMAN EQUATION (Oct 2003)

Book Two: THE ALIEN EQUATION (May 2004)

Book Three: THE RENEGADE EQUATION (Dec 2004)

Book Four: THE EARTHER EQUATION (July 2005)

Book Five: THE GENESIS EQUATION (July 2006)

Book Six: THE VENGEANCE EQUATION (July 2007)

Book Seven: THE NEMESIS EQUATION (July 2008)

Book Eight: THE DESTINY EQUATION (July 2009)

The Equations Novels are available in both print and ebook formats.

For more information, please visit

www.earther.net

ABOUT THE AUTHOR

Born in 1984 in St. John's, Newfoundland, Kenneth Tam holds both a Bachelor's and Master's degree in history from Wilfrid Laurier University in Waterloo, Canada. His MA thesis examined the creation and operation of the Caribou Hut, a hostel for Allied servicemen in St. John's during the Second World War.

In 2006, Kenneth received a prestigious Canada Graduate Scholarship from the Social Sciences and Humanities Research Council of Canada. He was also awarded a Balsillie Fellowship at the Centre for International Governance Innovation during 2006-07. In that capacity, he worked for Mr. Paul Heinbecker, Canada's former ambassador and permanent representative to the United Nations. Kenneth is presently an advisor at Sun Life Financial's Waterloo Wellington Financial Centre. He has also consulted for the Institute for Quantum Computing, and Kitchener-Waterloo's Member of Parliament, Peter Braid.

Since releasing his first novel in 2003, Tam has promoted his books across Canada, speaking with junior and high school students, delivering writing workshops, and doing book signings at bookstores and Iceberg-organized events. He frequently appears as a guest author at science fiction events across the country.

Kenneth remains very lazy about writing his author bios. When they told him to make this one longer, he mostly copied and pasted it together from the Iceberg website, www.icebergpublishing.com.

CPSIA information can be obtained
at www.ICGtesting.com
Printed in the USA
BVHW081708140219
540173BV00001B/87/P

9 781926 817118